Grand Theft Death
A Salty Sister Mystery
Ann Philipp

Salty Sister Publishing

Praise for *Grand Theft Death*

This cozy mystery is laugh-out-loud funny, and it's always full of twists and surprises. The characters, mostly old friends who bring a legacy of larceny to the story, are as quirky as they come, but the themes are modern and deeply human. Even if you're not a cozy fan, try *Grand Theft Death*. I can't imagine anyone not being completely delighted and looking for more.

Ana Manwaring ~ Author of *The Hydra Effect*, A JadeAnne Stone Mexico Adventure.

* * *

I was drawn into this story right away and entertained throughout by the foibles of the main character, Patricia, who, by merely borrowing a car, winds up in a world of trouble. She is aided by her recently deceased grandmother's friends who, by the book's climax, have upended all preconceived notions of what charming, elderly ladies are capable of. This is a well-crafted, fun book sparkling with whimsey that surprises in satisfying ways.

Laura McHale Holland ~ Author of the award winning novel *Reversible Skirt*.

* * *

This romp was fun from beginning to exciting end. The mystery is intriguing and the characters that solve it are truly amazing. These Salty Sisters are each a study in how to age without aging. Their spunk will charm you as each page finds a new adventure. Patricia, the young outsider who becomes an insider in spite of herself, is shocked to find that her grandmother had a risky history and her friends likewise. I can't wait for the next book.

Linda Loveland Reid ~ Author of *Touch of Magenta* and Past President of Redwood Writers, Sonoma County.

Acknowledgements

A big thank you to my husband John, and to all my critique group friends, who have encouraged and supported me over the years: Ana, Karen, Mona, Kerry, Kathy, Laura, Margery, Shelley, Diane, Geri, and Patsy. Thank you, thank you, thank you.

Chapter One

The Cadillac at the curb mocked me. I wanted to go over and kick the stupid thing, but I'd probably break a toe.

I paid the taxi driver and stepped out of the cab. My front door swung open, and Mrs. Betty Butterfield's small pudgy frame jogged across the lawn, her arms open wide. Two steps from me she stopped abruptly and folded up like a bat taking a siesta.

"Dear Patricia, what a traumatic experience," she said. "How are you?"

I reeked of *eau de jail cell*, my mouth tasted of vending machine coffee, and something icky was stuck to the bottom of my flip-flop. I appreciated her concern, but how did she get into my house?

"I need a shower," I said, running my fingers through my mop of curly blond hair.

She nodded in obvious agreement. "Of course you do. Come in dear, we have breakfast waiting for you."

We?

I followed her into the Spanish bungalow I'd inherited from my recently deceased grandmother. Then I heard the other ladies laughing. "The Ladies," as I'd always called them, had been good friends of Nana's. But why were they here? Was this an intervention to stop my supposed thieving ways?

Three smiling expectant faces greeted me. Mrs. Rita Miller and Mrs. Audrey Taylor sat at my sun-drenched kitchen table. Mrs. Sunny Russo stood at my stove.

"Good morning, Patricia," they sang in unison.

I slid into a chair and Mrs. Russo plunked a full plate of food in front of me—scrambled eggs, bacon, fried potatoes, plus a huge cup of coffee, and that was just the beginning. On the table were pancakes, fresh-squeezed orange juice, toast, and ham. I smiled meekly and took a huge bite.

"I remember my first time in." Mrs. Taylor's wide-brimmed, flowered hat flapped in rhythm with her speech. "I got picked up for shoplifting at Tiffany's."

"Shoplifting," Mrs. Russo scoffed. "Don't be so modest. A $100,000 diamond tiara and matching necklace is a major jewelry heist, and you know it."

"Mine was for check fraud," Mrs. Miller said, smothering her eggs with Tabasco.

"Mine was just like yours, dear," Mrs. Butterfield said, her bright yellow dress casting a warm glow onto her softly wrinkled face. "Grand theft auto." She smiled proudly at me.

In fact, they were all smiling proudly at me. I put down my fork mid-chew and looked from one sweet face to another, trying to grasp what was happening. Apparently I'd gone through a hazing ritual and joined their secret club.

"We'd given up on you, dear," Mrs. Miller said. A bright red hibiscus rested behind her ear, accenting her shoulder-length, salt-and-pepper hair. "Your grandmother was so pleased when you went into the art world. But this, oh, I wish she'd lived long enough to see you now."

I attempted to swallow but choked instead.

"Hands up, dear," Mrs. Taylor said, pounding on my back. "Open pathways are breathable pathways."

"Nana?" my voice was a whisper.

"Why yes, didn't you know?" Mrs. Butterfield asked.

I shook my head.

"She got sent up for counterfeiting. She was one of the best."

I instantly thought of the five dollar bills my grandmother had faithfully given me every birthday, always tucked inside a syrupy greeting card decorated with playful kittens or puppies.

"This is a joke, right? You're just saying this to make me feel better."

They glanced at each other, looking insulted.

Mrs. Russo had yet to disclose her transgressions and I looked at her serene face, haloed by a perfectly coiffed silver page boy. "I never got caught," she said, and The Ladies burst out laughing.

"I can't believe your grandmother never told you," Mrs. Miller continued. "She often mentioned that you were her favorite."

I gave Mrs. Miller a don't-patronize-me look. I was an only child of an only child.

"Look how similar Patricia's hands are to her grandmother's." She grabbed my arm and held it up like a trophy.

"And you're so tall and graceful," Mrs. Butterfield added. "I always thought you'd make a good cat burglar, like Cary Grant in *To Catch a Thief*."

"She never taught you how to pick a lock?" Mrs. Russo

asked. Her diamond tennis bracelet caught the morning light and shot starlight around the room as she gestured to my back door. "Or lift a wallet?"

These were such outrageous questions I didn't know how to respond. I started eating again, hoping the conversation was a hallucination produced by low blood sugar and a lack of sleep.

Mrs. Butterfield stabbed a pancake, plopped it on her plate and smothered it with syrup. "Well, thank goodness Sunny bailed you out," she said. "The jails are pretty rough these days."

Well, thank goodness I'd just swallowed, or Mrs. Taylor would have been slapping me on the back for a second time.

"Mrs. Russo, you bailed me out?" I asked.

She nodded, giving me a sly smile.

I'd called my parents twice during the night, but no one answered. "How did you manage that, Mrs. R?" I asked, falling back on my childhood habit of referring to The Ladies by the first initial of her last name. "It's only eight o'clock in the morning."

"I have some pull with the judge."

I picked up my coffee cup, held it with both hands, and peered over the rim at Mrs. Russo. Of all The Ladies, I knew the most about Mrs. Russo. She was a tall thin woman who radiated elegance. She lived life by her own rules and her past was littered with husbands. At least four from what I'd been told. Her most recent partner, the late Nico Russo, had been involved in organized crime. Arrested for tax evasion, he died in jail before the trial. I didn't know how Mrs. Sunny Russo could influence a judge, but she had connections to the mob, and now I was indebted to her. I wanted to ask her why she had done this, but a question like that smacked of ingratitude.

"Thank you, I'll pay you back," I said. "But I didn't steal that car." Their faces looked skeptical, like Officer Romano's had at the police station. "Really, I just went out for ice cream."

I took a deep breath. "I walked to the convenience store down on the corner, and ran into Julie Gordon, a friend from high school. She was drunk. So I drove her home in what I thought was her car. " I looked around frantically for reassurance. "How was I supposed to know the car was stolen?" My voice rose to a shriek. "I mean, come on, why would I steal a car and park it in front of my own house?"

"Rookie mistake," Mrs. Miller said, shrugging her shoulders. "It could happen to anyone."

"So you really had no idea about your grandmother?" Mrs. Butterfield asked, tactfully changing the subject.

I shook my head.

"Well, there's a lot more to tell you," Mrs. Butterfield continued, "but this probably isn't a good time." She reached over and gave my hand a squeeze. "All I can say is that we are so, so proud of you."

The beeping of a truck backing up interrupted the conversation. Mrs. Russo shot out of her chair and headed out front. We followed her onto the lawn with Mrs. Taylor relying heavily on a wooden cane. A yellow tow truck with the words 'Marino's Towing' on the door positioned itself behind the Cadillac.

Mrs. Russo stood on the sidewalk, hands on hips. The driver jumped out of the cab. Oil stains marked his dark blue slacks and shirt. An embroidered patch above the chest pocket said 'Mel.'

"On a Sunday?" Mrs. Miller said with alarm. "Why is he

working on a Sunday? But we haven't had enough time to—"

Mrs. Taylor elbowed Mrs. M in the ribs and gave her a stern look.

Mel hit a lever and the towing equipment lowered to the ground. The Caddy was one of the longest automobiles I'd ever seen. No wonder it felt like a bus when I turned a corner. Outside of needing a bath, it looked to be in pristine condition.

"It's breathtaking, isn't it?" Mrs. B whispered.

"What is?" I asked. "The car?"

"Oh, Patricia, it's not just a car." She raised her arms, palms up as if giving a benediction. "The 1959 Cadillac Eldorado Biarritz Convertible," she said, her eyes filling with tears. "Looks like a rocket, drives like a dream."

I imagined the massive automobile tipped up on end with the headlights pointing skyward. An arc of chrome running from tail to headlight mimicked the curve of an early spacecraft and oversized fins flared out like supports. I could almost see flames shooting out of the tail lights, propelling it into the ether.

"Mel, what are you doing?" Mrs. Russo asked the truck driver, bringing my attention back to earth.

"Police orders, Mrs. Russo. I'm taking the Caddy to impound."

Mrs. Russo stepped forward and grabbed his arm. "Oh, no you're not."

He hesitated. A look of compassion came over his face.

"I'm sorry, Mrs. Russo."

I leaned over to Mrs. Miller and whispered, "How does Mrs. Russo know the tow truck guy? And why is she so upset?"

"Sunny and Nico used to own the towing company," she

whispered back. She ignored my second question.

Mrs. Russo let go of Mel's arm and clenched her fists.

"How long until the owner can claim it?" Mrs. R asked Mel.

"I don't know. The police have to check for fingerprints."

I cringed. Mine were all over the steering wheel as well as the door. My cell phone rang from inside the house and I went back in to answer it.

"Hello?" I said.

"Patty?" A breathy voice replied.

I watched out the window as the Cadillac pulled away from the curb and eased down the street like a lumbering elephant. The Ladies flowed back into my house, talking nonstop. I put a finger over my free ear, blocking out the chatter.

"Yes."

"It's Julie."

I'd left her asleep on her bed. She obviously found my note telling her I'd slipped the Cadillac key off her troll doll key ring and used the car to get home.

"Sorry about last night," she continued. "I was pretty wasted. Could you bring my car over?"

"Your car?" I snapped. "After I drove it home I got arrested for stealing it. I spent last night in jail."

The Ladies quieted down, listening in on my conversation.

"Arrested!" she replied. "Oh, damn that Jimmy! I could shoot the guy."

"Who?"

"Jimmy Chang."

Ish. I shuddered. The name brought back bad childhood memories. Jimmy Chang liked to steal things from me. He stole my marking pens, my colored pencils, my drawing pads;

he even pulled a scrunchie right out of my hair one time. And then there was 'the incident.' Double ish, I didn't want to think about that.

"What does Jimmy have to do with this?"

"The car kinda belongs to him."

"What do you mean, kinda?" A combination of irritation and fear tighten my neck.

"It used to belong to my dad, and after he died I started driving it. Jimmy came by my work the other day and repossessed it. He said my dad owed him money."

"So, why were you driving it last night?"

"Jimmy was going to sell the car, so I swiped it from the Finley Hotel's parking lot. Patty, I'm really sorry about all this. I'll make it right. I promise."

I felt cold cell walls closing in on me and I broke out in a sweat.

She continued: "I'll ask my mom if she can drive me over to pick it up; just leave the key in your mailbox."

"The car's not here. It's been impounded."

The line was silent for a moment. "Jimmy's a dead man," she said, and hung up.

I turned to The Ladies. "Julie says her dad owed this guy some money, so he repossessed the car."

"Who repossessed it?" Mrs. R asked.

"Jimmy Chang."

"Jimmy Chang," Mrs. Miller muttered, shaking her head. "*Díos mío.*"

"How do you know Jimmy?" I asked.

Before she had a chance to reply, Mrs. R interrupted: "Patricia, what about the car?"

"Jimmy wanted to sell it, so—"

"Oh no!" Mrs. B exclaimed, her hand covering her mouth. "He's not going to sell the Cadillac!"

The Ladies turned in unison to Mrs. R.

Her jaw tightened and her eyes narrowed to slits. "We'd better go," she said.

The Ladies quickly gathered up their purses and headed out the door.

My phone rang again and I answered, only half listening to my mom as I peered out my living room window and watched The Ladies walk across the street. Mrs. Butterfield unlocked the passenger door to a bright yellow older model VW Beatle. Mrs. M hopped in the back, while Mrs. T leaned heavily on her cane, and slowly lowered herself into the front seat. Mrs. Russo lived in the apartment complex next door to me. She stood on the sidewalk until Mrs. B pulled away from the curb.

"So noon's okay?" My mother asked for the second time.

"Hmm?" I replied.

"Noon's okay for lunch?" she asked. "Patricia, what's wrong? You seem distracted."

"Yeah, that's fine."

"I'll meet you downtown then."

"Okay." I hung up.

I suddenly missed my grandmother. Her absence gripped my heart, and I let out a long sigh. If only she would walk in from the kitchen and tell me what to do, or more importantly, who to trust.

I plodded off to take my much needed shower, and pondered the irony, that after all the things Jimmy had swiped from me, I had been arrested for swiping something of his.

Ish.

Chapter Two

At noon I met my mother at Lombardi's, a family owned Italian restaurant that had been downtown as long as I could remember. We sat by the window watching shoppers stroll by in the warm June sun.

"Two coffees please," I told the waiter, ordering for both of us.

At first glance, my mother, Genevieve Schuster and I did not appear related. Her deep brown, shoulder-length hair contrasted with my light-colored, uncontrollable mane. I stood at five foot ten, a good three inches taller than her. But what we did share was fair skin that freckled easily and green eyes that took on a turquoise hue when we wore blue.

Ripping off a piece of sourdough bread from the loaf, I dug into the butter, working up the courage to tell her of my arrest. I delayed long enough for her to speak first.

"So are you going to sell Nana's store as a business? Or liquidate?" she asked.

Along with inheriting my grandmother's house, I'd also inherited her business, Elsie's Antiques.

"Neither, I thought I'd give it a go."

It had been three years since I received a degree in Graphic Design. Since then, I'd been laid off from two jobs and fired from another. I was a fine artist at heart, same as my mother and my grandmother. But I'd studied graphic arts, hoping to earn a living.

My mother raised her eyebrows.

"But, what about your graphic art's career?" She made it sound holy. Of course, for the price she and my father had paid for my education, it practically was.

I shrugged my shoulders. "Maybe this will carry me until I get my own design business going."

I was lying. Truth was I'd been bored with the work and bored with my life. What I thought would be an outlet for my creativity had turned into a game of trying to please executives who had no taste and took joy in tearing apart my work. I'd started my own business, but a few jobs here and there barely covered the rent. I was at the end of my financial rope. So when my grandmother left me her business, I moved from San Francisco back to my home town of Lakeville, forty-five minutes north.

The waiter came to take our order. Then we returned to safer topics of weather and food until I noticed my mother staring out the window; I followed her gaze. A meter maid driving what looked like a souped-up golf cart stopped outside the restaurant. A camera sat on the top of the tiny vehicle.

"What's that camera for?" I asked.

"It records license plate numbers and the time. If you're parked for more than two hours on the same street, you'll get a ticket."

"That's not very shopper-friendly."

"Welcome to downtown Lakeville," she said smiling. "You know, I've always believed that meter maids have a sadistic streak."

"Wouldn't you, if you went through police training, but your job description still had the word 'maid' in it?"

"They're called Parking Enforcement Officers these days."

I glanced outside again. The meter maid looked our direction. Her long, straight black hair partially covered her sunglasses. She tucked one side of her wayward locks behind an ear. "Well, that Parking Enforcement Officer is staring at us."

The woman turned her head and puttered off.

"That reminds me," my mom said. "I had an odd thing happen last night."

"You and me both."

"What's that?" she asked.

"You go first," I stalled.

"The police department called me," she said.

"Why didn't you answer?"

She paused and looked at me. "How did you know I didn't answer?"

"Because, I was the one calling."

"Oh no!" She put her hand to her throat. "What happened?"

"I was picked up for supposedly stealing a car." I hoped the statement sounded as if I'd just bought a new sweater.

Her mouth dropped open and her face paled. "What do you mean 'supposedly stole a car'?"

I paused, took a deep breath and explained. I waved my fork in the air, as if it would help to explain the complicated events.

My mother looked pained, and I had an odd feeling that

she didn't believe me. Her stare floated upwards and she mumbled something that sounded like, "I've always feared—"

"What?" I asked, leaning forward.

"Nothing," she said, looking back at me. "So they dropped the charges?"

"Mrs. Russo bailed me out."

My mother swallowed hard, took her napkin and blotted her upper lip. "Not Sunny Russo?"

"Of course, Sunny Russo. How many Mrs. Russos do we know?" I asked teasingly, hoping to lighten the mood.

She leaned over and whispered, "You know her husband died in jail a few months ago."

"I know. You told me when it happened," I whispered back.

"But she's still involved with *them*." She meant the mob. "For all we know, she could have taken his place. She could be their head-honcho."

"Mom, I don't think the mob hires women. They don't strike me as an equal opportunity employer."

Our lunch arrived and I cut open a cheese ravioli. My mother stared down at her soup.

"Look, it was all a mistake," I continued. "It will easily get cleared up. So why didn't you pick up the phone last night and what happened to your answering machine?" I popped a bite of pasta into my mouth.

"It's broken." Her voice returned to normal. "But I saw the name on caller ID." She turned away from me and stared out the window again. "Okay, okay, we can deal with this." She seemed to be trying to reassure herself, not me.

"I know we can Mom. I'm sure Dad has some lawyer friend that will get the charges dropped. Julie just wanted the car back, so she took it. See? So, it's probably nothing, just a misunderstanding."

"Maybe there's a twelve-step program," she mumbled, picking up her spoon and gingerly placing it in the minestrone.

"Mom, I wasn't the one drinking. Julie was." I searched her face, hoping for an ally. "I couldn't let her drive like that. She could have killed someone."

She nodded and sighed. "Well, call your father tomorrow at the office. He's been out of town all weekend." Then she leaned forward and looked around the room before she whispered, "You didn't enjoy, it did you?"

"Enjoy it? What do you mean? You know how claustrophobic I am."

'The incident,' that I so hated to think about, happened at the age of six, when Jimmy Chang locked me in his family's linen closet and ever since I've hated small spaces. Fluffy towels gave me the willies too.

I continued: "Enjoy sitting in a cell with some hookers? Enjoy being questioned by an officer who didn't believe a word I said? No, I wouldn't say I enjoyed it." I paused. "But it was interesting."

As I walked back to Elsie's Antiques, a voice called out: "Hey, Salty Sister!"

I turned and smiled, immediately recognizing my surfing buddies, Chris and Adam.

"Hey!" I called back, happy to see them.

The old beat-up van they drove had two surfboards strapped to the roof. Chris' tanned muscular arm rested on the open passenger window. He pushed his straight, shoulder-length, sun-bleached hair out of his face and grinned. Adam's locks were the same color but shorter with loose curls. Both wore T-shirts with ripped-out sleeves. I'd always considered them like brothers, despite their attractiveness, and they treated me like a little sister: protective, yet encouraging.

"What are you doing here?" Chris asked.

"I moved back."

"Really?"

"I'm taking over Nana's store."

"I was real sorry to hear about you losing your Nana," Chris said.

Adam nodded.

"Thanks, I miss her." My eyes started to tear up and I took a deep breath. "Where have you guys been? Every time I go by your store, the 'Gone on Surfari' sign's in the window." Chris and Adam's Surf Shop sat two doors down from Elsie's Antiques.

"Oh man, we were down in Texas, chasing supertankers," said Chris.

"Supertankers?" I asked.

"Yeah, the oil freighters that run in the gulf between Galveston and Houston send out great waves. A guy took us out in his boat, and we surfed the wake for miles. Totally juicy!"

"Killer on the quads though," Adam interjected.

"Did you see any tar balls?" I asked.

"Nope, not one," Chris replied. "Next time, you've got to come with."

I nodded. They'd been trying to get me to go on surfari with them for years. To Tahiti or Hawaii, even down to Half Moon Bay. But I'd always been working or in school.

"I'm also living in Nana's house," I continued.

"Wow, that's major," Chris said, his whole body nodding.

I glanced up at the meter maid who stared at us as she cruised by at a slow clip. The guys turned and looked.

"Oh man, that chick's crazy," Chris said, after she'd passed by.

"The meter maid?" I asked.

"She tried to run me down."

"Seriously?"

"Seriously. Right in front of our surf shop."

"I saw it," Adam said, holding up his hand, as if giving a sworn oath.

"Watch out for her," Chris warned, shaking his head. "She's a freakdudette."

Feeling a chill, I rubbed my arms. Chris wasn't a person who threw labels around lightly. I made a mental note not to leave my car parked on the street for too long.

I unlocked the front door of Elsie's Antiques and flipped over the sign in the window from closed to open. A woman walked across the street and headed my direction with a rather determined look on her face. She wore a blue and purple paisley dress that adhered to her large curvy figure. I judged her to be in her 60s, and her gray hair was pulled up into a beehive. As she got closer tiny bolts of light shot out from the sides of her head, like miniature sun flares. I had the distinct impression of a super-hero gone bad. She stopped in front of my door and I felt compelled to open it for her. Her arms went immediately to her hips and that determined look turned to anger.

"Elsie never closed up for lunch," she snapped.

I felt like a child being chastised.

"You know the merchants have an unspoken agreement," she said, pointing down the street, as if all the shop owners had suddenly lined up in front of my store. "We open by nine o'clock, we stay open until six, and we don't close for lunch."

I mulled over the irony of her speaking this unspoken agreement while I stared at what I could now see were two pink knitting needles sticking out of her hair. The beehive hid the X shape they made while the pointy ends hovered right above her ears. The round ends, with their shiny silver finish must have reflected the sunlight. My musings left a long silence and she started talking again.

"I've owned the Yarn Barn for twenty-four years. Plus I'm on the board of the Merchants' Association. And I will not have you," she said, thrusting her finger in my face, "ruining our downtown with your lackadaisicalness. You're as bad as those surf boys."

I wondered whether I should argue with someone who accessorized their hairdo with lethal weapons. Plus she'd used the word *lackadaisicalness* correctly in a sentence. I positioned myself behind the door so just my head was vulnerable.

"Do you understand?" she barked.

I nodded, which seemed to satisfy her. She turned and stomped away, muttering about how irresponsible youth shouldn't be self-employed, and that I'd probably be out of business in a week.

She'd made it to the center of the street when I noticed the meter maid traveling our direction. The little vehicle sped up, and the driver leaned forward over the steering wheel. For a terrible moment I thought the Yarn Barn lady might get mowed down, but she broke into a trot and made it safely to the sidewalk. As the wild driver zipped past, she turned my direction, tucked her hair behind her ear and gave me a satisfied smirk.

I shut the door quickly and had an overwhelming urge to lock it behind me. Maybe my mom was right. Maybe I should sell the store.

After a tiring day of sorting through accounting books and unpaid bills, I pulled into my driveway a little after six. My inherited house had a white stucco exterior, with classic terra-cotta colored roof tiles. A small palm grew out of a front lawn consisting mostly of crabgrass, and a bougainvillea climbed a trellis next to the front door. My grandmother had been the last hold-out against the land developers in the neighborhood. Condos and apartment buildings surrounded the house on all three sides. An elementary school sat across the street, which led to a lot of confusion around eight in the morning and two in the afternoon. Somewhere in the apartments to my right lived Mrs. Sunny Russo. I had come to the conclusion that she must be able to look directly into my backyard and with binoculars, probably into my house. It would have been the only way she could have known I'd been arrested the night before.

I let myself into the house, still trying to get used to the idea that it belonged to me. My grandmother passed away a month ago, and I'd been living here for a week. Practically everything in the house belonged to my Nana. I hadn't collected much furniture in my life, and what little I had, I left with my roommate in San Francisco. All I brought with me were clothes, a few plants, my computer, art supplies, and numerous finished and partially finished paintings on canvas.

For years I'd wanted to be independent, but it hadn't worked out that way until now. Because of my unstable work life I'd relied on handouts from my parents over and over again. I knew I could move back in with them, as so many of my friends had. But that wasn't the direction I wanted to head. Now I had a house and a business. On one hand I felt grateful and relieved, having a security that I'd never felt before. But on the other hand I was scared I'd blow it, lose it all to a bad decision or some unforeseen event. And last night I had run right into that fear. Now I was back in the position of needing help again. My independence waned and with it my self confidence.

I took some solace just being in my grandmother's house; it made me feel close to her. Her collection of tea pots decorated the counters in the kitchen and lined the tops of the cabinets. A large picture she'd painted of rolling golden hills broken by clumps of purple green trees hung over the fireplace. Every wall reflected her love of art with prints and reproductions of many wonderful artists: O'Keefe, Monet, Picasso, plus others I wasn't familiar with that could have been locals or friends of hers. She'd turned her extra bedroom into a studio. A blank canvas sat on her painting easel in front of still life of a vase and a stack of hardcover books. I hadn't touched a thing, hoping one day I'd finish the painting she'd never had a chance to start.

I went out back to the old garage that sat at the corner of the property. Two doors opened out to reveal a dirt floor that held parallel ruts from long-ago wheels and oil stains from long-ago leaks. On a homemade plywood workbench, along-side rusty trowels and weed pullers, lay gardening gloves that I'd given my grandmother as a birthday present when I was eight years old. I picked them up and slipped them on, remembering how my mother had taught me how to use fabric paint and I'd decorated the practical gift with yellow flowers and purple crescent moons, now faded from years of use.

Above the work bench, screw drivers and pliers hung from a peg board, while an assortment of rakes and shovels leaned in the corner. The opposite wall held something as dear to me as the gardening gloves, but in a different way. My surfboard. I'd stored it here since high school, after my father complained that it took up too much room in his shelf-lined immaculate garage.

I placed my surfboard fin down on two saw horses, opened an old tin of board wax and gave the surface a light coat. I craved surfing like a physical addiction. Especially during times like these, when the world seemed to be spinning away from me, out of my control.

Chapter Three

I woke to the sound of laughter. The Ladies were back, and I could smell coffee, plus something else buttery and wonderful. I shuffled into the kitchen wearing my light blue pajamas decorated with dancing sheep. Mrs. Russo turned from the stove top and smiled at me.

"I haven't started the Hollandaise sauce yet. So there's plenty of time for a shower."

Boy, I must really look bad if a seventy-two-year-old woman doesn't want to eat with me unless I've showered.

"Here dear, take this with you." Mrs. Butterfield held out a large mug of coffee with cream.

I nodded and shuffled back to my bedroom. I knew they wanted something and I felt ill-prepared. I guzzled the coffee, hoping caffeine would give me the courage to face whatever The Ladies had in store.

As expected, the Eggs Benedict were to-die-for. If I had been alone, I would have licked the plate. As Mrs. Butterfield poured me a third cup of joe, I couldn't take the suspense anymore and blurted out: "All right, why are you ladies really here?"

The question hung awkwardly in the air.

"Sunny has a favor to ask you," Mrs. Miller said.

We all looked expectantly to Mrs. Russo. She had just put a bite of egg in her mouth and I waited impatiently for her to chew.

"Well, as you know, my husband Nico died a few months ago." She explained after wiping her mouth. "And he made a request before he died. I thought you could help."

"Okay." I bounced one knee up and down, feeling the effects of the caffeine.

"As you may or may not remember, Nico and I used to own Russo's Towing. He sold the business back in the late 90s."

"And then there was the little problem with the stock market," Mrs. Butterfield piped in.

Mrs. R gave her a look that could wither a dozen roses, but Mrs. B's smile remained firmly intact.

"Back to the point," Mrs. Russo continued. "Nico wanted his remains spread at Russo's Towing."

"She means Marino's Towing and Wrecking Yard," Mrs. Butterfield chirped. "Victor Marino owns it now, and he expanded the business."

"What exactly do you want me to do?" I asked.

"Well, none of us drives at night, so we need a driver."

Mrs. Miller topped off my coffee with organic cream. She seemed to know the way to my caffeine-loving heart.

"Why does this need to be done at night?"

"Well, Victor wouldn't take kindly to us spreading Nico around. They weren't exactly the best of friends."

"You're not going to put him in the gas tanks are you?"

"No, of course not," Mrs. Butterfield replied, looking offended.

I let out a breath. Apparently that kind of vandalism was beneath them.

As The Ladies fell silent waiting for my answer, I glanced out into the bright morning sunshine. Maybe it was my full stomach, or my caffeine buzz, but I thought that granting someone's dying wish was a rather noble thing to do. Besides, Mrs. R put up my bail. How could I say no?

After The Ladies had cleared out of my house, I called my father.

"Bob Schuster's office, Attorney at Law," Natalie sang out.

"Hi, Natalie, it's Patricia."

"Patricia, how are you?" my father's secretary asked.

"Oh, I've been better."

"I heard. I'm so sorry. But I'm sure your father will be able to straighten it out in no time." I liked Natalie. She was an eternal optimist. "He's free; let me put you through."

"Sweetheart," my father said. "What's this about you getting arrested? I'm sorry I didn't call earlier; I've been out of town."

"Oh, it's so irritating." I explained the story and then added: "So I need a lawyer."

"Is it true that Sunny Russo bailed you out?" he asked.

"Yeah, thank goodness for Nana's friends."

"If you want to call people like that friends," my father shot back. He'd never liked my grandmother. Now it occurred to me that he knew about her past and her friends' pasts too. "Stay away from them. All of them. They're troublesome old bats."

I wanted to point out to him that Mrs. Russo was there for me when he wasn't but thought better of it. Then I heard giggling in the background. I knew it couldn't be Natalie; she wasn't a giggler.

"Dad, do you have someone there?"

"Um, yeah, a new client just came in."

I was shocked. He was lying to me. Natalie would never let someone in his office when he was on the phone. It was unprofessional. But who could get by Natalie?

"Look sweetheart, I've got it covered," he continued, "I already talked to Lenny Brunswick and he can meet with us on Wednesday; it was the earliest I could get him. When's the arraignment?"

"Not for a few weeks."

"We'll take Lenny out to lunch, and you can explain everything. I'm sure he can get the charges dropped." He paused. I heard a muffled noise, like he put his hand over the phone. "I'd better go," his voice came back on the line. "I'll see you on Wednesday. Come by the office before noon. We'll go from here."

"Okay, thanks Dad."

Late that night, I flipped the headlights on and backed my Honda Civic out of the driveway. Mrs. Russo rode shotgun and held a small black metal box with a white label taped to the top, I assumed it contained the remains of Nico, but I didn't ask. She wore all black including a wool shawl that draped her shoulders. Mrs. Butterfield sat in the back seat, holding a folded brown paper grocery bag on her lap. She was also dressed in black, except for a yellow scarf at her neck.

I drove the three of us to Mrs. Miller and Mrs. Taylor's house. Mrs. Russo went to ring the bell and while we waited, Mrs. Butterfield chatted about her run-in with the cashier at the market who had charged her for peaches instead of the oranges she'd picked up.

The three emerged huddled together, and when they got to the front of my car, one of them disappeared. I started to get out, alarmed someone may have fallen.

Mrs. Miller waved me back. "Just dropped something, dear. We're fine." I sat back down, but left the door ajar. Mrs. Butterfield tapped me on the shoulder, wanting my full attention while she told me about the tattoos and piercings of the tedious cashier.

Mrs. Taylor appeared at my door. "Could you open the trunk, dear?" she asked, leaning on her cane with one hand and carrying a small cooler with the other.

"What's in the cooler?" I asked.

"Snacks."

"Snacks?" Would we be observing Nico's passing with cheese and crackers?

After a moment the trunk lid slammed, the doors opened and they all slid in. I checked my rear view mirror, and I could see Mrs. Miller. She had on a knit cap with a tuft of yarn bobbing on top and a white carnation tucked behind her ear.

Marino's Towing and Wrecking Yard was on the north side of town next to the freeway. As I drove I sensed excitement amongst The Ladies, although there was little conversation.

Mrs. Russo pointed. "Turn here."

"But this is the entrance to the mobile home park."

"I know a short cut."

Most of the trailers, with their corrugated metal skirts, were dark, but a few TVs flickered here and there. A daisy whirligig, surrounded by white rock, spun in the soft night breeze.

Mrs. R pointed again, and we wound our way between a few houses until we were on a dirt road. The southbound freeway lay to our right and crickets called out from chest-high grasses still damp from yesterday's unusual early summer rain. The car dipped into an occasional pothole and I slowed my speed to avoid giving us all whiplash. The road curved to the left and my tires found asphalt. In the distance a sign read: Marino's Towing and Wrecking Yard, Enter Here.

"Pull over," Mrs. Russo said.

"What? Aren't we going to the wrecking yard?" I asked, pointing to the sign ahead.

"No, here's good."

I parked next to a chain link fence topped with barbed wire that surrounded rows of vehicles. The entrance was a sliding gate held securely closed by a padlock. Large overhead lights illuminated the lot and I could see the incarcerated Caddy parked one car in from the road.

"But this looks like the impound lot," I said. "I'm confused, I thought—"

"No time to explain." Mrs. Russo rolled down the window and the sound of the freeway grew louder. "Okay, keep the car running," she commanded. Then she turned and spoke to the three in the back seat. "We all know what we're doing?" she asked.

"Umm-hmm," they replied.

Mrs. Russo held out a whistle for me. "Now, if you see someone coming, give three short blasts."

I looked past her and saw two Doberman pinchers running headlong at the fence, barking and showing their teeth. "Oh, crap!" I recoiled, as if they could chew their way free. Then I felt a pat on my shoulder.

"Don't worry, dear. That's why we brought snacks."

I shivered in my seat and once again pulled on the lever that released the trunk lid.

The Ladies exited the car and I heard a whistle.

"Bruno, Daisy," Mrs. Russo called out.

The two dogs stopped barking and wiggled a hello. One stood on its hind legs and poked its long black nose through the diamond shaped metal wire. A moment later I heard an explosion of gunfire and breaking glass. I closed my eyes, covered my ears and ducked. The sound came a second time.

"Whoo, whee!" Mrs. Butterfield shouted, "I've still got it!"

I opened my eyes. The impound yard was dark. Mrs. B stood next to the car holding a rifle over her head. She'd shot out the overhead lights. I put my hand over my heart, willing it to slow down. She opened up the back door, threw in the rifle and grabbed the empty grocery bag.

Lights from the freeway lit up the area to some degree and after a minute of adjustment, I could see Mrs. Taylor struggling to cut the chain that held the gate closed with a pair of bolt cutters. "Help me, will you?" she called out.

Mrs. Miller ran to her aid and between the two of them the chain snapped and they slid the gate open. Mrs. Russo threw the mystery snacks into the yard sending the dogs scrambling after them. Then she came back to the car and grabbed the black box of ashes.

"Back in a minute," she said.

The Cadillac door squeaked open and the interior light clicked on, providing some illumination. Mrs. Russo slid into the front seat, but I couldn't see what she was doing. The trunk lid popped up, and then someone was at the rear. Mrs. Russo moved to the back seat, and it appeared she was pulling up on the seat cushion.

My fear turned to anger as I realized that unless they were sprinkling Nico's ashes onto the floorboards of the Caddy, I'd been had. I was about to get out when, in the distance, I saw headlights and the silhouette of a police car.

Like an actress who'd forgotten her lines, I started blowing on the whistle in one continuous shriek. The Ladies came running and Mrs. Russo wrapped the chain around the gate behind them. She sat down in the front seat and pulled the whistle out of my mouth.

"Put your lights on bright," she ordered, "and drive."

As we drove toward the patrol car I caught a glimpse of Officer Romano squinting. Just before we pulled up alongside the car, Mrs. Russo yelled, "Duck!" and we all bent forwards or sideways disappearing from Romano's view. I popped back up and looked in the rearview mirror. I saw brake lights and the car turning into tall weeds. The headlights did not reappear and I could only hope that he was stuck in the thick adobe mud.

"Go straight to your house," Mrs. Russo instructed.

Adrenaline blurred my vision and I drove on autopilot. When I turned into my driveway, Mrs. Russo directed me to open the trunk.

"Okay," she said. "Do you have any ice cream?"

A strange question, but I nodded as I thought about the coffee fudge ripple that I'd picked up the night before when this whole bizarre odyssey began.

"Change into your pajamas, turn on the TV and start eating.

If someone comes to the door tell them you went out for ice cream."

All of us bailed out of the car. I noticed that Mrs. M's grocery bag now contained something the size of a shoe box. The Ladies gathered their paraphernalia and scurried over to Mrs. Russo's apartment. Before rounding the fence, Mrs. R turned back to me.

"Pull the paper off your plates," she hissed.

"What?"

"The paper." She pointed to the back of my car. "Pull the paper off your license plates."

I looked down, newspaper obscured the small metal rectangles. "Oh crap!"

"It's on the front, too."

I tore off the paper and stomped into the house, still feeling angry, but also relieved. I clicked on the TV and stumbled into the bedroom in the semi-darkness. After hiding the crumpled newspaper securely under my bed, I put on my sheep pajamas, ran to the kitchen, and pulled out the pint of ice cream from the freezer.

Headlights flashed across the living room window, and a car door slammed. Footsteps crunched up my driveway. I ran to the window and peeked out at a police cruiser parked behind my Civic. I quickly sat down on the couch as the footsteps came up to the front porch and whoever was attached to those footsteps knocked softly on the door.

"Who's there?" I called out.

"Officer Romano."

I turned on the porch light and opened the door a fraction, as if I didn't believe the voice. His uniform was covered in mud up to his crotch.

"Officer Romano, what a nice surprise," I said, with as much sarcasm as I could muster. "Thought of something new to accuse me of? Dognapping maybe?"

"Ms. Schuster. Your car's warm, been out tonight?"

I eased my ice cream carton around the screen door and waved my coffee fudge ripple in his face. "You know how it is. When you got to have it, you got to have it."

Chapter Four

I woke up feeling a little giddy. I went to the mirror and laughed at my curly hair sticking out in odd directions. After I showered and dressed, I looked at myself again. Still smiling. It must be some sort of euphoric hangover after escaping arrest the previous night. I knew that The Ladies had lied to me and I didn't care. I grabbed my purse and headed for the door, deciding not to ruin my mood with too much psychoanalyzing. Once outside I heard Elvis singing *Love Me Tender*. The music came from one of the apartments next door. Then a sweet soprano joined him.

I opened my car door and noticed Mrs. B had left her scarf on the back seat. I checked the car clock; I still had time to swing by her place before opening the store.

Parked in front of Mrs. Butterfield's bright yellow house was a non-descript white van with dark tinted windows. Geraniums, agapanthus and roses lined a pristine green lawn. Bright yellow and green floral cushions on white wicker furniture decorated the front porch. I ran up the steps and knocked.

"Who is it?" her voice called out.

"It's Patricia, Mrs. B."

I heard laughing, a yelp and more laughing. The door finally swung open and Mrs. Butterfield's round head emerged. The tight curls of her salt-and-pepper hair haloed her face. She was grinning, a big grin that seemed inappropriate just for me.

"Patricia, what are you doing here so early?" she asked breathlessly, her eyes glancing past me. She wore a yellow silk kimono with tiny pink flowers. Her feet wore only bright pink toenail polish.

"You left your scarf."

"Thank you dear, that was very kind of you."

She grabbed my arm, yanked me inside, and slammed the door behind me.

"What's going on?" I asked, trying to regain my balance.

"Um, the cat might get out."

"You have a cat?"

She pushed me backwards against the door.

"It's the neighbor's."

With one hand on my arm she attempted to keep me pinned, while she twisted her upper body, straining to see out the front window. I broke free and I stepped around her to catch a glimpse of a tall man with gray hair in a dark blue suit and sunglasses disappearing around the van. It started up and pulled away from the curb. I turned to Mrs. B. She looked away, patting her tight curls.

"Why Mrs. Butterfield," I said in my best Southern accent. "I do believe you were entertaining a gentleman caller." I waved her scarf in the air, attempting to look extra-feminine.

She took the scarf and twisted it around her hand. I couldn't help it; I giggled.

"Well, I…well," she said.

Then I stopped giggling. "I can't believe it," I said, putting my hands on my hips, suddenly feeling very jealous, "you're getting more action than I am."

Mrs. B smiled, but still wouldn't meet my eyes, so I thought it best to respect her privacy and change the subject. I looked around the room; there were car parts everywhere. Her dining room table was covered with newspapers and an open red toolbox.

"What's that?" I asked, pointing to a screwdriver sitting next to a square chunk of metal.

"It's a carburetor for a 1966 Camaro. I'm rebuilding it." Mrs. B smiled sweetly. "It's an easy way to make extra money."

In the living room there was a chrome bumper lying on the sofa. The coffee table held five or six auto manuals. I walked over and looked down at a long bar with a flat end.

"Isn't that one of those things you break into cars with?" I asked pointing at the odd device.

"Oh, you know how it is. You lock your keys in the car." She shrugged. "Having one of those is so much quicker than calling a towing company."

Did that mean she carried it in her purse?

"So what happened at the impound lot last night? You ladies obviously had a very different plan than what I was told."

Mrs. B crossed her arms. "Some things are better off not known. This is one of those things." She continued to smile but I could see the determination in her eyes. It was then I realized she wouldn't be giving me an explanation for our trip.

When Jimmy Chang sauntered into Elsie's Antiques, I suddenly realized the immense peril of owning a retail establish-ment. People walked in unannounced. Annoying people.

Jimmy wore a navy blue suit and a silver tie. A pencil-thin mustache-goatee made an oval around his mouth. He clenched a toothpick between his teeth. Jimmy inherited his looks from his Chinese father, but he was tall, close to six feet, and lean like his Swedish mother. His father taught Martial Arts and his mother taught dance. Jimmy Chang was an expert at Kung Fu and I suspected he could do the Watusi as well as a Waltz.

Under certain circumstances I could see how he might be intimidating. At the moment, however, his fly was down and I was privy to the fact that Jimmy had on bright red boxers decorated with white hearts. He was wearing Valentine's Day underwear in June. This reduced his intimidation factor quite a bit. I gave him my best fake smile.

"Jimmy, good to see you," I lied. "How's the auto business these days?"

Jimmy owned Chang's Used Autos on the corner and a shiny black Mercedes was parked outside my front door.

He didn't smile, just stared. While I waited for him to speak, he picked up a large blue and white Oriental vase and tossed it back and forth from hand to hand. Since I hadn't examined the piece yet, I wasn't sure if he was juggling something worth five dollars or five hundred.

"I heard you took over your grandmother's business," he said.

I crossed my arms and nodded, "Yep, that's why I'm here."

He stopped tossing the vase and glared at me.

"You still practicing your, ah, artistic skills?" he asked and started juggling again.

"Yeah," I replied cautiously, unsure where this was heading.

"Good," he gave me an evil grin and took a step forward. "You know I had a little problem this morning."

"Oh?" I asked, feigning interest.

"I went to pick up my Cadillac at the impound lot. It wouldn't start."

I shrugged my shoulders, trying to ward off the panic that was creeping up my spine. "Ran fine when I took Julie home."

He took another step and slammed the vase down onto a nineteenth Century pine blanket chest that I had just finished dusting. Luckily, neither broke.

"Then what happened to it?" he demanded through gritted teeth.

He was close enough now that I could see words printed above the white hearts on his shorts.

"Well, I didn't do anything to it."

"Was it making any odd noises when you drove it?"

What was I? A mechanic? I shook my head.

He looked outside, his toothpick bobbing up and down. I took the opportunity to glance down at his drawers. The words 'Be Mine' come into focus. He looked back and took one long stride forward, putting his face only inches away from mine.

"Then what's wrong with it?" he asked, spewing minty-fresh breath at me.

"Seriously, Jimmy, I don't know."

"Well you'd better find out, 'cause it's costing me a hundred bucks a day to have it sit there and I'm expecting you to pay for it." He pulled back a bit and smiled around his toothpick. "Not that I can't afford it; Reno paid out pretty good for me yesterday."

"Look," I said, pointing my finger in his face. His peek-a-boo red undies were making me gutsy. "I didn't steal that car."

"Really? For all I know you could have been trying to get me back for that little linen closet incident."

I wanted to hit him, but he'd have me hogtied like a calf in less than five seconds if I tried. He fondled his toothpick, but it remained in his mouth.

"Since we're old friends," he continued. "I'll consider dropping the charges. But before I do, you're going to have to do a few things for me." He looked me up and down. "You're going to be a lot more fun to work with than your grandmother."

My bravado shifted to nausea.

Jimmy's cell phone went off, and he reached into his pants pocket to retrieve it, looking down at the same time.

"Oh geez," he said, quickly turning around and zipping up while his cell phone continued to sing.

Oh geez? I smirked.

"What?" he snapped into the phone. He stepped sideways and looked out the front door. I leaned forward to follow his gaze and saw a young Asian woman with long straight dark hair, sitting in the front of a Mercedes, also talking on a phone. She blew him a kiss.

His voice dropped an octave, "I told you not to interrupt me."

Not being able to read lips, I had no idea of her reply. But her pouting mouth gave me a good idea.

"The wineries aren't going anywhere," he continued. "Okay, okay." He slammed the phone shut, slipping it back into his pocket. He walked to the door and barked over his shoulder, "This isn't over."

After he pulled away from the curb, I locked the front door and turned my open sign to closed. Risking the Yarn Barn lady's wrath, I spun my fake clock to explain I'd be back at two and stuck it back on the window. Jumping in my car I headed over to Mrs. B's, hoping we'd have enough time before lunch to undue whatever The Ladies had done to the Caddy.

Mrs. B knelt on the grass, weeding around an agapanthus in her front yard. Her gardening gloves were bright yellow, as was the handle of her weed puller. I stepped out of my car, slammed the door and stood facing her with my hands on my hips.

"Patricia, so nice to see you again." She reached into the plant, pulled out a snail and held it up for me to see. "Escargot?" she asked. "I'm thinking of selling these to the French restaurant downtown."

I stood silent.

"What's wrong?"

"What did you do to the Cadillac last night?"

She lowered her hand and the snail slowly emerged from its shell, as if sensing a potential for escape.

"Why?"

"'Cause Jimmy can't get it started, and he's blaming me."

"Jimmy? He's back already?" She looked down at her capture.

I paused. "How did you know he was gone?"

She shrugged, her eyes hidden behind yellow-framed sunglasses.

"Anyway," I continued, "he can't get the car started and wants me to pay for his impound fees."

She tossed the snail aside and nodded.

"We can fix this, but I'm going to need your help."

* * *

From the front seat of my Civic, Mrs. B and I stared into the depths of the wrecking yard side of Marino's Towing business. Tall grass encroached on rusting autos, as if making an attempt to reclaim their territory. Walking paths between the rows of cars allowed some access to the vehicles. A young man walked out carrying a dented hubcap. Must be slim-pickings if that's all he could get.

"So what's the plan?" I asked.

"You distract the guy, and I'll handle the car," Mrs. B said.

Her red tool box sat on her lap, along with a bag of doggie treats for the Dobermans.

"Distract him? How?" I didn't like the sound of this.

She looked at my outfit. I wore a light gray silk skirt and a matching tailored jacket with a modest scoop-neck blouse underneath. I was hoping to make a positive impression on the lawyer I'd be meeting at lunch.

"You look too professional. You should have worn a button down, so you could, you know…" She wiggled her eyebrows up and down.

I returned a raised eyebrow in indignation.

"No matter," she continued. "But, you'll need to lure him out into the yard with you."

"How am I going to do that?"

"I don't know. Act helpless."

Ish. "So what should I get?"

"There's an old VW bug. Ask for the top of an air filter. That means you won't need these." She put the toolbox on the floor.

I stared at her. I had no idea what she was talking about.

"It looks like an upside down fry pan with a handle on the

side." She held her hands up to indicate its size. "You'll see it, right dead center on top of the engine. It's held on with clamps."

"Okay."

I hoped that what I didn't understand would become clear to me in the moment. I got out of the car and my high heels sank into the soft dirt. I walked tippy-toed up to the small building. On the far side an open gate led to the impound yard that held the Cadillac. Of course, the street access was padlocked closed, and I'd rejected Mrs. B's idea of, once again, using bolt cutters as a means of entrance.

The two Doberman pinchers stood at the open door. They gave me a blank stare and then retreated. Today, doggie treats would be unnecessary. I leaned against the jamb. The interior was as dreary as the yard. Two desks and a couple of file cabinets took up most of the small room. Mel, the driver that had towed the Cadillac, sat behind one of the desks and looked up from a crossword puzzle.

"Hi, can I help you?" He showed no signs of recognizing me.

"I'm looking for the top to an air filter," I smiled, pleased that I had remembered my quarry.

"What kind of car?"

"VW bug."

"What year?"

We hadn't discussed a year. I stared down at the worn vinyl floor, like I was searching for the right answer and not making something up.

"Late 60s."

"We have a '68 down this first row."

I smiled again, pleased that I had guessed correctly.

"Help yourself. It'll be fifteen bucks if there's still one left."

The phone rang and Mel picked it up. I had no choice but to venture out into the yard alone. The window next to Mel gave him a good view of the path to the impound lot, so Mrs. B wasn't going to be able to sneak past him. I shrugged as I walked by her. What could I do?

The VW bug had seen better days. The front windshield was cracked and the upholstery was torn and sun-beaten. The hood faced the path and I reached down and grabbed the handle, pushing in the button. It opened with a screech and stayed propped open on its own. I looked down into an empty compartment. Damn! The whole engine was missing.

"It's in the back."

I turned and Mel lit up a cigarette as he walked down the steps. He was pointing to the rear of the car. Mrs. B dashed behind him tossing the unneeded doggie treats at the pinchers as she ran.

"What?" I asked.

Mel came up next to the car. "The engine. It's in the back."

"Oh," I said, giving him an embarrassed smile. "I didn't realize that. I'm getting it for a friend."

"Yeah, I got that when you didn't know the year." He opened up the back end of the car. "Yep, still here." He reached over and pulled up on the clamps, easily popping off the top of the air filter and handing it to me. "That should do the trick." He slammed the trunk lid closed and stood staring at me.

"Oh, right, the money." I handed back the air filter and walked slowly over to my car. Mrs. B leaned up against it like she'd been there all day.

"Good job playing ignorant," she said. "I knew you could think on your feet."

"Ha, ha," I said, giving her my best sarcastic look. "You got any cash on you?" She shook her head. I opened my purse, pulled out the correct amount and took it over to Mel.

"Thanks for your help."

He shoved the bills into his pocket. I guess I wouldn't be getting a receipt.

"So what did you do to it?" I asked Mrs. B on the drive back to her house.

"There's a kill-switch under the dash."

"How did you know that?"

"It's a long story." She turned her head away from me.

"And why bother to turn it on?"

She looked back. "Jimmy is…how do you young people say? He's fun to mess with."

I laughed. "And what was in the bag?"

She gave me a ditsy smile. "What bag?"

"The grocery bag that you had last night."

"Some things are better off not known—"

"And this is one of those things." I said along with her. "You said that this morning," I replied to her questioning face.

"Did I? Well, I guess I'm starting to repeat myself in my old age."

Yeah, and I'm growing a third ear.

Chapter Five

Looking around the restaurant I saw designer ties and white dress shirts. This was the hot spot for the movers and shakers of the community. The cutlery probably cost more than I made in a month. Even dressed in my best silk suit, I felt out of place. Only those who spoke of mergers and stock market trends belonged here. I was thankful my dad would be picking up the tab, not only for lunch, but for my defense.

"Just to warn you, he's a little rough around the edges," my father said, as he glanced at his watch. "And not punctual, but that's the way it is with criminal lawyers, they're busy people. I want you to have the best, Sweetie."

"Thanks Dad," I said, as I ran my hand over the soft fabric napkin. "I bet you never thought you'd have to find me a defense attorney, did you?" I smiled, trying to make light of the situation.

My dad had removed his dark blue suit jacket and had rolled up the sleeves of his white shirt. The navy tie he wore was decorated with navy colored stars in a contrasting diagonal weave that had been a Christmas present from my mother. He rubbed his wrist over the spot where his watch usually sat, and then ran his hand through his thick curly hair. I did the same when nervous or tired. His mane was sandy blond and had just recently started to show some gray at the temples. His nose was straight and he had a half inch scar over his left eyebrow that came from a skateboarding accident in high school. He smiled easily when pleased, but he wasn't flashing his pearlies this afternoon.

He looked down at his iced tea and busied himself by using a long teaspoon to fish a lemon seed off the bottom of the glass.

"So Dad," I said, wondering if this was the best time to broach the subject of my grandmother. "How come you never told me about Nana?"

"What about her?" He emptied a packet of sugar into his tea.

"That she spent time in jail."

He stirred his drink at such a quick pace that a funnel of air appeared in the center of the glass. "That was a long time ago. No need to dig up the past." His eyes darted around, not meeting mine. Then he seemed to change his mind, and he focused on me. "Why? What else did you hear?"

"That she was an art counterfeiter."

"Well, there's not much more to tell than that."

He pressed his lips together, a sure sign he wanted to end the topic of conversation. His eyebrows creased into a V shape and he tapped his fingers on the table. I glanced at the time on my phone; our lunch guest was over fifteen minutes late.

"Oh, here he is," my dad said, standing up.

"Bob, how the hell are you?" Mr. Brunswick said as they shook hands. He pulled out a chair for himself and put down a half-finished drink.

"And you must be Michelle," he said, reaching out his hand to shake mine. "Lenny Brunswick."

"Patricia," I corrected him. I smiled, waiting for an acknowledgement and when none came, I murmured, "Nice to meet you."

Lenny Brunswick's black hair, at least what was left of it, was held down by heavy-duty hair gel. A layer of sweat made his large forehead reflect the overhead lights. Gold framed glasses sat on a flat ruddy nose. He was overweight and wore a perfectly tailored deep gray suit with a light gray tie. His gold cufflinks matched his tie clip, and the face of his gold watch was encircled with diamonds. He wore a pinky ring with a ruby stone. Everything about him sparkled like the inside of a casino and I had a sudden urge to hold onto my purse.

The waiter appeared and looked to me for my order. "What can I get for you today?"

"I'll have—"

"I'll take your Surf and Turf," Brunswick interrupted, "as rare as possible. And the lobster bisque."

"Yes, sir," the waiter said, lowering his eyes and gluing them to his notepad.

"I'll have the Caesar with chicken," I said.

"Crab salad," said my father.

I handed the waiter my menu, but not before noticing that our guest had ordered the most expensive item the restaurant offered.

"Oh, there's Manuel," Mr. Brunswick said, quickly standing and grabbing his drink, leaving us alone again.

I felt uneasy and I stared out the window. A black stretch limo pulled up and parked in front of the restaurant. The chauffeur, a stocky Asian man with thick-framed dark glasses, jogged around the vehicle to open up the rear door. The well-dressed passenger who emerged was one of the tallest men I'd ever seen. I estimated him to be close to seven feet, with a brow that jutted out from his forehead giving him a Neanderthal appearance.

The waiter distracted me for a moment as he placed a bowl of soup in front of Mr. Brunswick's empty chair. When I looked back up, the chauffeur leaned casually against the car, sharing a laugh with his passenger. I was struck by the unusual familiarity of their body language.

Mr. Brunswick noticed the arrival of his first course, and only then, did he once again grace us with his presence. He sat down with a grunt and picked up his spoon.

"The easiest way to handle this is to have Chang drop the charges," Lenny Brunswick said, in between slurps of his creamy soup. "It's not like you intended to keep the car." He looked up at me. "Did you?"

"No, of course I didn't," I responded, instantly irritated. "I left a note with Julie telling her I'd taken it."

"Well, I'm sure your note's in a garbage heap by now." He looked at my father as if he had grown weary of me already. I thought for a second he might roll his eyes.

"If Chang tells the police it was a misunderstanding, it won't matter what the evidence says," he continued.

I took a deep breath, resisting the urge to push his head into his bisque.

"Jimmy Chang's not a big fan of mine," I told him. Jimmy's vague threats danced around in my head. "I don't think he's willing to give on this."

"This woman should be able to verify your story."

I didn't like that he was referring to my dilemma as a *story*.

"I have her address."

I picked up my purse and started to dig. When I found Julie's information I glanced up at Mr. Brunswick who was looking at my father with a raised eyebrow.

"Sweetie, you're going to need to go talk to her yourself. Mr. Brunswick is doing this pro bono."

So my dad wasn't picking up the tab for my defense. That wasn't good. The waiter replaced Mr. Brunswick's soup bowl with a steak the size of my head. His lobster tail came on a separate plate. I hoped Dad was still paying for lunch.

"Okay," I said, putting down my purse. "How does this work?"

"You'll need to convince Julie to go down to the station and tell her side of the story," Mr. Brunswick said.

"Isn't that Officer Romano's job?" I asked.

"Officer Romano is a very busy man," Mr. Brunswick said in a condescending tone. "Besides the car was parked in front of your house." He stared at me over his glasses.

My mouth opened, but nothing came out. This guy didn't believe me. I scowled at my dad.

Mr. Brunswick looked beyond me and his hand shot a greeting up into the air. He waved someone over to our table. A shadow blocked out the afternoon sunlight, and I felt a cold presence next to me. I looked up, craning my neck to see.

"Mr. Finley," Mr. Brunswick said, reaching out to shake hands with the man. "Have you met Bob Schuster?" He pointed to my father. "Bob's in Estate Law." The man walked around the table.

It was the tall passenger from the limo. His hard angular facial features gave him a cruel demeanor that I found repellent. His enormous hand swallowed my father's as they shook.

"Roger Finley," the man said, nodding his head just once.

He glanced at my chest, and then up to my face. In a second his eyes delivered the message: Not interested.

I fought an overwhelming desire to bolt from the room.

My father gestured to me and started an introduction, but Finley interrupted him.

"Nice to see you again, Lenny." He slapped Mr. Brunswick on the back and walked off.

"Now, there's a hell of a business man," Mr. Brunswick said, looking around the room, apparently to see if anyone had noticed Finley at our table. "He owns the Finley Hotel and Convention Center." He shoveled a piece of steak into his mouth and kept talking. "Four star accommodations and that restaurant! Classy, very classy."

My dad nodded in agreement.

"And the convention center he opened is going to bring in a lot of revenue for the city." Brunswick's head turned and he followed the huge man with his eyes, probably making a mental note of who else he talked to. "He runs a tight ship over there at the Finley Hotel."

My father took a bite of his crab salad. He chewed slowly, gathering his thoughts to change the subject. I'd seen him do it a thousand times in conversations with my mother. But before he got a chance to swallow, Mr. Brunswick continued.

"He has access to all his employee's e-mail accounts." He raised his eyebrows three or four times to drive home this hidden gem of insight as to what makes a good business man.

"Plus he won't let the men on his staff wear facial hair." He took a gulp of his drink. "He owns tons of property: a beach house out in Bodega, a winery over in Napa. I've heard he's even a member of the Bohemian Club." Mr. Brunswick leaned over to my father. "You know he travels to the Orient quite often," he whispered. "I hear he's got a thing for the young Asian girls."

My father's face paled and he glanced at me with apologetic eyes. I picked up my ice tea, placed the glass against my cheek and took a deep breath. The coldness reassured me that the anchovies in the Caesar salad dressing hadn't mysteriously rendered me invisible.

"Where's that waiter? I could use a drink," my father said, looking around the room.

"And you know he's adding another wing to the Finley Hotel, thirty-six more rooms. Yep, he's one hell of a business man."

Taking a sip of tea, I weighed my options. I didn't have enough money to hire another lawyer. Letting a public defender represent me might work, but he or she probably wouldn't believe me anymore than this slime-ball did. I could represent myself and probably sit in a claustrophobic jail cell for four or five years. Or I could let this disgusting weasel do his job. I tried to look on the bright side. At least in jail I'd get caught up on my reading.

The afternoon sun exposed floating dust mites inside Elsie's Antiques, so I'd opened the front door hoping the fresh air would suck them outside. I took inventory while giving myself a crash course on antiques using Nana's reference books that

I'd found in her office.

Checking the condition of a pine highboy, I squatted down to pull out the bottom drawer and felt a sneeze coming on. Turning my head sideways I closed my eyes, but not before seeing legs wearing blue jeans and Italian loafers sans socks. Male, definitely male, I thought as I sneezed right on them. Damn! I am so bad at first impressions.

"Oh, I am really sorry," I stood up quickly and looked into a beautiful set of brown eyes. He was laughing. Whether he was laughing at me or with me I couldn't tell.

My height matched his and I stood a little closer than necessary. A whiff of soap and sweat acted like an ember landing on a pile of dried kindling, igniting my animal instincts. I wanted to close my eyes and savor his bouquet.

He wore a button-down white cotton shirt with the sleeves rolled up to the elbows, his hands stuffed casually into the pockets of his blue jeans. I guessed he was of Mediterranean decent: dark curly hair, dark eyes and a natural tan. His shoulders and biceps strained slightly against the fabric. I assumed he was one of the other shop owners, not an antiquer, since he seemed more interested in me than my armoires.

I repeated slowly, "I am really sorry."

"It's okay, no harm done. But if my loafers catch cold, they'll expect chicken soup." His smile never left his face. "I'm Jake Romano."

We shook hands and I didn't want to let his go, and for an extra second, I didn't. Fortunately, or unfortunately, depending on how you look at things, I was pretty sure he noticed.

"I'm Patricia."

"Welcome to the neighborhood," he said.

"Thanks. Do you work down here?"

"Yeah, I own the body shop on the corner." He pointed in the general direction, his eyes glued to mine. "Looks like you have your work cut out for you."

"Yeah, I'm working on inventory. My grandmother didn't keep very good records, so I'm pretty much starting from scratch. She did leave me some reference books." I gestured to the table where they sat. "I'm brushing up on my antiques." There was a slight pause in the conversation.

"I'm sorry about Elsie," he broke the silence. "I'm going to miss her."

"Thanks. Me too."

Another pause and I started to feel nervous.

"Do you know about the Merchants' Breakfast Meeting tomorrow?" he asked.

I nodded, "Yeah, I saw the flyer."

"Good," he smiled and nodded also.

We probably looked like bobble heads in the back of a car window.

"Well," he continued. "I'll let you get back to your work." He ran one hand through his hair and turned to make his way to the door. He looked as good from the back as he did from the front. "See you at breakfast."

There was something about him that seemed familiar. What was it?

"Okay," I said, and as an awkward pause hung in the air, I realized to my horror, I'd forgotten his name.

"Jake," he said turning back to me, "Jake Romano." He flashed that beautiful smile again and left.

Then it hit me. Son of a cop! I slouched down onto a

low-back Windsor chair. Damn it! I'd just fallen in lust with the son of a cop.

I spent the rest of the day cleaning Elsie's Antiques. Not only the basic dust and dirt but also some worthless items left in the store room. As I was dragging my garbage out to the alley I heard yelling. I walked past the back entrances of the jewelry store and Chris and Adam's Surf Shop. Crouching down next to the dumpster, I listened into the conversation.

"How was I supposed to know it was you who'd taken it?" The voice sounded like Jimmy's.

The office of Chang's Used Autos was housed inside a portable trailer which sat three or four feet off the ground, supported by metal cross-beams that created a temporary foundation. From my vantage point I could see Jimmy Chang's navy blue slacks standing close to a woman's straight-legged jeans that covered pink leather cowboy boots. A guy with spiky black hair sat in a black sedan with the passenger window down watching the two.

"Whatever, Jimmy, but you still have to tell the police it was a mix-up." It was Julie speaking. "Patricia doesn't deserve this."

Jimmy grunted. The silence dragged on and imaginary cell walls started creeping toward me.

"So did you sell it?" Julie asked.

"No, after you took it the buyer backed out. Surprise, surprise."

"So it's still for sale?"

"Of course it's still for sale."

"How much did my dad owe you?"

Jimmy did not reply.

"How much, Jimmy?"

"Ten grand."

"I'll give you fifteen."

"It's worth ten times that, or more."

"Right, Jimmy," Julie said sarcastically. "Okay, I'll give you twenty."

He made a huffing sound.

"My dad's dead, Jimmy. It's the only thing I have of his. Can't we work something out?" Her voice turned pleading and I winced. I hoped she wasn't offering what I thought she was offering.

"Hmm," he purred. "Maybe."

I saw his feet take a step forward, and suddenly I felt the need to take another shower.

"I want it tonight." He told her. "Call me when you have it. I'll come over and pick it up."

The guy in the sedan stepped out of his car, pulled on his tie and unbuttoned the top of his dress shirt. "Come on Julie, let's go."

I arrived home that night feeling defeated. I reached out to put my key in the lock, but the door was ajar. I froze. Do I push it open and look? Or call the police? I smelled garlic. If a burglary had taken place, I doubted the thief would have left me a lasagna. I pushed open the door and heard a female voice singing in the kitchen. The same voice I'd heard that morning coming from the apartment next door. Now I smelled butter and basil too.

"Patricia, is that you?" Mrs. Russo called out.

"Yes, Mrs. R."

"Good, I didn't want to frighten you. I made you some dinner."

My kitchen was a mess, pots and pans everywhere.

"Are you hungry?" she asked.

"Very," I replied.

"Come, sit."

I slid into a chair. Steam rose from a basket of garlic bread. In front of me, Mrs. Russo plopped a mound of spaghetti that would last a week. I dug in greedily. She joined me. We didn't say anything for three or four minutes.

Finally Mrs. Russo said: "I heard you met with Lenny Brunswick."

"How did you know?"

She shrugged noncommittally.

"Jimmy Chang's not dropping the charges," I said.

"Jimmy Chang," she spit the words out, "he's nothing but a two-bit thug."

"Yes. Exactly. But since he couldn't get the Cadillac started this morning he wants me to pay for his impound fees."

She stared at me, "Damn, we should have seen that coming."

"I took Mrs. B over to the impound lot today and she flipped the kill switch." I leaned forward and lowered my voice. "So, what else did you do?"

"It's not important." Mrs. Russo gave me a hint of a smile.

I sighed. I had more pressing things to think about than The Ladies tampering with Chang's car. "I can't stomach this Brunswick guy."

"I'm not surprised."

"You know him?"

"Enough to know you've got to be in pretty deep to tolerate him."

"Do you know anyone good?" After it came out of my mouth I wanted to take it back. "I'm sorry, I didn't mean to imply that…"

She waved my apology away. "Actually, I do." She passed me another piece of garlic bread.

"Brunswick says I need to talk to Julie, so she can corroborate my story." I used air quotes around the word *story*. I had no idea if Julie would confess to the police she'd stole Jimmy's car, but at this point it seemed to be my only hope of easily getting out of the theft charges.

"I'm sure Julie's a reasonable person. I'll go with you. In fact, let's go tonight."

I shook my head, "You've done enough." I meant that on many levels.

"No, really, let me. I can be very persuasive."

I swallowed hard. "Yes, I can imagine."

Mrs. R insisted on washing all the pots and pans before we left, so it was close to 9:30 by the time we arrived at Julie's apartment building. I parked my car at the curb and pointed out Julie's second-story bedroom window. We walked into a dark courtyard.

"I can barely see," I said, using only the slivers of light that came from the occupant's windows to find my way to the stairs. "Why aren't the lights on?"

When my eyes adjusted I could make out that the area was concrete, the monotony broken only by a few lounge chairs and yucca trees growing out of raised brick planters. A wrought iron fence, with an open gate, surrounded a swimming pool. A dark raft floated on the water's surface. Rock music filled the space and bounced off the walls.

A circle of light appeared at my feet. I glanced over my shoulder to see Mrs. R holding a flashlight. We were halfway up the stairs when her light shot around the enclosure. She grabbed my arm from behind and squeezed tight, stopping me from moving forward.

"We've got to get out of here," she said and pulled me down one step.

"Ow, you're hurting me." I said.

"Shhh!"

"What are you shushing me for? I don't think anyone will hear us over that music," I replied.

"Come on."

"Why?" I asked.

"I don't think Julie's going to be much help to you."

"Why not?"

"Did Julie own a pair of pink cowboy boots?" she asked.

"Yeah, how did you know?"

Mrs. R slapped her hand over my mouth.

"Don't scream," she said. "That's her."

Using her other hand she shot the flashlight at the pool. What first registered as a floating raft morphed into a floating body. Julie lay face down in the water, her brunette hair haloed around her head. My stomach lurched and I felt nauseous. Mrs. R slowly removed her hand from my face.

"Oh God, that is her," I whispered.

"Let's go!" Mrs. R said, again pulling me down the stairs.

"Shouldn't we get her out? See if she's still alive?"

"Believe me, she's not."

"How do you know?"

At the bottom of the stairs she stopped.

"Okay, but go start the car. I'll be there in a minute."

I ran to the car, turned on the ignition and automatically locked the doors. I turned on the heat and rubbed my hands together in front of the vent until the warm air finally came. Mrs. Russo knocked sharply on the window, startling me. I unlocked the door.

"Well?" I asked and handed her a towel from my beach tote. She shook her head. "Let's go."

Glancing in my rear view mirror, I saw a teenager on a mountain bike under a light pole watching us. Damn, we should have covered the plates first.

Chapter Six

Once again I drove on autopilot while Mrs. Russo gave me detailed instructions. I pulled into the driveway of Mrs. Miller's dark house.

Mrs. R pulled a clicker from her purse and the garage door rolled up. I drove in slowly. Mrs. R used the remote again and the door rattled down behind us. I stepped out of the car and stood, unable to move. The second half of the two-car garage was walled off, save for a doorway. Through the opening I could see rows of delicate plants bathed in a florescent green glow. Mrs. Miller and Mrs. Taylor had a pot farm in their garage.

Mrs. R took me by the hand and led me up a few steps into the house. She pulled me through a laundry room and into a large family room. The house smelled of marijuana and garlic. Mrs. M and Mrs. T sat on an overstuffed suede couch watching a huge flat screen TV.

Mrs. M sat up quickly, her eyes wide as she switched off the television. A bag of potato chips sat on her lap.

"What happened?" she asked, her mouth full.

"Julie Gordon's dead," Mrs. R replied. She led me to the

couch, and Mrs. M moved over to make room. "Give Patricia a drink, will you? She's had quite a shock."

Mrs. Taylor bustled to the counter where two porcelain cups waited with a matching tea pot. I nodded. Yes, that's what I needed, some nice calming herbal tea. She poured me some and I took a sip. It was tea and rum, or should I say rum with a little tea in it. I started to cough, my eyes watering.

"Sorry," she said, "I forgot."

I slouched backwards onto the couch, feeling exhausted.

"You know how it is," Mrs. R said, letting out a sigh. "The first murder is always the hardest."

"The first?" I sat back up. "There'll be more?"

"Oh, I remember my first murder," Mrs. Miller said, smiling broadly.

"Rita, not now," Mrs. R interrupted her, giving her a stern look.

I felt warm as the rum found its way to my extremities. Maybe it would find its way to my brain and blot out the image of Julie floating in the pool.

"Mrs. M, you grow pot?" I asked, trying to find a less gruesome subject.

"Purely for medicinal purposes. I have customers up and down the coast. Glaucoma, cancer, AIDs. I provide a valuable service," she stated proudly.

I looked at a blue glass bong on the table. She followed my glance.

"Well, I have to test the product."

I nodded as if this all made perfect sense. Mrs. R went into the kitchen. I could hear her talking on the phone.

"Where were you tonight?" she asked. After a brief pause

she continued in Italian.

Mrs. Miller offered me the bag of chips, and I took one, wondering if I was getting a contact high.

Mrs. R came back into the room. "You know this ratchets things up," she spoke to the other ladies, not me. "There's no way Jimmy Chang is getting away with this."

"You think Jimmy killed Julie?" I asked, horrified by the thought.

She nodded, "I'd bet on it."

Despite the rum-laced tea, I suddenly felt cold.

Before I was fully awake, I smelled coffee. What a wonderful, comforting aroma. I opened one eye and looked at a low table with an open bag of chips, the bong and a small bottle of rum. All I needed now to completely resurrect my college days would be for an unknown guy to try and kiss me with stale beer breath.

I sat up and shuffled into Mrs. M's kitchen.

"Good morning, *mi hija!*" she sang. Over her clothes she wore a black apron decorated with red chilies and a yellow daisy tucked behind her ear.

"Hmm," I said.

"Here's some coffee. You can use the bath down the hall."

I grabbed the mug and kept shuffling. After showering and dressing I noticed the numb feeling of Julie's death receding and anger taking its place. A woman dying at such a young age just shouldn't happen. The conversation I'd overheard between Julie and Jimmy tape-looped through my brain. Chang had paid a visit to Julie the previous evening. He held a theft charge over me and may be a killer. The base of my neck started to ache with anxiety and a sense of foreboding. I took some deep breathes before heading out to the kitchen to have breakfast with Mrs. M.

"Mrs. T still asleep?" I asked, putting scrambled eggs on my plate.

"She didn't come to bed till about one. She loves to stay up and watch old movies, but she'll be up soon."

"Could you tell me about my grandmother?" I asked, wanting to talk about anything but Julie's death. "I'm having a hard time imagining her as a counterfeiter."

"Well, she was really an artist at heart, printing money was just for kicks. She called it her green period. Unfortunately, that's when she got caught. But she specialized in counterfeit artwork. You know, reproducing artwork and passing it off as the real deal." Mrs. Miller's eyes narrowed. "You ever try that?" she asked. "Reproduce artwork?"

Looking down at my plate I shrugged. "All art students do that, copying the masters is a great way to learn."

"You any good at it?"

I nodded. "Yeah, you could say that."

She looked pleased. In fact, I felt a little uncomfortable with how pleased she looked.

"So how did art counterfeiting work?" I asked, drizzling honey over a piece of sourdough toast.

"Elsie would research artists in Europe that had their artwork stolen or had gone missing. Picasso was one of the easiest to copy. She'd paint a replica and we'd take it down to South America. Selling them to government officials was easy. They never knew the difference. Sometimes we'd say that it was found in someone's attic, or we'd allude to knowing a thief and let them draw their own conclusions. Rudy, your grand-father, acted as our art dealer."

"So that little Monet in my living room may not be real?" I meant it as a joke.

"Oh, I think it's real all right."

I sucked in air, glad there wasn't food in my mouth.

She continued: "Your grandmother traveled to Europe and she frequently posed for Picasso. I believe he gave the Monet to her as a thank you gift."

I tried to take this all in. Nana traveling the world, selling fake art, posing for Picasso; it was a bit much. Plus I might have a real Monet hanging in my house.

"How did she have time to raise my mom?" I wrapped my hands around my coffee mug and took a sip.

"Mrs. Taylor helped. She took care of your mother when we traveled, or when Elsie was in jail."

"How long was she in for?"

"A little over two years. That was a hard time for your mom. She must have been around eight when Elsie went in, and by then your grandfather had already passed on."

"I wonder why my mom never told me."

"She probably wanted to protect your relationship with your grandmother."

Mrs. R joined us, wearing a casual black suit over a lavender silk blouse. Today's over-the-top adornments were rectangular amethysts earrings and matching necklace. She poured herself some coffee and handed me a slip of paper.

"Maria Sanchez? Who's that?" I asked after reading it. The paper also said: Thursday @ 9, plus an address at the Lakeville Marina Business Center.

"Hopefully, your new lawyer," Mrs. R said, sitting down and helping herself to breakfast. "I made an appointment for you. I told her about your situation and Julie's death. Don't be late; she's squeezing you in."

"But I can't pay for this," I said. Except I might have a real Monet hanging in my house; if I sold it, I could pay for a high-priced lawyer. I wondered how my grandmother would feel about that.

"Don't worry, everything's arranged," she said, stirring sugar into her coffee.

"But Mrs. Russo, I already owe you for my bail."

"Patricia, your grandmother did me a big favor. This is my way to repay it."

Before I could ask: What favor? Mrs. R continued.

"But we might need more funds," she said.

Mrs. M smiled eagerly. "Have something in mind?"

Mrs. Russo looked at me. "Well, Elsie's Antiques is right next to Yvonne's Jewelers. There used to be a door connecting the two stores."

I started to choke and put my hands up without being told to.

"Gosh, I wish I could get through a meal without doing that," I said, acting like it was the food, and not the conversation that caused it.

"Kinda messy though, isn't it? Going through sheetrock?" Mrs. M responded.

I looked back and forth between the two. "You're not going through my wall," I said.

Mrs. R went on talking as if she hadn't heard. "We'll probably only need twenty-five grand. I can call up Louie. He usually knows someone who's in the market for diamonds."

"You are not going through my wall!" I repeated firmly, hoping they'd get the message.

"But, bail's going to be set a bit higher for murder, if we can get it at all."

"Murder?" I asked.

"Who's the first person that the police are going to think of?"

"Who?" I asked, my voice a whisper.

"You, dear," Mrs. R replied softly.

"But why would I kill Julie? She was an old friend. Plus she could explain what happened with Jimmy's car." I broke into a sweat. The idea of being charged with another crime petrified me.

"You know that," Mrs. R continued, "but no one else does. For all Officer Romano knows, Julie Gordon may not have corroborated your story at all. She may have said otherwise, and that's why you hit her on the head and pushed her in the pool."

"Hit her on the head? Pushed her in the pool? Where did you get that idea?"

"I don't have that idea, Patricia," Mrs. R said. "But the police will look for the obvious."

"But Jimmy's the obvious one. I heard him fighting with Julie."

"What? When? What did they say?" Mrs. R asked, looking angrier by the second.

"Yesterday. Julie tried to buy back the Cadillac."

Mrs. R gripped her coffee mug so hard her knuckles turned white. "Tell me everything you heard."

"Julie's dad owed Jimmy ten grand, but Jimmy wouldn't take ten, so Julie offered him fifteen."

"What else?"

"Jimmy said it was worth ten times that. Then Julie offered herself as part of the deal, and Jimmy settled for twenty."

Mrs. M's lip curled up in disgust.

"Damn it!" Mrs. R swore.

"He was going to her apartment last night."

We sat in silence for a moment, digesting information as well as breakfast.

"I wonder where he came up with seed money to loan?" Mrs. Miller asked.

"He must have gone into business with someone new," Mrs. R said.

"Someone new?" I asked. "Then who was the someone old he was in business with?" I looked from one to the other. "Oh no. Not Nana?" I could see it on their faces. I slumped in my chair. So Jimmy Chang had been in business with my grandmother. "Tell me. I need to know. What was she doing?"

"He wanted her to paint reproductions, and he'd find the buyers. Like the old days, but she refused," Mrs. R said quietly. "But Jimmy did give your grandmother items to sell for him. Jewelry, watches, trinkets."

"But Elsie's Antiques is a legitimate business. I looked through her books, she bought stuff, she sold stuff, that's the way it works."

"It matters where the stuff comes from, dear."

"You know this is ancient history," Mrs. M piped in, waving her hand in the air, as if trying to shoo away the memory. "Water under the bridge."

"Well," I said, "the water's still flowing, if Jimmy expects me to pick up where she left off. He's going to hold that car theft charge over my head to do who-knows-what."

The two ladies again exchanged glances, and for a second I thought they almost looked pleased.

"For the time being, you may have to do what he says," Mrs. Miller said. "We have to find out what he's up to."

I looked at her, my eyes wide.

"Within reason," she clarified.

I hung my head. Ish.

I'd forgotten all about the Merchants' Association meeting until I pulled out of Mrs. M's pot garage. Hurrying home I changed into a straight black skirt and a casual blue jean jacket. I didn't want to look as bad as I felt.

The gathering took place in the party room at Tony's Pizzeria. The meeting was already underway when I arrived. Four big screen TVs hung in the corners above fake walnut paneled wainscoting. The space was probably used for kid's soccer tournament celebrations and Super Bowl Sundays. It smelled of pepperoni and beer.

I found Jake in the crowd immediately. We made eye contact and exchanged smiles. Grabbing a cup of coffee, I examined the picked-over pastries that were being passed off as breakfast, glad that I'd already stuffed myself.

Looking around the room, I didn't see Chris or Adam, they were probably out surfing. The tables were laid out picnic-bench style and I saw an empty spot directly in front of Jake. I sidled my way over giving him another smile as I sat down. Suddenly, I became acutely aware of the back of my head and

I ran my hand over my hair, hoping it wasn't sticking up in funny directions.

Turning to give my neighbor a smile, I realized too late that I had sat down next to the Yarn Barn lady, who withered my silent greeting with the 'You're Late' glare. This morning her knitting needles were sea foam green and appeared even more lethal close up. Then I heard someone call my name. Surprised, I looked up. Jimmy Chang stood in front of the room gesturing for me to rise. It never occurred to me that Jimmy would be at this meeting or that I'd be asked to speak. He introduced me as the new owner of Elsie's Antiques.

I reluctantly stood, gave the crowd my best parade wave, and settled back into my seat. Jimmy motioned me up again.

"So Patricia, what are your plans for Elsie's Antiques?" he called out across the packed room, a grin plastered on his face.

I was completely unprepared for this, and I could feel my face turning pink.

"Well, I'm probably not going to change much," I said, my voice trailing off.

Jimmy didn't pick up the ball and I could see his grin turning wicked as he relished my embarrassment. I looked down and ran my finger around the edge of my coffee cup, trying desperately to think of something to fill the awkward silence.

I heard a whisper behind me: "Tell them you're taking inventory."

"I'm not quite done with inventory yet," I said to the group.

At the word *inventory*, eyes glazed over, scowls appeared and heads turned away. Apparently inventory was a painful subject. This time Jimmy did pick up the ball.

"Okay, next item on the agenda," he said.

And just like that, I was off center stage. I sat down quickly and spun around. There were those big luscious brown eyes staring into mine. I mouthed the words 'thank you' and was rewarded with a smile.

My heart rate returned to normal along with my breathing. Jimmy rattled on about vandalism and an automobile being stolen from the parking garage, and how we should all be careful. But I didn't want to listen to him, or even look at him for that matter. All I could think of was Jake's sweet face.

Jimmy introduced the Yarn Barn Lady to the group, and after we endured a fifteen-minute talk on the do's and don'ts of the upcoming sidewalk sale, the meeting finally broke up. I turned to Jake again.

"Thanks for throwing me a life line. I wasn't prepared to talk."

He smiled.

"I didn't realize the word *inventory* would have that kind of effect," I continued.

Jake laughed. "Yeah, it's pretty much a forbidden subject around here."

"Why is Jimmy running the meeting?"

"He's president of the Merchants Association."

My mouth must have been hanging open because Jake was staring at it.

"You look surprised."

"He doesn't strike me as the civic-minded type." And after considering Mrs. R's accusation of Jimmy committing murder, that was quite an understatement.

Jake shrugged. "I don't know him that well."

Glad to hear it, I thought.

He glanced at his watch. "I've got to get back to work. But I'm having a barbeque after the sale on Saturday. Would you like to come?"

"Sure." I smiled.

"Here, I'll give you the details." He scribbled some words on a napkin, gave it to me and then waved goodbye.

I held onto the paper tightly. It felt good to have something to look forward to. I refilled my coffee cup and was contemplating a buttermilk donut, when I noticed the Yarn Barn lady setting her sights on me. Leaving the pastry table behind, I made a beeline for the door. I couldn't bear to hear another lecture about what supposed infractions I had committed against the Merchants' Association. Luckily, I was quicker on my feet, and made it out the door before she could. I let out a breath and headed to Elsie's Antiques. But I'd relaxed too soon; Jimmy Chang was suddenly walking beside me.

"Got a thing for the police officer's kid, huh? Think you're going to screw your way out of the auto theft charges?" He gave a snort. "Oh, it's going to take a lot more than that." He picked up his pace and left me staring at the back of his head. I felt like I had just been splattered with used motor oil. Shaken by his threat, I thought again about Julie in the pool. Was Jimmy capable of such violence?

By the time I got to Elsie's Antiques I'd decided to search through all my grandmother's files. I wasn't sure what her bookkeeping could tell me, but I felt I was missing something. There were too many secrets, too much I didn't know.

After an hour all I'd found were the typical bills of sale from venders she bought from and customers she sold to. I also discovered an overdue tax bill, which I put in my to-do pile. But there weren't any obvious links between Nana and Jimmy Chang. I wished my grandmother was around to point a finger and say 'Look over here. This is what you're after.'

I didn't like the idea of waiting around for Jimmy to come up with some sordid task for me. I shivered, hoping those teeny-tiny jail cells didn't have fluffy towels.

The smell of grilled steaks and fresh cucumber met me at the door of my parent's home. They lived in an old Craftsman style house, with hardwood floors and crown molding. The kitchen had been expanded and remodeled with modern maple cabinets and black-speckled granite countertops. My mother stood at the island using a long wooden spoon and fork, tossing a dinner salad with extreme exuberance. Every once in a while a stray vegetable took flight. She enjoyed cooking, and she rarely let me assist, but I always asked.

"Do you need any help?"

"You could pour us some wine," she replied.

The glasses stood ready and as I uncorked the bottle I thought about my jailbird grandmother. I vacillated between curiosity as to Nana's life and irritation that my mother had kept family secrets from me. I also wanted to discuss Julie's death, even though I was unsure how much to tell her. The news hadn't been reported yet, so how would I explain what I knew? But she leveled a bomb shell on me before I had a chance to mention either.

"I have something to tell you," she said, her green eyes unfocused. "Your father and I are getting a divorce."

I had just taken a sip of chardonnay and started to choke.

"Hands up dear, open pathways are breathable pathways," my mother said, putting down the salad bowl and rubbing between my shoulder blades.

"Why?" It was the only thing that would squeak out of my mouth.

"He says he's having a midlife crisis. I guess I am too, since I'm not too upset about the whole thing."

I stared at her with my mouth open. She had resumed her tossing and lobbed a slice of red bell pepper onto the floor.

"So that's it?" I asked. "No shot at counseling? No trying to work it through?" I couldn't believe what I was hearing. "Mom, how many years have you been married?"

"Twenty-seven." She slammed the wooden fork down on the counter top.

"Twenty-seven years," I dragged out the words.

"It's quality dear, not quantity that's important. You don't go on living with someone because you were with him the day before. That's not a reason. That's an excuse." She popped a carrot slice in her mouth. "More wine?"

"No thanks." I had drained my glass without even realizing it. "I can't believe he didn't say anything to me. I just saw him yesterday."

"Well, that's your dad. He's not one for confrontation."

"Where is he?" I asked, suddenly uneasy.

"I don't know. I'm not sure what he's doing." She picked up the salad bowl and held it in the crook of her arm. Holding the spoon in her other hand, she started stirring the lettuce vigorously as if it were cake batter.

"So, he's still living here?"

"He's in the process of moving out. He took the answering

machine." She used the spoon to point at an empty spot at the end of the counter. "He wanted to move in with his new girlfriend, but he says he doesn't want to rush it. So he found an apartment." A mushroom slice flew through the air and landed on my arm.

"Girlfriend?" I asked, picking off the wayward vegetable.

"You know your father's a very attractive man. He had no problems finding someone new."

"How long has he had this girlfriend?"

"Oh, a few days."

"And when did you two decide to break up?"

"About a week ago."

There it was—the starting bell. My mother was out in the ring with her boxing gloves on, fighting off the truth of my father's infidelity. I feared that when reality landed a punch, she'd go down hard.

"And you'll be staying here?" I asked.

"Yep. Could you put this on the table?" She handed me the salad bowl. The lettuce leaves had turned to mush.

Chapter Seven

The Marina Business Park overlooked the serene Lakeville River. Small yachts, sailboats and kayakers dotted the dark blue turning basin that flowed south emptying into San Francisco Bay. Maria Sanchez's corner office was filled with morning light and sparse modern furniture. My new lawyer flipped her long dark hair over her shoulder and spoke with a confidence I found reassuring.

"Ms. Schuster, have you ever been arrested before? DUI? Drug possession?"

"No."

"Anything before the age of eighteen?"

"No."

"Pretty boring life, huh?" She smiled easily.

"Yeah, up until now."

"Tell me about the night you drove the car."

"Well, it was late and I was craving ice cream. So I walked down to the store on the corner."

She took notes on her computer as I spoke.

"I got my ice cream and was walking back to the counter when I saw Julie Gordon stumble in the front door. She came up to me and wrapped her arm around my shoulder. It was pretty obvious she was drunk."

Ms. Sanchez nodded and continued typing.

"She stumbled to the register, almost knocking over a candy rack. I asked her if she was driving, and she said, 'Yeah. Want a ride?' So, I suggested that I give her a ride. I drove her home in the Cadillac and helped her up to her apartment. She immediately fell asleep. I took the car home because I didn't have enough cash to call a cab. I left her a note with my phone number so she could call me, and we could make arrangements for her to get the car back."

"Did she talk about the car on the way to her place?"

"No, she sang most of the way."

She glanced at an open file folder.

"And Jimmy Chang reported the car stolen."

"Right. But the next day Julie told me that the car was her dad's, and she started driving after he died. She thought it should be hers. Later I overheard Jimmy and Julie talking."

"Really? When?"

"The day she died."

"Oh?"

I recounted the conversation; ending with Julie telling Jimmy she'd give him twenty grand and implying that she'd sleep him.

Ms. Sanchez wrinkled her nose, like she'd smelled some-thing rotting.

"So, some time back Jimmy loans Julie's dad some money. And after he dies, Jimmy takes the car back as payment. He should have asked Julie to make payments or pay off the loan before he repossessed it." Ms. Sanchez leaned back in her chair.

"And I assume that there wasn't a contract to prove how much her dad owed Chang," she said.

"Not that they talked about."

"What kind of car is it?"

"A '59 Cadillac. Convertible. Big fins. I can't remember the name."

"How long have you known Jimmy Chang?"

"Since I was a kid."

"How about Julie?"

"Same thing; we all grew up together."

"Do you think Jimmy Chang has something against you?"

It'd crossed my mind that Nana owed him something and he was taking it out on me, but until Jimmy made his intentions clear, there was no way to be sure. "Not that I know of."

She jotted down another note.

"Mrs. Russo told me about you finding Julie in the pool. What time was that?"

"Just before ten o'clock. We wanted to convince Julie to go to the police, and tell them the truth about the car. But when we got there she was face down in the pool. Mrs. Russo checked to make sure she was gone." I paused, realizing that the image of Julie floating in the pool would be with me forever. "Then we left. I didn't want the police to know I was there."

"Why not?"

"Because they didn't believe me about the car." I put my hands out, palms up, as if showing her all my cards. "What if they thought I killed Julie to keep her quiet?"

Ms. Sanchez tapped her red polished nails on the desk.

"What do you think happened to her?"

"Maybe Jimmy Chang did it."

"Possibly he went to her house and she didn't have the money, or changed her mind about sleeping with him?"

I nodded. "But then again, I don't have a very high opinion of him."

"Why's that?"

"He came into my store and implied that if I did stuff for him he'd drop the charges."

"Sexual stuff?"

"He didn't say. But he did want me to pay for his impound fees."

"Sounds like a peach."

I smiled. I liked her sarcasm.

"Hey, you can't park there," Jimmy yelled, running toward me.

"Well, duh, Jimmy," I muttered to myself.

A car carrier blocked the entrance to the alley. As I looked at the back side of it, I had a sudden urge to drive up its ramp, mostly because it would irritate Jimmy. Unfortunately, an older model two-door compact was backing up, blocking my impulse.

Mrs. Butterfield stood on the sidewalk waving. I returned the greeting before putting my car in reverse and backing out onto the street. The downtown parking garage was a block away so I drove there and hoofed it back to the car lot.

A string of triangular red and blue plastic flags flapped above my head. Chang's Used Autos represented the extremes in previously owned vehicles. Edging the lot, next to the street sat three Mercedes, an Audi and a few cars I didn't recognize. A Vega and Pinto were backed up against the brick wall, each with a price tag of $888. A couple of motorcycles, cocked sideways with attitude, filled in the space up to Jimmy's office.

I walked past Jimmy as he stood next to a short, husky fellow, who I recognized as Roger Finley's chauffeur; he was wearing the same thick-framed glasses.

"Kwan, I can't find the invoice to the Vega," Jimmy said, gnawing on a toothpick as he flipped through a stack of papers.

"It's there; keep looking," Kwan replied.

Mrs. B had the trunk open on a VW Bug. It was painted like a cow with a white background and asymmetrical black spots. I joined her to examine the engine compartment. She gazed up at me, her eyes dancing.

"Look what Jimmy found for me," she said. "Ain't she a beauty?"

"It's very nice," I replied, walking around the car.

On the front end, a copper cowbell tied with twine hung from the bumper and painted-on eyelashes circled the headlights. I walked around to the open driver's side door.

"Hey, give the horn a toot," Mrs. B said.

I leaned in and pressed the center of the steering wheel, it sang a plaintive 'moo.'

"Ain't that a hoot?" She slapped her hands on her thighs, giggling with pleasure.

"Yeah, the toot's a hoot." I laughed, joining in her fun.

She slammed down the rear hood and a braided white yarn tail tied with a pink ribbon bounced on the back end, partially covering the car's paper plates.

"How do you like my new set of wheels?" Jimmy called out. I turned to see him swaggering our direction with his chest sticking out. He hoisted up his pants and pointed behind him with his thumb. An older sedan sat next to the car carrier. The trunk of the car looked like it had been cut off at an angle with a cheese slicer.

"What is that?" I asked. "A Cadillac?"

"That's a 1979 Seville," Mrs. B explained. "They belch a horrible smoke—"

"No," Jimmy said, looking irritated. "I mean yes. That's a Seville." He pointed again. "But I'm talking about the car carrier." His toothpick shifted from one side of his mouth to the other. "I'm going international."

I gave him a fake smile and nodded. "Are you shipping cars to Mexico?"

He tipped his head back and gave a hearty laugh. "Oh, Patricia, you don't know anything, do you?" He walked away snickering.

Kwan opened up the driver's side door of the car carrier and hoisted himself into the cab.

"Any idea what those cost?" I asked Mrs. Butterfield.

"A lot," Mrs. B replied. "They can run as high as $200,000 brand new. But for a used one like that I'd say thirty or forty thousand."

The engine came to life and he drove forward down the alley.

"Do you know that guy?" I asked Mrs. B.

"Not by name, but from what I gather he and Jimmy are partners." She slid in behind the wheel of her new bovine-mobile. "Want to go for a spin?"

"No, thanks. I'd better get the store open. The Yarn Barn lady's been watching me."

Mrs. B looked puzzled as I waved goodbye.

* * *

After work I went by my father's office to tell him I was using another lawyer. His secretary greeted me warmly.

"Patricia," Natalie said, "so nice to see you."

"You too. Is dad busy?"

"He just got off the phone; I'll let him know you're here." She buzzed him and after a moment, he opened the door.

"Hi Sweetheart, come on in."

My father enjoyed redecorating. A few months ago his office was ultra-modern; today it was 1960s retro. What possessed him to do this, I'll never know. My theory was that he liked taking time off to golf, while painters and decorators occupied his work space. A large area rug in geometric patterns of brown, burnt orange and beige decorated the floor. A sun burst clock hung on an oak-paneled wall. He came out from behind his large walnut desk and sat with me on a crinkly chocolate brown vinyl couch.

"So what brings you here?"

"I wanted to let you know that I'm going with a different lawyer."

He nodded. "I thought you might. Lenny's a bit rough around the edges. So do you have someone else in mind?"

"Maria Sanchez."

He nodded again, "She's gotten a few guilties off. You'll probably be fine."

As I sat there staring at my Dad, I realized the only person who believed in my innocence was Jimmy Chang. I took a deep breath, trying to keep my anger in check.

"I had dinner over at Mom's last night," I said.

He looked down. "So, she told you about the divorce."

"Yeah," I replied. There didn't seem much else to say. "So how do you like your new place?" I asked, feeling a shift in our relationship.

"It's okay," he shrugged his shoulders. "It's on the small side, but it's just temporary. You know, until things smooth out."

The phone beeped and he jumped up to answer it.

"Okay, thanks," he said into the receiver.

"Sorry, I have to take this call."

I stood up to leave.

"You know, I'd love you to meet Cassandra," he continued.

"Cassandra?"

He paused, smiling uneasily. "My new friend."

The anger came back, and I was glad the conversation was over. But, it was his life and not my place to judge. I decided to take the high road.

"Okay," I said, forcing a smile.

"Would you like to come to dinner with us on Sunday? We'll be at the Finley around six. She has to eat early. She works in the evenings."

"Oh, what does she do?"

"Some kind of home parties." He took me by the elbow, steering me to the door. "You know, woman stuff."

"I can't wait to meet her," I lied. "I'll see you at six."

Chapter Eight

My grandmother's newspaper subscription service continued to drop a paper on my front doorstep every morning. Over cold cereal I read this small article in the Empire section.

> LAKEVILLE – An accidental drowning took the life of a young woman Tuesday night at the Arroyo Apartments. Julie Ann Gordon died after slipping, bumping her head and falling into the swimming pool.

This made me wonder why Mrs. Russo was so sure Julie's death was murder. Could Jimmy Chang really have killed Julie and made it look like an accident? I thought about him bobbing his arrogant toothpick in my face. But arrogance by itself didn't drive people to kill. I needed to find out what Mrs. R knew.

I called ahead and asked Mrs. Russo for her apartment number. Freshly clipped grass lined a concrete walkway that curved through the complex. At the third unit, two miniature roses planted in cobalt blue pots flanked the entry. I knocked, and she opened the door holding a large mug of coffee.

"Good morning, Patricia."

Dressed for the day, she wore a steel gray pant suit, which complimented her gray bob perfectly. A gold serpentine necklace accented her outfit. Before letting me in, she looked to the left and right, as if checking for spies. I followed her into the kitchen.

"Did you see the paper?" I put it on the table. "They're saying that Julie's death was an accident."

She waved a dismissal.

"Why do you think it was murder?" I asked.

She poured me a cup of coffee, topped hers off and sat down. Picking up a piece of junk mail, she flipped it over and grabbed the pen she'd been using on a crossword puzzle. She drew a rectangle indicating the shape of the pool.

"Because the odds of someone walking around a pool, slipping, and falling in," she explained, while using the pen to make a circle in the air above the sketch, "so their head hits at exactly the right angle to cause death is very low." She put a line across a corner of the rectangle, indicating how a body would have to fall.

"Okay, so do you have a theory?"

"Well, if she didn't have an injury to her head—"

"How do you know she did?"

"Because the papers say she hit her head. They're making that assumption based on some kind of wound."

I nodded. That made sense.

She continued, "So, if she didn't have a bump, we could assume it was an accident. She'd been drinking, she stumbled, fell into the pool and drowned. But because she did have a bump, it definitely wasn't an accident."

I folded my arms in front of me. "But it still could have happened."

"Our debating the fact isn't going to matter. In a case like this, the coroner will do a complete autopsy, and then we'll know for sure."

I cringed at the thought. "How will they know? If they find water in her lungs?"

"Well, water would be in her lungs even if she was dead before she went into the pool. But there are chemical changes that happen in the body when death occurs from drowning. They'll know."

I walked back to my house and saw the Caddy parked at the curb. When I got to the porch, I could hear cartoons playing on my TV. I turned the knob and the noise stopped. Pushing the door open I found Jimmy Chang leaning back on my couch, clenching a toothpick between his teeth and holding a shoebox on his lap. His feet were on my coffee table. He wore one beige sock and one brown.

"Jimmy," I said flatly, as I stood in the doorway.

"Patricia. Come. Sit." He patted the cushion next to him.

"I prefer to stand."

"Suit yourself; it's your house." He smiled. "I was hoping you could do me a little favor."

"Is this the favor that's going to get me out of the theft charges?"

"Depends on how good you do."

My first instinct was to turn and run, but I held my ground.

"Shoot," I said.

"I want you to sell these."

He opened up the shoebox and I could see a jumble of pearl jewelry in a variety of colors—white, gray and pink.

"Are they real?" I asked.

"Are they real?" he shot the words back at me. "Of course they're real. I expect a thousand for the lot." His long praying mantis-like legs folded up to his chest before they hit the floor. He stood up and put the box of pearls on my coffee table.

"A thousand?" I asked. "You mean now?"

He walked toward me and I backed onto the porch, pushing the screen door open as I went. He stood on my threshold looking down at me, his toothpick dancing up and down. Sticking one hand in his pocket, he adjusted himself. I made a mental note to burn my remote control.

"Nah, I'll catch up with you in a few days," he smirked. "I know where you live." He walked past me snorting like a rutting pig.

I turned to go into the house. Mrs. Russo was standing in my living room. I really needed to get an alarm system installed, or maybe a large dog.

She held out a pile of hundred dollar bills.

"What's that for?"

"It's a thousand for the pearls."

My mouth fell open. "How long have you been here?"

She walked over to the window and watched Chang drive off. She sighed and rubbed her forehead.

Since I didn't take the money, she turned, dropped it on the coffee table, and grabbed the box. "Hold off giving it to him for as long as possible." She paused. "And make up some stories about the people that bought the pearls, in case he asks."

"Mrs. R, are you sure?" I pointed to the wad of hundreds.

"That's a lot of money."

She gave me her dismissive wave and looked out the window again. "Damn," she said and headed for the kitchen. "The police are here."

Panicking, I picked up the cash and followed her.

"Don't tell them anything," Mrs. R said, as she exited through the side door and closed it behind her.

Where could I hide the money? In the oven? No, I'd forget and fire it up. In the freezer? No, too obvious, they'd definitely look there. I opened up a tea pot decorated with hand-painted pansies, one of many from my grandmother's collection. I dropped the money inside and put the lid back on. The doorbell buzzed, jangling my nerves as if I didn't know it was going to happen. I ran back to the front door and opened it. I was breathing hard, which I'm sure the officer could see.

"Patricia Schuster?" he asked.

"Yes."

"Did we catch you at a bad time?"

"No," I lied.

"I'm Detective O'Reilly, this is Detective Evans." He gave a quick nod to the tall stocky blond woman next to him, who looked like she could handle herself in a fight. "We're from the homicide department. Mind if we ask you some questions regarding Julie Gordon's death?" He tilted his head down and peered at me over his sunglasses. His military-cut red hair clashed with childlike freckles sprinkled across his nose. He wore a dark suit and tie, and she donned a black tailored jacket over a white blouse with black pants.

"Sure."

I opened the screen and they stepped inside. I gestured to

the couch and he sat, while she stood, her thumbs hooked on her waistband. Her gaze circled the room and she inhaled deeply, probably checking for marijuana.

I sat down across from them in Nana's rocking chair.

"You were friends with Ms. Gordon?" he asked, removing his sunglasses to reveal facial features that were hard and angular.

I nodded and looked down at my hands.

"And you were picked up last Saturday for stealing a car Ms. Gordon claimed she owned?"

I looked up and nodded again. His eyes turned to slits as he stared at me.

"When was the last time you saw Ms. Gordon?"

I took a deep breath, trying to remain calm. They weren't accusing me of anything, just asking questions, contrary to what Mrs. Russo thought they would do. And they weren't going to put me in a small room with no windows, at least not yet.

"Saturday, when I drove her home." I wasn't really lying. I'd only seen her shoes in Jimmy's car lot.

He looked up to his partner and then down to his clipboard.

"Where were you on Tuesday night?"

The conversation was taking a turn. If I raised the question of wanting a lawyer it could send up a red flag.

"Here."

"Anyone with you?"

"Sunny Russo."

The Officer's head popped up from his notes. Suddenly he was interested.

"When did she leave?"

"Around nine-thirty."

His focus went back to his missive.

"Sunny Russo, nine-thirty," he repeated softly as he wrote.

"How do you know Sunny Russo?" This time it was Detective Evans who spoke. Her partner gave her a dirty look. I guess he wanted to ask the questions.

"She's a friend of the family."

"Didn't she post your bail?" Detective Evans asked.

I was impressed; she'd done her homework.

"Yes," I replied.

"Must be a good friend."

I looked back and forth between the two and then shrugged my shoulders. I wasn't sure what they were after, but I was starting to get angry, and that, mixed with anxiety, left me mute.

"Do you know of anyone who would wish to harm Ms. Gordon?" Officer O'Reilly asked with a sigh, looking down at his clipboard.

I blinked a few times, collecting my thoughts. What was I so worried about? These officers didn't think it was murder, these questions were just routine, something to fill up their day.

"Hmm," I said, staring at the floor, as if the answers were written there. It was more like Julie wanted to harm Jimmy Chang, not the other way around. But Julie promised him money and maybe more. I was scared to mention Jimmy's name, in case he heard that I'd pointed the finger his direction. I decided to take that chance.

"Not harm necessarily. But Julie wanted that Cadillac. Maybe there's something there."

O'Reilly glanced up at his partner who snorted and crossed her arms. He clicked his pen closed, dismissing my insight. Their minds were made up, about Julie's death and about me. Anything I said would be ignored. They thought I was a car thief and I associated with a mob widow. In their eyes I couldn't be trusted.

"Thank you for your time," he said, standing up and giving me a synthetic smile.

I closed the door behind them and let out a breath.

I felt an urgent need to get Mrs. R's thousand dollars out of my house. Hiding it somewhere in my store seemed a safe bet. After unlocking the front door to Elsie's Antiques I turned the closed sign to open and hurried into the office.

"Patricia," a curt voice called out to me from the hallway.

I jumped. It was the Yarn Barn lady. In the corner sat an antique safe, about three feet square. I pulled open the door, threw in the money, slammed it shut, pushed the handle into the closed position and spun the dial.

When I turned, the Yarn Barn lady stood in the doorway glaring. She reached up and gave one of her knitting needles a downwards push. The pointy end then appeared on the opposite side of her head. As her hand hovered there for a moment, I imagined her pulling it out at lightning speed and stabbing me like a sword fighter in one smooth motion. Again, I had spent too much time staring at her instead of speaking.

"You're supposed to have this up in your window to advertise the sidewalk sale." She shoved a bright yellow flier at me. "You'd have known that if you showed up to the meeting on time." She turned and briskly walked out.

I looked down at the flier and then back to the safe. My stomach flipped, I didn't know the combination.

My parent's backyard had changed drastically since the last time I'd visited. My mother had rototilled what was once my father's prize dichondra lawn. Now there were only rows and rows of deep dark dirt ready for planting. She was on her hands and knees digging a hole with a small trowel. The sharp stench of manure burned my nose. I blinked a few times and took a step backwards, hoping a breeze might find me.

"Mom, what kind of fertilizer is that?" I waved my hand in front of my face.

"It's a special blend of compost I got from an organic farmer." She turned to me, sitting back on her heels. I could see that the rims of her eyes were red. "He mixes it with bat guano and something else. He was a little vague about what was in it."

I eyed the three trays she had in front of her. I did the math; there were seventy-five plants. The leaves looked like a squash.

"What are these?" I asked.

"Zucchini."

"I didn't know you could buy zucchini in flats," I said. Or that you'd want to, I thought to myself.

She'd returned to digging.

"Oh, if you know the right people you can get anything," she answered.

"I met with Maria Sanchez today. Have you heard of her? I'm going to use her for my legal defense."

"I thought your dad was going to find someone for you?" She changed her grip on the trowel and stabbed at the earth in short, staccato motions. I had a feeling that my mother had moved out of the denial phase of her grief into the anger phase.

"Didn't I tell you? I met with Dad and Lenny Brunswick."

"Lenny? Ish, the guy's a prick."

"Yeah, that was my opinion, too."

I decided to skip the part about Dad not picking up the tab for my defense. She might dig all the way to China over that. She popped an infant plant from its plastic womb and put it in the ground.

"I can help you pay for your legal bills, dear. I have money."

Just like a mom, reading my mind.

"That's sweet of you, but it's a moot point, the charges should be dropped."

She gingerly moved a few feet over, being careful not to disturb one of the many soaker hoses she had running up and down each row.

"So why haven't they been dropped?" she asked.

"Jimmy Chang is why."

"Jimmy Chang?" She shook her head. "He was always hanging around your grandmother's store. He sure seemed to have a lot of time on his hands for a guy running a business." She stood up and brushed dirt off her knees. "Well, I'd ask you to stay for dinner, but I have a class to get to."

"Oh, what class is that?"

"Tae kwon do."

I nodded my head. Yep, she was definitely in the anger phase.

Chapter Nine

My first Saturday sidewalk sale proved to be my best day since I opened. A hankie collector bought a dozen embroidered handkerchiefs, and a woman renting an old farm house bought a picture of grazing cows in a gaudy frame that she thought would 'go great' with her living room couch. Two nightstands and a tea cart sold also. But the most interesting part of the day occurred just before I closed.

A young couple came in dressed in what I would describe as 1950s Beatnik. He wore a long-sleeved black T-shirt, even though it was way too hot for that, and a beret. She wore a black short-sleeved turtle neck, black Capri pants and flats. They had dark sunglasses which they kept on as they examined my jewelry case.

"Do you have any pearl necklaces?" the woman asked in a thick German accent. Her short-cropped, jet black hair looked as if she'd just come from a salon. She ran her fingers over the tops of her ears.

"No, sorry," I replied.

"No pearls?" she asked again.

I shook my head.

"You sold already?"

I didn't know how to reply to that. How did she know? They must be connected to Jimmy Chang. But how?

"Nein." The man grabbed her hand, said something in German, and tapped on the glass.

"Could I look at that?" he asked, as he pointed to a piece of vintage costume jewelry—a brooch with a fake ruby in the center surrounded by small rhinestones.

A thirty-five dollar price tag dangled from the clasp. I placed the pin on a velvet covered pad. He removed his sunglasses and pulled a jewelry loupe from his pocket to give the brooch a closer inspection. For a moment my heart leapt into my throat. Could the jewels be real?

The woman asked to use the restroom and I pointed down the hall. Her partner tapped on his watch, giving her a dirty look.

"Thank you," he said, replacing the brooch on the pad.

The front door jangled and Mrs. Russo and Mrs. Butterfield came into the store. Mrs. Butterfield had on a white dress with a bright yellow belt that matched her bright yellow canvas bag. Mrs. Russo looked elegant as always in a pale peach pantsuit.

"Mind if I use your bathroom?" Mrs. Russo asked.

"Sure, it's…," I said, pointing down the hall. "But there's someone in there."

She was already walking, waving me off. "I know where it is."

The German man wandered over to my freshly polished 1940s mahogany secretary. Mrs. B sauntered up next to him.

"Oh, this is such a pretty piece, don't you think so?" she asked.

He gave her a pained smile and glanced at his watch. She pulled down on the desk top and laid the writing surface out flat. The inside was full of small drawers and vertical slots for letters and mail.

I walked over to the two of them. "They don't make furniture like this now-a-days."

"Really? Do tell," Mrs. B responded.

"Like here." I wanted to share what I had learned from the antique books I'd been reading. I tugged on what appeared to be molding detail, but slid out to reveal a secret compartment.

"Oh my!" Mrs. Butterfield exclaimed, fully engrossed with the secretary. She smiled at me as I went on to show her the dovetail construction and explained that the direction of the grain indicated whether it was made in America or Europe. Even the guy seemed impressed with my knowledge, as he leaned in close while I pointed out the attributes of the old-fashioned desk.

The front bell jangled again and I looked up to see the German woman standing in the door way, ready to leave.

"Thank you," the man said and followed her out.

Mrs. R emerged from the hallway dialing a cell phone. "Did you get it?" she asked Mrs. B.

Mrs. Butterfield held up a man's wallet and then opened it quickly. "There's not much in here."

"What?! You stole that?" I was mortified.

"Oh, look at this!" she said, holding up a condom.

"Put that back," I hissed at her.

"But it's yellow."

"And go give that back to him." I pointed out the door. "Before he drives off!"

"Okay," she said, turning away from me, but I saw her slip something into her pocket.

She tottered over to the couple's silver BMW and knocked on the dark tinted window. The man was all smiles as he took his wallet back and opened it to reward her.

Mrs. B returned waving a hundred dollar bill in the air.

"Dinner's on me," she sang out. "Did you get one?" she asked Mrs. R, who was looking at her phone.

"Yes," she replied.

"Did you take a picture of that woman?" I asked.

Mrs. Russo nodded and headed out the door.

"Good to see you, dear," Mrs. Butterfield said as she exited, still waving her new-found wealth in the air.

I checked my makeup in the visor mirror three times while driving to Jake's party. My lust buzz hummed and I hoped I'd make a better impression than the first two times we'd met.

His neighborhood consisted of houses that ranged in age from the late 1800s to the present. Jake's home was a single-story Victorian, painted completely white. Street parking was limited, so I parked a block away and hoofed it back. I walked up the driveway that ran along side the house, following the sound of a sweet jazz tune. I carried my obligatory bottle of wine into the backyard.

Jake stood at a large gas barbeque. A puff of smoke temporarily obliterated my view of him. When the air cleared, I could see a young woman standing at his side and next to her was Jake's father, Officer Romano. My lust buzz immediately went into hiding.

A tall, burly man stepped in front of me. I tilted my head

up to see his face. From the neck up he looked like Elvis from the 1970s, with long sideburns and yellow tinted sunglasses. From the neck down he looked like a tourist. His green and pink Hawaiian shirt was unbuttoned to the waist and he held up a large tomato inches from my face.

"What do you think?" he asked, smiling and flashing me a gold front tooth. "Does it look like Elvis?"

I took a step backwards to focus. Sure enough, there was a semblance of a face on the tomato, brought about by the dirt sticking to the fruit as it grew. Two spots for eyes and a line for a mouth. I tried squinting, but I didn't see Elvis.

"I'm going to sell him on eBay and buy me a SUV!" he stated with enthusiasm.

I smiled indulgently. "I'm sure you'll make a mint."

"Me and Elvis need a drink." He turned and headed for the refreshment table.

Jake had seen me by then and passed a long spatula to the young woman next to him and headed my way. I gave him my best smile.

"Patricia!" He leaned in and kissed my cheek. I tried returning the favor, but he pulled back too quickly and I puckered into the air instead. "I'm glad you made it! I see you met Uncle Pete."

"He's going to make a killing on Ebay," I stated.

"He always is. Come on, let me introduce you." He took my hand and led me to a group of people clustered around the grill. Mostly strangers to me, but I recognized a few faces: the couple who owned the Italian restaurant downtown, an acquaintance from high school, and an older gentleman who said he knew my grandmother well and missed her.

Jake introduced the young burger flipper as his sister Lily. She was in her late teens, dark hair and eyes, and a button-up blouse that wasn't buttoned up very far. She barely looked at me and with a pout handed the BBQ utensil back to Jake. "I can't do this," she said and slunk off.

"This is my dad, Marc." Jake gestured to his father. "This is Patricia; she's running Elsie's Antiques."

"Officer Romano, nice to see you again," I lied.

Drippings from the burgers sent flames shooting into the air. The three of us took a step back. Jake reached out and nudged the meat out of harm's way.

"Ms. Schuster." He shook my hand firmly, his face grim.

"You two know each other?" Jake asked, obviously surprised.

"Our paths have crossed," Officer Romano responded noncommittally.

"Dad, why don't you take Patricia over to get her a drink?"

Officer Romano gestured to the drink table. We walked together and I added my wine to the mix. Pulling out a beer from a metal tub full of ice, I twisted the top off and took a long drink.

"So you know Jake," he said, studying my face as if he'd have to recall me in a lineup later on.

"I think most of the downtown merchants get to know each other eventually."

"Is that all it is? Fellow shopkeepers?"

I took another large swallow, realizing that the burgers weren't the only things being grilled tonight.

"You know, Marc," I put the emphasis on his first name. "I recently moved back into town and just met Jake. He was kind enough to invite me to his party. That's all; don't read something into it that isn't there."

From a few yards away the barbeque again erupted into flames. We both turned to look and then turned back to each other.

"There have been a few car thefts at the downtown parking garage." He stared at me intensely, his eyes never leaving my face.

"So I hear," I said. "I'll try and keep my hands in my pockets." Taking another sip of beer, I knew I was drinking too fast. I was a lightweight when it came to alcohol and I hadn't eaten since lunch.

He paused for a second, "That's not what I meant. I just meant for you to be careful." He sounded irritated.

"Hmm," I replied, not believing him.

"I'm sorry about your friend," he said.

"Thanks. Any idea who did it?" I couldn't help myself, I had to ask.

"Did what?" he replied quickly.

My beer-numbed brain responded slowly. Of course, the police would keep up a united front, maintaining that Julie's death was an accident. They all had to keep up the same pretense. But if I explained I'd been questioned by the homicide department he'd want to know why. Did I really want Jake's dad thinking I was involved in a murder?

"Did what, Ms. Schuster?" his eyes narrowed to slits.

"Oh, can you believe this?" A voice came from behind him. It was Lily, standing by the drink table holding up my bottle of wine. "Someone brought Napa wine. Who doesn't know that in Sonoma County we only drink Sonoma County wine?" She looked around for the culprit, her eyes resting on me for an uncomfortably long second. "How rude!" She slammed the bottle down and walked off.

Officer Romano had turned to look, his demeanor changing from interrogating cop to embarrassed dad. I took advantage of his momentary distraction, took two steps backwards, and promptly bumped into someone.

"Elvis!" A deep male voice cried out.

Spinning around I was eye level with Uncle Pete's prized tomato, which was now squished into his hairy chest. I felt the back of my head; it was wet and slimy.

"Oh, I'm so sorry!" I said, wiping my hand on my jeans. But I wasn't sure he heard me. His eyes flashing anger and his non-tomato juiced hand closed into a fist. I was overtaken by panic. Power walking, I bolted for the exit.

Passing the grill, which was now fully engulfed in flames, I heard Jake call my name, but my flight instinct had taken over. When I hit the street, my gait turned to a full-out run. I reached my car with the beer bottle still in my hand. I tossed it over a small wooden fence where an overgrown daisy was also trying to make an escape through the pickets.

"Hey!" A woman called out from her porch.

I hadn't even seen her. I jumped in my car and gunned it, hoping the neighbor wouldn't take down my license plate number. That's all I'd need right now, adding littering to my list of offenses.

After my hasty retreat, I paid a visit to my favorite Chinese restaurant. The comforting aromas of broccoli beef and steamed rice poured out of the small take-out containers that sat next to me on the passenger seat of my car. As I passed the

Finley Hotel and Convention Center, I saw my father's black Jaguar sedan turn into the parking lot. I followed him, finding a dark spot to park with full view of the front of the building.

The Jaguar pulled under the portico and a man in a black vest ran to the driver's door to open it. My father got out and hurried into the hotel. The valet left the car at the curb, indicating my father would return soon.

Curious, I decided to wait and opened up my bag of food. Using chopsticks I was about to take a bite of broccoli when my passenger door opened. My heart immediately jumped into second gear. Mrs. Miller picked up my bag of Chinese food and slid in next to me, a spray of Baby's Breath behind her ear. She smelled of marijuana.

"Want some company?" she asked. "Stakeouts can be so boring."

"What are you doing here?" I looked around for the other Ladies. "You scared me."

"Sorry."

"Were you following me?"

"No, I was out doing a little shopping." She didn't have any bags, only an oversized canvas tote, which bulged in odd directions. "Mmm, Chinese food. What did you get?"

"Broccoli beef and rice."

"Anything else?"

"A bag of fortune cookies."

"Oh, can I have one?" she asked expectantly.

I pulled out the bag and passed them over. She ripped the top off and snapped open the first one, wiping the crumbs from her lap onto my floor.

"Hmm, I can't make this out without my glasses. Can you

read it for me?" She asked while crunching on the cookie.

"Don't sneak up on your friends; someone might get hurt."

"Ha-ha, it doesn't say that."

"Okay, it says 'The early bird gets the worm.'"

"Humph. That's not a good one. Let's try another." She shoved the last piece of cookie in her mouth and broke open another one. She handed me the fortune.

"Keep your options open."

She made a face. "These are terrible fortunes. Confucius should be rolling over in his grave. What happened to 'Great riches are about to be bestowed upon you?' Or 'A stranger will make your life more exciting?'"

I put the thin slips of paper on the dashboard and pulled the second container out of the bag.

"I see you haven't been arrested for murder," she said casually.

"No I haven't, and I don't appreciate Mrs. Russo assuming that I would be. I went and stuck my foot in my mouth to Officer Romano by implying that Julie was murdered. But he's sticking with the story that it was an accident." I stabbed my chopsticks down into the rice and came up with three grains. "But I wouldn't be surprised if he wanted to arrest me for being stupid."

Mrs. Miller ignored my ramblings and pointed to the front entrance. "Who's that?" she asked.

A stretch limousine pulled up under the portico behind my father's Jag. The valet ran to open the door for the passenger. He smiled and nodded as a man exited the vehicle. It was Finley, the cold man I'd met at the restaurant, his size was unmistakable.

"He owns the hotel," I said.

"Kinda late to be working."

"I heard he's really strict with his employees; maybe he's checking up on someone."

"Oh, there's your father," Mrs. Miller said. She reached into her tote, pulled out a pair of binoculars, and handed them over.

My dad wasn't alone. I peered through the glasses and gasped. On his arm was an Asian woman with long dark hair, wearing a very short and very tight white dress. It was the pouter from Jimmy Chang's car.

"Oh, I can't believe it! My dad's dating Jimmy Chang's girlfriend!"

"Oh my," she said. "Let me see." She looked. "Oh dear."

"What?" I asked.

"She's a professional."

"What?" my voice went an octave higher.

"Yep, she's from a service. I recognize the look."

"Oh no!" I was horrified.

"Boy, those gals can wring you dry. They pretend they want out of the business and get a guy to rent them an apartment, or a suite at a nice hotel." She gestured to the building. "And the guy thinks they're doing something noble. Then the woman uses the place for their other johns."

I looked again. The two were holding hands, talking close and my father looked almost giddy. The valet moved to open the passenger door, but my dad beat him to it. I couldn't look anymore. I handed the binoculars back to Mrs. M and leaned my head against the side window, closing my eyes.

"No wonder my dad isn't paying for my defense," I said.

"Maybe they're going down to San Francisco," Mrs. M said excitedly, "to see a show or go dancing."

I turned and stared at her.

"What?" she said. "I don't get out much. I have to live vicariously through someone."

I put my head back on the window and watched my father's car drive out of the parking lot. A hotel security guard suddenly appeared between the rows of cars walking toward us. I sat up straight.

"Busted," Mrs. Miller said.

The guard came up next to the car and made a circle with his hand indicating I should roll down my window.

"Good evening, ladies." His black baseball hat was decorated with embroidered words that read 'Finley Hotel Security'.

"Good evening," I replied.

"Were you planning on going inside tonight? The management would prefer if you didn't just sit in your car." He smiled sweetly.

Mrs. M spewed at him: "We'll do whatever we damn well—"

I reached over, put my hand on her arm and squeezed tightly, never taking my eye off the guard.

"Sorry about that. She's had a bad day." I lowered my voice and leaned over a little closer to him. "She found out she's going blind and wanted to come over and look at the pretty hotel lights."

He looked over at Mrs. Miller and whispered, "I'm sorry to hear that." Then he spoke louder, as if she was going deaf too. "You two sit here as long as you want." He gave my door a pat.

He walked away and I turned to Mrs. M, she broke open another cookie.

"Why do you want to draw attention to yourself?" I asked.

"You smell like pot."

"Oh, those security guards, they're just want-a-be cops, strutting around in their uniforms, wearing those stupid hats, telling people what to do."

"Well, you get more flies with honey."

"Yeah, well I'll remember that the next time I want a fly." She paused, "Oh, look who's here."

Jimmy's long white Caddy drove past us and around to the back of the hotel.

"*Vamos*," Mrs. Miller said and jumped out of the car.

"But I'm not done with my broccoli beef," I called out after her.

She ran hunched over between the cars, occasionally popping up like a meerkat to look around. She glanced back and waved for me to follow. When I caught up to her, she was crouching next to an SUV, looking around its bumper.

"What about the security guard?" I whispered.

She turned to me holding her index finger to pursed lips and pointed. I peered around the car to see the back of the guard's white windbreaker. He stood in the shadows with the valet, just past the hotel entrance. A pinpoint of light danced next to the valet as he gestured with his cigarette. Mrs. M sprinted to the sidewalk and into the bushes near the building. I followed close behind hoping that she would scare away any spiders that might be lying in wait for their prey. Visions of black widows with their shiny, plastic-like bodies danced in my head. I swatted at every leaf that brushed against my bare legs. My heart rate was in fourth gear by the time she stopped and squatted down.

From our vantage point we could see that Jimmy had parked

the car in an area by a sign that read 'Employee Parking.' He was talking to Finley and Kwan, the man I'd seen at Jimmy's car lot, who also acted as Finley's chauffeur.

Jimmy's trunk stood open and he gestured to its interior.

"It's amazing how big the trunks of those old cars are," I said.

"Yeah, we used to call those six-packs, 'cause you could get six bodies in there."

I couldn't see her face to tell if she was kidding or not. Probably not.

Jimmy closed the trunk lid and went to the front of the car, opened the hood, and gestured to the engine compartment. The two men didn't move. Jimmy opened the driver's side door, reached inside and the roof folded back, disappearing behind the back seat.

Finley said something, and Jimmy shook his head. Finley spoke again, his voice louder, but I still couldn't hear the conversation. Jimmy crossed his arms in front of him.

"Jimmy must be trying to sell the car," I whispered.

"That would be my guess," Mrs. M replied.

The three men stood perfectly still for a minute.

"Stalemate," Mrs. M whispered.

Jimmy was the first to move. He shrugged and got into the car. His backup lights came on and the other two men moved aside as Jimmy pulled out of the parking space. As he drove the Caddy's convertible top slowly made its way back into the up position.

The two men returned to the building and disappeared inside.

We crept back to my car, watching for the guard. I slid into the driver's seat and Mrs. M grabbed her purse, stuffing the binoculars inside.

"Thanks, dear. It's been fun."

"Do you need a lift home?"

"No, I'll catch the bus. You never know who you're going to run into using public transportation."

She closed the door and waved goodbye. I looked down to assess my food situation. The broccoli beef and rice were cold, and there were five fortune cookies left. I started the car and looked around before backing out of the parking space. Mrs. M was nowhere in sight.

By the time I arrived home, I was exhausted and plopped down in front of the TV to eat. I watched the end of a 1960s horror flick and went to bed.

I stared into the darkness and thought about my father dating a hooker.

Could he be paying for her room at the Finley? If he was, I really didn't want to know. I finally fell asleep, waking up three or four times during the night, always from the same dream. I was being chased by a giant tomato with a creepy look on its face.

Chapter Ten

The front door bell jingled, announcing Elsie's Antiques' first customer of the day.

"Hello? Ms. Schuster?"

I poked my head out of my office. Officer Romano strode confidently through the store dressed in jeans and a polo shirt.

"Good morning," he said. "May I speak with you a moment?"

Ish. I'd gotten up late and had only one cup of coffee that morning, definitely not enough caffeine to face my lapse of judgment from the night before. Guilt and humiliation need at least two cups.

I stifled a sigh and forced a smile. "All right."

"I'm sorry to bother you. I wanted to apologize for yesterday. You asked me a question and I overreacted. You were obviously upset, so I wanted to say I'm sorry."

"Okay." I replied, surprised.

He gave a single firm nod. "Okay." He took a step back. "But, I have to ask you. Why do you believe Julie Gordon was murdered?"

After experiencing the skepticism of the detectives I was hesitant to offer my opinion. But Officer Romano had gone out of his way to apologize. I wasn't ready to trust him yet but I felt a sliver of optimism. I hoped my instinct was valid and not fueled by lust for his son.

"Odds." I pointed my index finger down and made circles over an imaginary pool, just as Mrs. R had done.

He raised a questioning eyebrow.

I continued. "What are the chances of someone hitting their head on the side of a pool? The angle would have to be perfect." I made a chopping motion with my hand.

His questioning eyebrow stayed firmly intact. "But, no idea who? Or a motive?"

"Well, there were a few things that had changed recently in Julie's life. One was that she owned the Cadillac and then she didn't. Plus something caused her to start drinking again. Usually the idea is to check out the boyfriend or follow the money, right?" His head moved just enough that I took it for a nod. "In this case I think you should follow the car."

Officer Romano's face stayed impassive. But I sensed he was in detective mode.

"Two officers came to see me yesterday morning," I continued.

"O'Reilly?" he asked.

I nodded, "And Evans."

His shoulders slumped just a bit.

"Did you tell them your theory?"

"Yes. But, I don't think they believed a word of what I did say, no less an insight as to what might have happened. I'm a car thief remember? Plus I cavort with criminals."

The Officer lowered his eyes. Was he embarrassed?

"Thank you, Ms. Schuster."

"Patricia," I replied.

As he left Jake came in. The two stopped to speak to each other. Jake looked my direction and strode toward me with the same confident gait as his father.

"So, my dad came by to apologize," he said.

"Yeah."

"I wanted to apologize, too. I shouldn't have thrown you in with my family before we got to know one another a little better. Of course, I didn't know you'd met my father." He left that last part hanging.

"It's a long story." Hoping to put him off a little longer, I'd need at least three cups of caffeine to explain a felony.

His eyes searched my face for a moment before he spoke. Then he smiled and asked: "Would you like to go out to dinner?"

"Sure."

"Tonight?"

"Can we make it tomorrow? I'm having dinner with my dad tonight."

"Tomorrow then."

I felt my lust buzz resurfacing.

Cassandra, my dad's new girlfriend, wore a gold dress that sparkled in the light when she moved. I guessed her age to be around twenty-two, a few years younger than me. We sat in a round booth, the center decorated with a softly glowing candle surrounded by white gardenias. My dad left the two of us to say hello to one of his clients across the room.

"My father says you're in sales?" I asked.

"Sure am." She reached into her large gold lamé purse and pulled out an oversized, neon pink dildo. It waved hello.

I reached out, grabbed it from her, and pulled it down behind the white fabric table cloth and threw my napkin over the beast. In horror I looked around the restaurant. The maitre d' had seen it; I could tell by the smirk on his face. As well as a woman sitting at a table across from us who'd let out a yelp.

"Ah, so it's been awhile." She grinned at me slyly. "If you're that desperate, I can give that to you at ten percent off. A special deal for you since your dad's such a good friend."

"Oh no," I exclaimed, waving my free hand at her.

"No? Okay, how about this?" She reached back into her bag and brought out another dildo made of a clear material. She banged it on the edge of the table top as if she was trying to open a biscuit tube. "Acrylic, practically indestructible." She held it up above her head, shooting light around the restaurant like a disco ball. "Isn't it beautiful?"

The maitre d' laughed out loud. The yelper dabbed her forehead with her napkin. Again, I reached out and yanked her arm down.

"Cassandra, you can't pull stuff like that out in a restaurant!"

"Patricia, there's nothing to be ashamed of; human sexuality is completely natural."

"People are eating," I hissed at her.

"Like food and sex don't go together?" She smiled, her eyes big. "Like this one time—"

"That's okay." I said, stopping her before she went any further. "Why don't you put those away before my dad comes back?"

"Oh, you should see the one that he likes." She turned back to her purse to dig.

Now it was my turn to yelp. She looked at me rather

surprised. I took a deep breath.

"Cassandra, it's always been my motto not to know anything about my parents' sex life."

She shrugged and put the sex toys back in her bag, but not before the pink one gave me a final wave. She handed me a gold business card with black letters. It read 'Delectable Dildos—Your one stop vibrating shop.' Her address was a room at the hotel.

"How are my two favorite girls getting along?" My dad said, as he slipped back into the booth.

I cringed. He never would have made such a chauvinistic statement in front of my mother. Cassandra was all smiles.

"Oh, Patricia and I are getting along just fine. I know exactly what your daughter needs."

Now it was my dad's turn to cringe.

"Waiter!" he yelled out. The waiter appeared and my father ordered himself a scotch on the rocks. He then gestured for us to order.

"A martini," Cassandra said, "with two extra olives."

"White wine." I smiled at the waiter, but he wasn't looking at me. He was leering at Cassandra.

As she reached into her purse I pulled up the edge of the table cloth. One more waving sex toy and I was diving for cover. Instead she handed the waiter a business card.

"Thank you." He grinned like he'd just received the keys to the city.

"I have to tinkle," Cassandra said, her eyes darting back and forth between my dad and me. We had her hemmed in. My dad stood up to let her out. She was halfway across the room when I decided to join her.

I waved my hands under the automatic faucet as Cassandra emerged from one of the stalls pulling down the skirt of her dress. I reached for a towel, but they looked to be real cotton and a little too fluffy for comfort. I shook the water off and held my arms awkwardly in front of me while my hands air dried.

"You know Jimmy Chang, don't you?" I asked her.

Under the harsh florescent lights she looked tired as she washed her hands.

"Yeah, so what?"

"I don't like my dad looking like a schmuck."

"Daddy's little girl doesn't like someone else getting all the attention?" Her pretense at friendship had disappeared.

"No, that's not it at all. I don't like him being played for a fool."

"You just said that," she snapped at me.

"I'm going to tell him." I sounded like a snotty sister, but I couldn't help it.

"Tell him what?" She turned to face me, one hand on her hip. "That I know a guy?"

"I know what line of business you're really in."

"And what would that be?" She spit the words at me.

I opened my mouth, but couldn't bring myself to say it. What if Mrs. Miller was wrong? She looked me up and down.

"Are you upset he's spending your inheritance?" she asked rather matter-of-factly while turning back to the mirror to apply more lipstick.

It took all my resolve not to pick her up and dunk her head first in the toilet. I settled on my meanest glare.

"Look," she said, throwing her lipstick into the black hole

of her purse. "Your daddy's a big boy; he knows what he's doing." She gave her dress one last tug and left.

I looked at myself in the mirror. Yeah, that's what worried me.

Chapter Eleven

Mourners outnumbered seats at the Gentle Hills Memorial Park and Mortuary for Julie's funeral. My mother and I arrived early and sat in the second row of the small chapel. Hushed voices mixed with organ music bounced off the white stone walls. Next to a modest podium stood a table covered with crisp white linen. Pink and white roses surrounded a framed picture of Julie shot in the desert. In the photo she wore sunglasses and an uneasy smile.

The minister obviously didn't know the family and the service was straight from the hymnal. An old girlfriend from our high school spoke, as well as Todd, Julie's older brother.

After the service we drove to the Gordon home, located in a neighborhood of houses built in the post-war '50s. The front lawn had recently been mowed, but the house needed paint and looked as gloomy and tired as I felt.

We stepped into the living room, filled with subdued adults and boisterous children. My mother waved to a friend and then disappeared into the crowd.

A group of photographs decorated the wall above the couch. I looked at Julie through the years: A baby picture, a kindergarten picture, a photo taken during our third grade field trip to a local farm, where I stood out with my freckles and wild blond hair, her graduation picture and the most recent photo taken at a friend's wedding when the two of us had been bridesmaids. We grinned into the camera, cheek-to-cheek, wearing gaudy hunter green taffeta dresses. My eyes laughed, but her eyes showed pain under the smile. I'd never seen the picture before and teared-up, overwhelmed with sadness at the loss of my old friend. Julie never healed that pain; I'd seen it the night I drove her home.

Soft murmurs from the dining room drew my attention to the buffet table. I joined the group, put a few carrots sticks and some cheese on a dessert-sized paper plate, and poured myself a cup of coffee. After finding a wall to lean up against, I put the coffee down on an end table and popped a chunk of cheddar into my mouth. Next to me two women sat in matching Queen Anne chairs, plates balanced on their laps. Both looked to be in their seventies. One leaned over to the other.

"You know she'd gone off the wagon," she whispered loudly to her friend. "My neighbor's brother's sister-in-law was her sponsor. Broke her mother's heart and now this."

The woman next to her stiffened, pulled at an earring and looked the other direction. Maybe she hoped the side of her head would dissuade continued conversation. It didn't.

"And she'd just got that new promotion. Now, Mary Belle, you know she'd have to be making good money with that." She clucked her tongue.

"Janie, please."

"All I'm saying is her mom could have used a little help."

Mary Belle squirmed in her seat.

Janie didn't acknowledge the discomfort she was causing and forged ahead. "After all that poor woman has gone through. First, the death of her no-good gambling husband and now this."

"I need some fresh air," Mary Belle said and abruptly stood up.

"Me, too," Janie stated, following Mary Belle out the front door.

After making myself comfortable in one of the abandoned chairs, a man with spiky hair walked over to me and smiled awkwardly.

"This seat taken?"

"No, go ahead," I replied. "I'm Patricia."

"Matt."

He wore a dark navy suit with a pink tie.

"How did you know Julie?" I asked. As soon as the words were out of my mouth I realized I'd seen him at Jimmy Chang's car lot. He was Julie's ride the day Julie and Jimmy were arguing.

"I worked with her at the Finley." He took a bite of a lemon bar, leaving powdered sugar on his upper lip. "In the Accounting Department."

"Oh," I nodded at him. "I thought she worked as an Events Coordinator."

"She did, but before that we worked together."

"Well, she always was really good at math."

"She was beyond good," he said proudly, as if he could take credit for her intelligence. "This one time she found an error that our auditors couldn't even find. She even joked on how she could cook the books if she wanted to."

I gave him a questioning look, hoping he would continue.

"She found a glitch in the software, where you could make money look like it was going to pay off a vendor, when in fact it was going somewhere else, without a trace." He laughed, pleased with Julie's cleverness. "She even talked to the owner of the company about it, trying to get him to update our system." He paused taking a gulp from his soda can. "That's when she got promoted. Seemed like it happened so fast. One day she was there, the next day she was down the hall in her own office." He shrugged, "Yeah, I really missed her when she left. We got new software though. Yep, Julie was a whiz." He sighed.

I found work relationships interesting. People often spent more quality time with their coworkers than their spouses. How close had Julie and Matt been? I didn't see a ring on Matt's hand, but that didn't mean he wasn't married.

"How did you know her?" he asked.

"We went to school together," I explained.

"Ah," he said, nodding his head, as if I let slip a telling secret.

I stared at a small bouquet of pink roses that sat on the table between us. Matt's eyes followed mine.

"You know pink was her favorite color," he said.

I nodded. "I'm surprised she didn't have that car of hers painted pink."

"Oh no, she never would have done something like that." He looked at me as if I'd suggested something criminal. "She loved that car. It was a sad day when it was repossessed."

"Oh?"

"Yeah, some guy showed up at work and handed her some

papers. In fact, I just saw him a few minutes ago."

We both looked around as if Jimmy would suddenly appear.

He continued: "Said her dad owed him money and the car was used as collateral. We followed him out to the parking lot and watched him tow it away. Julie started to cry. She said it was the only thing she had left of her dad's." He stared down at his shoes and lowered his voice. "The guy was a real jerk. He kept pointing a toothpick at her." Matt looked up and gestured toward the front door with his soda can. "There's our boss now."

"Who?" I asked, turning to look.

"The owner of the hotel, Roger Finley."

He came in shoulder first and he ducked his head under the door frame. I remembered my first meeting with him and how uncomfortable I was with his dismissive attitude. Now it was he that looked uncomfortable here in the Gordon's modest home with his perfectly tailored suit and a hundred dollar tie.

So Roger Finley knew Julie. The thought of that left me uneasy. A woman with short dark hair and wearing a navy blue suit slammed into Finley on her way out the door. He gave her a quick nod.

"Excuse me," Matt said, putting his plate down and striding across the room. "Mr. Finley."

The man's massive paw completely engulfed Matt's hand. Finley leaned over and spoke quietly.

To avoid being forced into polite chitchat with big Finley, I finished off my coffee, dumped my empty plate and cup in the trash, and went looking for Julie's mom. I was surprised to find her alone at the kitchen table, a plate of untouched food in front of her. She clutched a tissue in one hand.

"Mrs. Gordon," I said, reaching down and putting my hand on her arm. She looked up at me and smiled. Her graying hair was cut short and she wore a dark blue suit that hung loose on her thin frame.

"Patricia, how good of you to come."

"I'm so so sorry about Julie. I'll miss her."

"Thanks," she said, her eyes unfocused.

"Is there anything I can do for you?" I asked.

"No. Todd's here, have you seen him?"

I shook my head.

"He'll be cleaning out Julie's apartment."

I was going to offer to help, realizing it might be a way to look through Julie's things, but a little boy ran up to her, calling her "Grandma" and tugging on her arm. Apparently she was urgently needed somewhere else. She smiled at me and allowed herself to be pulled away. I went out into the backyard and found Todd, overlooking a brood of kids playing tag on the lawn. He greeted me warmly.

"Patricia, it's good to see you."

We hugged.

"It's not supposed to happen like this, is it?" I said.

He shook his head and sighed. "When Julie started drinking again after dad died, I thought she'd get through it. I just never imagined this."

"Is there anything I can do?" I asked. "Do you need help at her apartment?"

"No thanks, Jennifer and I can handle it," he said, referring to his wife. He watched the rambunctious children intently, obviously welcoming the distraction. It seemed a difficult time to try and catch up, so I gave his arm a squeeze.

"It was good seeing you," I said softly.

"Yeah, you too."

Easing through the crowd, I went back inside and down the hallway to the guest bathroom. The restroom door was shut and as I stood waiting, I couldn't help but peek into Todd's old bedroom. The only light came from a high squat window showing a stripe of blue sky. Mrs. Gordon had transformed the oak paneled room into a craft room. A scrapbook lay open on a long built-in counter top, along with scissors, colored paper, ribbons and glue sticks. Then I noticed a fluff of pink caught in the closed sliding closet door. I recognized the fluff as hair belonging to a naked troll doll that hung from Julie's key ring.

I looked down the hallway. I was alone. The toilet had yet to flush, so I assumed I had a minute to myself. I went into the room, slid open the closet door, grabbed Julie's keys which were sitting on top of her purse, and tried to stuff them into mine. Unfortunately, when I was choosing my accessories for the funeral that morning, I went with fashion over function. And because of that choice my teeny tiny black bag now sported a pink mane. I removed my loot and wrestled with the doll hook attempting to free it from the key ring. I could hear kids playing outside and one of them yelled "Monster! Monster!" followed by squeals of laughter. The toilet flushed and the keys slipped from my grasp, falling to the hardwood floor with a thud.

As I bent down my hands started to shake, and I was overcome with the frightening feeling of being watched. I looked to the high window and saw a tall shadow moving away. The bathroom door opened and I finally pulled the doll from the key ring. I dropped the pink haired troll back into Julie's purse and the keys into mine. A small girl ran from the bathroom. I closed the closet door and I poked my head out into the hallway. I made the three steps to the bathroom and was about to close the door when I glanced down the hall. Jimmy Chang stood in the opening to the living room, bobbing a bright green toothpick between clenched teeth. I took a quick breath. He grinned and turned away.

I locked the bathroom door behind me and removed my plunder. There were two dead bolt keys and a small one that could be for a mailbox. But the Cadillac key was missing. Did Julie's mom still have it? Or did someone else take it?

Ten minutes before my date with Jake, I paced nervously around the house. Hope had a way of doing that to me. At this point, my feelings about Jake were just lust, and they should have stood alone, since I knew very little about him. But leaning up against lust was potential, and potential was holding hands with hope. This didn't always happen, but it definitely had this time. And that hope stood there looking at me, imploring me with its big, round eyes that this time I'd make it work.

The living room looked the same as it had two minutes earlier, so I walked back to the bedroom. I was worried. I didn't want to appear desperate—desperate to have a boyfriend, desperate to please. Desperate wasn't attractive. I jumped up and down a few times trying to release some energy. I was starting to think that maybe Cassandra had the right idea with her waving pink dildo.

I checked my makeup in the mirror and thought about what

I was up against. I'd sneezed on Jake's shoes the first time I'd met him. He had to save me from making a fool of myself at the merchant's meeting. Then I made a scene at his barbeque, when I crushed his uncle's tomato and his dreams. What witty banter could undo all that damage? But then again, he did ask me out. Maybe he liked my eyes. Yeah, like that's going to sustain a relationship. Ish.

The maitre d' at the Finley gave me the same smirk I'd seen the night before and then looked Jake over head-to-toe. As he walked us to our booth, I noticed Kwan tending bar. I waited until Jake and I had placed our order before I threw out the first question.

"So, how long have you lived here?"

"Three years. I grew up in San Francisco and worked for an auto body business. My dad transferred here, and he told me about the shop downtown going up for sale, so I thought I'd give it a shot. I bought it, moved up here and it's been working out."

"If you don't mind me asking, why is your father working the night shift?"

"My dad's an alcoholic. It cost him his marriage and seniority as a homicide detective at the police department in San Francisco. He got sober, but pretty much had to start over here. My mom still lives in the City, she works for a publishing house." He paused and took a roll from the bread basket. "So how do you know my dad?"

I took a sip of wine. Dang, I didn't want to go there yet.

"Grand theft auto."

"Your car was stolen?"

I paused and stared at him. "No, that's the charge against me."

He laughed, "You're kidding. You were arrested for stealing a car?" When he saw I wasn't returning the laughter he stopped and became serious. "What happened?"

I explained the strange events and hoped that he wouldn't bolt from the room. He listened without interruption.

"That's a tough situation," he said, shaking his head. "I met Julie. She was in AA with my dad. My Uncle Pete lives in her complex. He complained about Julie's music, said she played it too loud." He sighed. "It sure is sad."

The waiter brought our salads and I thought about the loud music we heard the night we found Julie in the pool. Was it loud enough for Uncle Pete to kill her for it? Seemed a little excessive, even for someone with an unstable personality, especially in an apartment complex where a complaint to the manager could easily end a dispute.

"You know, Jimmy Chang called me about painting that car," Jake said.

My eyebrows went up in curiosity, but before I had a chance to ask specifics, a commotion at the entrance caught my attention. I glanced over to see The Ladies, all four were talking to the maitre d' at once. Mrs. Russo wore a white silk pant suit, Mrs. Butterfield had on a light yellow shift with matching jacket and Mrs. Taylor and Mrs. Miller's outfits were a blur of pastel flowers.

"Patricia?" Jake had asked me something.

"Hmm?" I turned to him.

"How's your salad?"

"Fine." I looked down and went back to eating, hoping they

wouldn't see me.

"Patricia!" one of them called out.

They were upon us within moments. Ish. There went the evening.

"Oh look! Patricia is having dinner with her new beau," Mrs. Miller said. Tonight she sported a small purple orchid behind her ear.

I felt like a monkey in a zoo. Jake looked at me and then back to The Ladies.

"Hello," he said, rising from his seat.

"Don't get up on our account," Mrs. R said. She had on four or five strings of pearls that looked exactly like the ones she had taken from me yesterday.

"We just wanted to say hello," she continued.

All four faces beamed unrelenting smiles.

"Would you like to join us?" Jake asked. I would have kicked him under the table, but that wave was already breaking.

"Oh no," one said.

"Oh, we couldn't impose," another said.

"Are you sure?" Jake smiled politely.

"Okay, maybe one drink," another replied, as they turned to each other nodding.

I gave a muted smile. Jake and I started scooting sideways, toward each other, until we touched shoulders. His arm felt warm and his thigh leaned into mine. For a moment I wanted to lay my head on his shoulder and close my eyes. The Ladies sat two to each side of us. We made our introductions.

"So Jake, tell us about yourself," Mrs. B asked, reaching out and patting his hand.

"I own Jake's Body Shop downtown."

"Really?" Mrs. Butterfield replied with eager interest. Her face looked like someone had just offered her a two-pound box of chocolates. "You must love it."

"It can be routine. Just smoothing out dents and painting."

"Oh, but the artistry that goes into creating such beauty," Mrs. B said, her face glowing. "Chrome that shines like a full moon. Perfect paint without a blemish. And the touch! The touch that's a breathtaking combination of both smooth and hard."

"Phew, is it hot in here?" Mrs. Miller waved at her flushed face with her hand. "Where's that drink waiter?"

"Why don't you go get us some champagne?" Mrs. R asked. "I feel like celebrating."

"Oh, good idea," Mrs. Miller said, hopping out of her seat and heading for the bar.

While Mrs. B and Jake continued to talk shop, I watched Mrs. Miller chatting with Kwan. Her hands became animated and Kwan appeared completely engrossed. He opened the champagne bottle and popped the cork, turning heads of the other patrons. Mrs. M clapped and continued to talk. Kwan reached into his pocket and handed her something. Then came out from around the bar and grabbed the tray to bring to our table.

"This is Kwan," Mrs. Miller introduced the bartender, like he was a long-lost friend.

"Hello," he smiled broadly, as he slid the tray onto the table. An Armani logo decorated the wide arms of his eye glass frames.

"Kwan has an import/export business," Mrs. M said, holding up a business card like she had found the answer to a pressing problem. "He's saving his money to bring his family here from Korea."

As we offered words of encouragement and support, Kwan poured champagne for each of us. He glanced at me and then Mrs. Butterfield. But if he recognized us from Jimmy's car lot he didn't acknowledge it.

"What's the occasion?" he asked.

"We usually don't need a reason," Mrs. T offered. "But we did make a killing in a business deal." The Ladies laughed a private-joke kind of laugh.

Our food arrived, and Kwan gave a small bow before returning to the bar.

"Oh, that looks good," Mrs. M said, as the waiter slid my salmon plate in front of me.

"Would you like to order?" the waiter asked.

The Ladies hesitated.

"Go ahead," Jake offered. He glanced at me, surrender and apologies written all over his face. I smiled back at him. It really was the polite thing to do.

After dinner, the six of us went into the Beastly Lounge, a small venue for up-and-coming singers, musicians and other live acts. A Bette Midler look-alike performed first. She and her three backup singers belted out songs from the 1950s and Mrs. Miller danced in the aisle. A comedian followed and we laughed until we cried. I had a great time that evening, even with four chaperones.

"I'm sorry I asked them to stay," Jake said, as he walked me to my front door.

I smiled. "It's okay, I had a nice time. Plus, they're starting to grow on me."

Pulling open the screen door, I put my key in the lock, and

turned around. Jake stood close enough for me to smell his heady aroma. He waited for me to make the first move. I took a step forward and he leaned in and kissed me passionately. I returned his enthusiasm. The combination of his taste, smell and touch made my mind go to places I wasn't ready for.

I wanted to ask him in. I wanted to grab the front of his shirt and drag him into the living room. I wanted to fall backwards on the couch and pull him down on top of me. I wanted him to stay the night. But I took a mental step back from the potential both of us felt. I'd lost out on that proposition often enough to know: sex without a relationship equals no relationship at all. And tomorrow morning I wanted to look at myself in the mirror and tell hope I'd given it my best shot.

I broke away from him and he opened his eyes and gave me a sweet smile, without a hint of disappointment.

Chapter Twelve

The next morning, three new pieces of furniture magically appeared inside Elsie's Antiques. My back door had been locked when I entered. I checked the front door; it too was locked. Both were fitted with dead bolts, meaning whichever Santa had brought me these presents came down my non-existent chimney, or had a key. I voted for the latter.

I took a closer look at the new furniture. A tilt-top table had a large scratch across the surface, sometimes that's called character, but in this case it just looked bad. The fake Chinese Chippendale chair had a back leg made from a ripped two-by-four, still in need of finishing. Not a look that is highly sought after by antiquers. The third piece, a pretty settee with brass inlay accenting rosewood legs and arms, had fabric so stained it would have to be professionally cleaned.

"How do you like 'em?" the voice came from behind me.

I jerked and spun around. Jimmy Chang stood there looking smug. He had a toothpick in his hand and he was using it to point at the mystery furniture.

"Did you bring these?" I asked.

He smiled.

"How'd you get in?" The thought of Jimmy having a key to Elsie's Antiques made me shudder.

"You have the thousand, Patty Cakes?" he asked, ignoring my questions and using my childhood nickname. A name I hated.

"Um, I need more time." I thought about the safe that I had slammed shut the day before and took a step back.

He strolled over to the jewelry case and looked in. Then turned to me and folded his arms.

"Funny, I don't see the pearls. You lose them?"

"No."

"You selling them online?"

"No." I stared at him, wondering how scared I should be. I thought again about Julie floating in the pool. Could Jimmy really kill someone? The few times I'd been alone with him he'd never made a move to physically hurt me. But maybe I was worth more to him with all my appendages in working order.

"Then what?"

"I sold them."

He didn't move except for one eyebrow that went straight up.

"But, I locked the money in Nana's safe." I spoke fast and took another step backwards.

With three long strides he stood a foot from my face.

"The safe in her office?" he asked with minty breath.

"Yeah and I don't have the combination. I've looked."

"Well," he said, giving me a satisfied, evil smile. "They say that criminal intent is in your genes, maybe you should take a crack at opening it. Let's see what you got."

My brain and body seemed to be working independent of each other. While my body walked to the back of the store, my brain yelled: 'Run!'

I entered the office and pulled on the handle to the safe door just to make sure, but it was still locked. Jimmy hovered over me and I fought the desire to push him back to give me some breathing room.

He popped the toothpick into his mouth, tilted his head toward the safe and through clenched teeth said, "Go ahead."

The large black box looked antique. The numbers on the dial were worn and rusty.

"Try spinning it to the right first." He leaned against the desk with his arms folded, acting like he could wait all day.

At first the dial turned smoothly, but then I felt a resistance and heard a faint click. The knob stopped on the number twenty. I couldn't believe my luck. I spun it the other way, hoping against hope that I could do it a second time. Again the dial stiffened, and then stopped, this time at thirty-two. I was on a roll and Jimmy was now on his feet leaning over me. I spun it back to the right until I felt another spot of resistance and the knob stopped at five, again with a slight click. I pulled on the lever and the door opened. I grabbed the wad of money, passed it over to Jimmy, and stared at the back of my hands.

"My God, I'm a natural." I smiled with relief and amazement.

"You are so gullible," Jimmy said, sneering at me.

"What?"

He leaned his head back and laughed. "It's a fake, Ms. Patty Cakes. Anyone can open it."

I took a closer look at the safe. The painting of the logo on the side appeared distressed, but in a consistent manner. I looked at my fingers and they were clean, no orange grit. I leaned in closer to the dial and what I originally thought was rust was spray paint. I cringed, feeling like a fool to be taken in by such a simple trick.

Jimmy continued to snicker as he counted the money.

"Okay, here's the deal," he said, turning serious. "You've just hit your first number on the combination to your 'get-out-of-jail free card.' Let's see you go for a second."

His confusing metaphor irritated me and I started to correct him, but Jimmy raised his hand, indicating he would not tolerate an interruption.

"I want $1,500 for the three pieces of furniture. I'll give you three days." He turned and left, his laughter stopping only after the front door closed.

Since I always liked to get in the last word, I poked my head out of the office door and yelled: "But they're crap!"

I used Julie's key to let myself into her tiny apartment. The place was hot and stuffy and needed cleaning. There were magazines thrown about, dirty pans on the counter, and coffee mugs on every horizontal surface. I'd just started leafing through a small stack of bills when I heard a knock. Looking through the peephole I saw a teenager with straight, dyed black hair hanging down into his eyes. I opened the door enough to show my head and saw the same outfit I'd seen on the kid that stood under the streetlight the night Julie was killed: a tattered black leather jacket, a black T-shirt, and black jeans.

"Hi," I said.

"Hi." He looked down.

"Can I help you?" I opened the door a little wider. He stood as tall as I and had the lanky body of someone growing faster than the calories he consumes.

"I have Ferris."

The statement sounded like a threat. Had this guy kidnapped someone named Ferris? Was he asking for ransom?

"Who?"

"Ferris. Julie's rat."

"I didn't know she had one," I replied, relieved I wasn't being dragged into another crime.

"I take care of him when she goes away. I was just wondering…" He started picking at paint flakes on the door jam. "I was just wondering if I could keep him."

"Oh, I don't know." I thought about Todd's kids, but they seemed a little young to care for a rat. And I couldn't see Julie's mom wanting it.

I made an executive decision. "Sure, why not." The kid would go away and Todd would never know what happened to the rat.

He made eye contact for the first time and almost smiled.

"What's your name?" I asked.

"Jason."

I didn't offer mine.

"What apartment are you in?"

He turned and pointed directly across the complex. It provided a perfect view of Julie's front door.

"There in 2H."

In front of closed drapes, a purple and blue tear-drop crystal hung in the window.

"Did you ask your mom about keeping Ferris?"

He rolled his eyes away from me, like all adults are so stupid. "Yeah, she's okay with it."

I thought the conversation was over, but he didn't move.

"I saw you," he said.

"What?"

"I saw you. The night that Julie…" He half turned and pointed to the pool.

"Oh." Now I was the one who didn't want to make eye contact. Then something connected. "Did you see anyone else?"

"Maybe."

His brow furrowed and he crossed his arms. I waited for him to speak. He unfolded his arms, shifted his weight from one leg to the other, and folded his arms again.

"I want some weed." His eyes narrowed.

"Okay," I replied slowly.

"Then I'll tell you who else I saw."

So, he wanted to barter. I caved immediately.

"Okay. You want to give me your phone number?"

"No, no phones." He backed up a step. I wasn't sure if that meant he didn't have a phone or that he didn't want to use it. "Come by the apartment any time after four." He turned and walked away. I realized how much I was pushing my luck, showing up during daylight hours. I should have sneaked in after dark, like any self-respecting criminal.

It was seven o'clock when I pulled into my driveway. I was hoping that Mrs. Russo would be standing in my kitchen preparing some wonderful meal for me, but she wasn't. Since I'd eaten all the leftovers, I decided on soup and salad.

After dinner I expected a boring night of TV, but when I

sat down on the couch, I could easily see my maybe-Monet. The light wasn't good, so I took it down from the wall and held it under a table lamp. The brush stroke looked right, as did the signature. It could be real, but who was I kidding? I wasn't an expert. I started to hang it back up, but instead took it into the kitchen, placing it on the table.

"I could do that." I spoke confidently, as if Monet stood next to the sink. I went to my bedroom closet where I'd stashed my unpacked boxes and looked for the one that said 'oils' on the side. I lugged it to the kitchen and set up my easel. All my blank canvases were too large, so I selected a picture of a sunset I'd painted in watered-down acrylics. Since paints work on the science of fat-over-lean, I knew my oils would stick without a problem.

I popped the Monet from its frame so I could see the colors all the way to the edge. I dug in and lost myself in recreating a sailboat with two passengers at sunset. Blue and gray created the sky, while pink and orange mimicked the sun on the horizon and again on the water's surface. Hours later as I was painting the *t* in *Monet*, I heard footsteps behind me. I turned to see Mrs. Russo admiring my work.

"Like grandmother, like granddaughter, I see."

I felt a combination of embarrassment and pride. I turned back to the painting.

"Don't you ever knock?" I asked.

"I did, but you ignored me."

"Sorry, I didn't hear you."

She took a step closer and leaned over my shoulder, whispering in my ear. "Sotheby's would never be able to tell the difference."

"Oh, please," I said flatly.

She came around and sat down across from me. "But it would be fun, wouldn't it?" Her eyes lit up. "We could take the real one in first, have it authenticated, and then switch it with yours right before the sale."

I shook my head. Mrs. R grinned at me.

"You can't tell me that you wouldn't like to see your artwork sell for half-a-million dollars?" She paused, waiting for a reaction. "The auctioneer's opening offer at a $100,000. The bids jumping up fifty grand at a time." She looked off into the distance. "It's really a thrill, knowing all that money is yours."

I sighed and swirled my brush in a jelly jar of turpentine. I decided not to point out that she was short a zero on her estimates.

"I saw Jimmy today," I said.

"Did he give you another job?"

"Yeah, how did you know?"

She shrugged. "He's predictable. What is it?"

"He wants me to sell some furniture for him."

She wrinkled up her nose, "Oh, that's going to be tough. We'll have to get some help to move them out of the store."

"Maybe I should try to sell them."

"How much did he want?"

"Fifteen hundred."

"And I suppose they're not worth that?"

"Not by my estimate."

"I'm starting to think he's playing you for his own perverse kicks. Plus, he has no idea what he's doing; he's a terrible business man."

"He says after this, he has one more job for me, and then

he'll drop the charges."

Mrs. R's mouth turned into a thin line.

I put down my brush. "Oh man! Jimmy's right. I am gullible."

"Patricia, we need to nail him for Julie's death. Then his credibility will tank, the charges against you will be dropped, and you'll come out smelling like a rose."

I didn't share her belief that muddying Jimmy's reputation would magically make the charges disappear, but she did seem sincere about helping me. I reached for my purse and pulled out the keys to Julie's apartment. "Maybe we should start at the scene of the crime."

"How did you get those?"

"I found them lying around at Mrs. Gordon's house."

"Well, imagine that," Mrs. R gave me a sly smile.

"Yes, imagine that." I thought of Jason. "Do you mind making a stop at Mrs. M's before we go?"

"No, why?"

"I need to pick up some weed."

Chapter Thirteen

A white rose adorned Mrs. Miller's ear, which I thought a little formal for breaking and entering. She pointed at two large black boxes that flanked Julie's couch.

"What are those?" she asked.

"Stereo speakers," I replied.

"Humph," she snorted. "I've owned refrigerators smaller than that."

Mrs. M had insisted on coming with us to investigate Julie's apartment. She said she didn't want to watch *A Street Car Named Desire* with Mrs. T, but I think it was because she didn't want me to get caught with an illegal substance while out on bail. I appreciated the sentiment.

Julie's living room felt cold. Even with the lights on, the shadowy corners held secrets. To the left sat a dining area and a small galley kitchen. A butcher block table at the end of the counter held the telephone and mail. A cork board hung above it, with pictures and phone numbers. On the far wall a doorway led into the hall.

"I'll go with you," Mrs. Miller said, referring to the delivery of the weed.

"Jason said he'd talk only to me," I replied, hoping that was a strong enough argument.

"Are you sure he's not an undercover cop?"

"I'm not even sure he shaves yet."

"Well, you can't be too careful." She slowly pulled the bag from her pocket and handed it to me.

"I'll be fine," I said, giving her my best trust-me smile. I left her standing in the living room looking disappointed.

Jason answered his door wearing a dirty white T-shirt, jeans and holey socks. His jet black hair stuck out in odd directions. The apartment smelled faintly of marijuana. Without a word I followed him into his room.

Dark blue walls displayed music posters featuring bands I'd never heard of. A pile of clothes lay on an unmade bed. Just inside the door were two grocery bags sitting on the floor. Ferris' cage sat on a chest of drawers. I couldn't see the rat, but I assumed he was in there somewhere, hiding under cedar chips and ripped up newspaper.

"How's Ferris doing?"

"Fine."

I turned and smiled at Jason. He moved hair out of his eyes and looked at the floor. I pulled the weed out of my pocket and handed it to him. He stared at the small bag.

"That's it?" he said, sounding irritated.

"What were you expecting? A shoebox full?"

He grabbed the weed and shook it at me. "Shit, more than this!"

I raised an eyebrow, surprised by his craving for the drug.

He sat down on the bed, opened the bag and inhaled; then closed his eyes for a moment and sighed. "I guess it's better than nothing."

"So, are you going to tell me what you saw?"

"Oh yeah," he said, sealing up the bag. "Some lady in a yellow dress."

"Old? Young?" I asked, thinking that really didn't help me much.

He shrugged, everyone probably looked old to him. "It was dark. And a guy."

"Could it have been Jimmy?"

"I don't know. I didn't see him. They were going into the passageway that goes out to the back parking."

"Anything else?"

"They were speaking in Chinese or something like that."

"How long between when you saw them and when you saw me?"

Again he shrugged. "Half hour, maybe. I don't know."

"Did you see Julie that evening?"

He shook his head.

Ferris emerged to take a spin on his exercise wheel which emitted an annoying squeak. I watched his trip to nowhere for a few moments before remembering that Jason mentioned he took care of Ferris when Julie traveled.

"When did you get Ferris from Julie?"

"I don't remember, a day or two before she died."

"So she was going out of town?"

"I guess."

"Did she tell you where she was going?"

"No."

I rubbed my temples in frustration. Conversing with this guy was torturous.

"How long was she going to be gone?"

He finally looked up at me. "She said a while. That's why she brought so much cedar and food." He gestured to the bags on the floor. "Even though I had enough left over from her last trip. I guess she forgot."

I looked back to the cage, a bag of cedar chips leaned up next to it with a twist tie keeping it closed.

"Jason," a woman's voice called out.

Jason jumped up and headed out the door.

I knelt down next to the bags and dug around hoping to find a receipt. I knew it was a long shot, but a date of purchase might provide an insight into Julie's trip plans. The first bag held rat food. I pulled the cedar chips out of the second bag and found a sealed envelope, with Jason's name written on it in longhand. I felt something unbendable inside, like a credit card, and something else small and hard.

I heard the female voice again. "Who?"

"I don't know what her name is, Mom," Jason said.

I leaned sideways and looked into the hall. A pale woman dressed in sweats, a head scarf and a baggy T-shirt leaned on the door jam. Pale skin and dark circles around her eyes suggested a serious illness. She looked at me unblinking before Jason pushed her gently into the room and closed the door behind him.

I dropped the envelope back in the bag and replaced the rat food, scrambled to my feet and returned to the living room. I was flooded with guilt for stereotyping Jason as a stoner. He didn't want the weed for himself; he needed it for his mother.

Jason emerged from the bedroom, went into the tiny kitchen and put water on the stove.

"My name's Patricia," I said.

He picked up a mug from the dish drainer and dropped in a tea bag.

"Is your mom getting chemo?" I asked.

He nodded.

"Was Julie your supplier?"

"Yeah." He turned, resting a hip against the chipped Formica counter top with his arms folded across his chest. He suddenly looked much older than his years. "Julie was cheaper than the dispensary." He took a deep breath as he rubbed his forehead with the back of his thumb, blinking back tears. "It's the only way my mom will eat. Those anti-nausea drugs are a joke."

"I know someone you can get it from."

He turned back to the stove and moved the kettle over half an inch on the burner. "I can't afford to get in trouble, I'm the only one—"

"Don't worry. I'll be right back."

He shrugged, looking as if he couldn't get caught up in hope. He probably didn't have the strength.

I let myself back into Julie's apartment with her key. Mrs. R sat at the kitchen table going through Julie's mail. I heard a faint buzzing sound and followed it to the bedroom. Mrs. M sat on Julie's bed, eyes closed, holding a small beige vibrator against the side of her neck. She was purring.

"Mrs. Miller?" I whispered.

"Oh, I need one of these. Do you think anyone would miss this?"

"Mrs. Miller, those aren't, ah, necessarily used for sore

muscles." She stopped purring and her eyes popped open wide. She quickly pulled the vibrator away from her neck and held it out in front of her.

"Really?" She looked at me and then back to the vibrator. "Oh my goodness." She started to grin. "Now I have to have one." She put it back to her neck. "And maybe one for Mrs. B too. Her birthday's coming up. Do you think I could get one in bright yellow?"

"Oh, I think you could get one in any color you want."

She closed her eyes again and as much as I hate to come between a woman and a vibrator, I needed to get back to the task at hand.

"Mrs. Miller, I have a favor to ask you."

"Anything, dear."

"The kid I took the weed to?"

She pulled her new found friend away from her neck, and I finally had her full attention.

"Yes? Did you get some information?"

I heard a rustling behind me and turned to see Mrs. R.

"First," I said, "I found out the weed is for his mom. She's going through chemo."

"Oh?" Mrs. M inquired.

"And Julie was his source."

"Say no more." Mrs. M's hand came up, as if stopping traffic. She stood. "What apartment are they in?"

"2H. But I don't think they have a lot of money."

She nodded. "Most of my clients don't. I'll go talk to him," Mrs. Miller said and left the room.

"Did you find out anything else?" asked Mrs. Russo.

I repeated that Julie said she'd be gone for a while. When

I told them Jason had seen a woman wearing a yellow dress and heard a guy speaking in an Asian language, her eyes narrowed.

"What?" I asked, wanting to be included in her thought process. I waited for an explanation, but she didn't say a word. She went back to the kitchen, and I thought about Mrs. B's trademark yellow. She was a crack shot and could probably steal a car out from under someone as he changed radio stations, but I couldn't imagine her as a killer. Especially in this case, why would she? But Mrs. B was the one person I hadn't seen the night Julie died.

I picked up the vibrator. The blunt end had a small round gold sticker with black letters reading: 'Delectable Dildos.' So Julie had crossed paths with Cassandra. Since Cassandra lived at the Finley Hotel and Julie worked there, it really wasn't surprising. Tossing the sex toy on the bed, I went back to the kitchen.

"Find anything?" I asked Mrs. R.

"No." She opened a cabinet door and slammed it shut.

"What should we be looking for?" I asked.

"Any evidence of Julie's relationship with Jimmy."

"Like?"

"Pictures, letters, cards."

"We're a paperless society, remember?"

"Did you find a computer?"

"No," I said, looking around as if she'd have one set up next to the sink. "But if Julie had a laptop, it could be anywhere."

"What about an address book?"

"Her address book would be in her phone, which is another thing we haven't found."

I returned to the living room, and as I sat down on the couch my knee bumped a magazine, tipping it off the coffee table and onto the floor. I picked it up and noticed a toothpick tucked into the dark brown shag carpeting. Using a clean tissue I gently extracted it from the long fibers. It smelled faintly of mint. It had to belong to Jimmy Chang.

"Hey, look what I found," I said, returning to the kitchen. "A toothpick." I held it up proudly for Mrs. Russo to inspect.

"It's not much to go on."

"But its minty, the kind that Jimmy Chang likes. It's DNA evidence."

"Evidence that he was here isn't evidence of murder," she replied, bursting my bubble. She opened a drawer. "Here's a baggie, put it in that." She obviously wasn't impressed with my find. "We should also be looking for drugs, prescription or otherwise."

Mrs. M returned, her mouth set in a straight line. "It's all taken care of."

After an hour of hunting, our only find had been my toothpick. No computer, no drugs, no incriminating evidence linking Jimmy to Julie.

"It's odd that we didn't find anything useful," Mrs. M said, as we were leaving.

"Actually it's not," Mrs. R replied, shaking her head. "We just got here too late."

At the front curb I used my remote to unlock the car.

A gruff voice came from behind us. "So you're back."

The three of us turned. Out of the shadows stepped Jake's Uncle Pete. He wore khaki shorts and a Hawaiian shirt, unbuttoned to the waist, just like the night I'd met him.

Mrs. Russo jumped into the front seat, but Pete grabbed the door before she had a chance to close it.

"I knew you'd come back. They always do." He let out a low chuckle and his gold tooth reflected a headlight of an oncoming car.

"You're mistaking me for someone else," Mrs. R said.

Mrs. Miller had snuck up behind Pete, her purse high in the air, ready to smack him over the head. I rapped my knuckles on the top of the car. She looked my direction and I shook my head. She slowly lowered her arm, scowling.

"I don't make mistakes over beautiful sophisticated women," he continued. "Especially one I owe a favor to. That blaring music the other night was driving me crazy."

Short drive, I thought.

"Whoever you think I am, I'm not," Mrs. Russo said, tugging on the door handle.

Uncle Pete backed up and let her close the door. Mrs. Miller and I got in the car and I hit the automatic locks. He tapped on the window.

"Being coy only makes you more attractive," he said, wagging his finger at her.

I turned the ignition over, pulled away from the curb and glanced in the rearview mirror. Uncle Pete stood on the sidewalk waving goodbye.

"You'll be back," he yelled.

Mrs. R turned her face away from me. I gave a quick look over my shoulder to Mrs. Miller. Her brow was furrowed.

"So you want to tell me what that was all about?" I directed the question to Mrs. R. "You've met Julie?"

"I wanted to buy the Cadillac from her; that's all." She gave me her dismissive wave. "And as I was knocking on Julie's front door, that guy came running at me yelling about her music." She turned to me. "Julie turned down the music before she let me in. He was pleased and obviously a little too grateful."

"I can't believe you never told me that you met her," I said.

"There's nothing to tell. I tried to buy the car; she wouldn't sell it; end of story." Her mouth was set in a thin line.

Leaning forward I looked at Mrs. Miller in the rear view mirror. She was biting her lower lip. They had to be withholding information. But why?

On arriving home, I flipped on the light in my kitchen and immediately saw that my Monet was missing. Not my grandmother's, but the one I painted that evening. In its place was a napkin with sloppy writing on it that said: 'We're back in business!'

"We? We who?" I asked the remaining Monet.

I looked around, wondering if anything else was missing. But why take a wet painting? It would be a week or so before it dried.

I walked through the rest of the house. Everything seemed to be in its place. For a moment I considered calling the police, but since I didn't know who had keys to my house, I didn't want to waste their time. I assumed that whoever took the painting would contact me. Apparently to do business.

Chapter Fourteen

The next morning I turned on my cell phone and listened to the one message I'd received the night before: *Patricia, this is Cindy Gordon. I was wondering if you could come by when you get a chance. There's something of Julie's I'd like you to have.*

My neck tightened, which made me realize how guilty I felt about going through Julie's apartment.

When Mrs. Gordon opened her front door, she gave me a strained smile and welcomed me inside. I followed her into the dining room. On the table was a mahogany jewelry box decorated with flowers made from mother-of-pearl. She opened the lid and it played a tinny version of Beethoven's *Fur Elise*. I hadn't seen it the previous night, which meant that Todd had already been through Julie's apartment, probably collecting valuables and keepsakes, and I assumed her computer and phone.

Mrs. Gordon pulled out a silver bracelet inlaid with three pieces of turquoise and handed it to me. "Why don't you take this? I'd like to see it go to a good home."

I smiled and slipped it on my wrist.

"Thank you, it's very pretty."

"Julie picked it up on a trip to Arizona this spring. She was so happy then." She paused for a moment. "That was before her dad died and she started drinking again." She took a deep breath and pulled a tissue from her pocket, dabbing at her eyes. "I don't know what I'm going to do with that Cadillac. I told her to get rid of it, just sell the damn thing. I sure didn't want her driving it."

Bewildered, I stared at her.

"You know," I said, speaking softly. "Jimmy Chang claims he owns that car."

"Really? Julie sold it?"

"Chang said he had a lien on it."

"A lien? Well, how would that—" she stopped mid-sentence. "So does Jimmy have the car now?"

I nodded.

"Well, good riddance. It brought us nothing but trouble."

Hmm, you and me both.

As I pulled out of Mrs. Gordon's driveway, I thought about our conversation. Mrs. Gordon's ignorance about the lien on the Cadillac didn't surprise me. Mr. and Mrs. Gordon had been divorced for years and there was no reason for Julie to tell her mother. But what confused me was her distaste for the Caddy. Why wouldn't she want Julie to drive it?

Based on what I overheard of Julie's conversation with Jimmy, there wasn't any contract to pay off the Cadillac. But, it made me wonder about Jimmy's bookkeeping in general. Had he filed the correct paperwork with DMV to go through the repossession process? It was a long shot, but I thought I had better check with the police, just in case. I couldn't be charged with stealing the car if Jimmy didn't legally own it.

As I turned into the police station's parking lot, Officer Romano was pulling out, driving a little pickup truck. He turned back around and parked next to me. He stepped out of the car wearing jeans and a polo shirt.

"Ms. Schuster," he greeted me formally and looked me over. Not the way a man does to a woman he's attracted to, but like a cop does to a suspect.

"Officer Romano." I mirrored his formality.

"Can I help you?"

"I just spoke with Cindy Gordon, Julie's mother. She was under the impression that Julie, or maybe her ex-husband, owned the Cadillac that I supposedly stole. Julie had a key for it; I used it the night I drove her home. Jimmy Chang says he owns it, but if he had a lien on it, wouldn't he have to submit paperwork to repossess it?"

He stared at the ground. "I thought we ran it through DMV, but I can look again."

The Lakeville Police Department was a low, squat building with a flat roof. The interior was modern but sparse, with a small waiting area and bulletproof glass dividing the officers from the public. A woman spoke Spanish through a circular grouping of holes in the see-through barrier to an officer on the other side.

Officer Romano gestured to a wooden bench for my waiting pleasure. He used a keypad to unlock a door leading to the inner sanctum of the department.

Instead of sitting down I examined a cork bulletin board showing the FBI's Ten Most Wanted list. Thankfully, I didn't see any pictures of The Ladies. When I did sit down, the seat was cold and hard. They obviously didn't like people loitering.

After a few minutes, Officer Romano returned to the lobby. Just before the door slammed shut behind him, I saw a female officer in the hallway. Her short black hair looked familiar, but I couldn't place her.

"The DMV records show Jimmy Chang was a lien holder and he repossessed the car legally," said the Officer. "He filed all the proper paperwork. The car belongs to him."

"I wonder why Julie still had a key."

"You can tow a car without the key, and a locksmith could make a new one. Or Chang already had a key and didn't need hers."

I sighed at the obvious answers. Of course, Mr. Gordon could have given Jimmy a key to the Caddy as collateral for the loan.

I thanked Officer Romano and left.

The furniture in Elsie's Antiques needed rearranging. And I hated moving furniture, mostly because I didn't have the strength to do it. I made an attempt to shove a six-foot long buffet, but my feet slid on the floor like I was wearing socks on hardwood.

A pounding at my backdoor interrupted my cartoon antics. The noise kept up, and I was ready to give whoever it was hell, until I opened the door and saw a burly man standing there, wearing an undershirt, dirty jeans and a lot of hair. The man's onyx colored eyes squinted at me.

I was instantly on alert.

"Mrs. Russo sent me," he grunted and reached out his greasy paw to push the door open further.

My instinct was to slam it in his face. So that's what I did. But it didn't shut. I looked down at a steel-toed boot holding the door open about five inches shy of the jam. For a big man he had pretty quick reflexes. Did Mrs. Russo send this goon to have me whacked? But why now? Could it have been because I found out that she'd met Julie?

Putting my shoulder to the door, I leaned into it with all my weight, knowing full well if he wanted in, there was no way I could stop him.

"Now, this is exactly what we've been talking about in group." A reedy male voice said from the other side of the door. "What's the impact of your actions?"

The grunter grunted.

"You've scared the woman," the other voice said. "Plus you didn't achieve your objective."

"I know, I know. I can't help it," the grunter said. "It's a habit."

"That's all right," the other man gently replied. "Go ahead, try it again."

"Ma'am, we've come for the furniture."

"Better, that's better."

"You think so? 'Cause it still kinda sounds like an order."

"Okay, how could you say it differently?"

"Maybe I should start with 'hi'?"

My panic morphed into a mixture of irritation and curiosity. I peered around the edge of the door.

The grunter smiled awkwardly at me. "Hello," he said. "How are you?" His eyebrows went up and he nodded, as if to say 'Okay, your turn.'

I stared for a moment. "Fine."

"Mrs. Russo sent us to pick up—"

"I heard," I said, interrupting him and slowly opening the door.

A tall thin man wearing jeans and an oversized hooded sweatshirt stood behind the grunter.

"Hello, ma'am," the thin man said, hiking up his pants.

"Hello," I responded and stepped aside.

The grunter charged past me into the store.

"How are you today?" the remaining man asked and stood staring and grinning until I motioned for him to enter.

"Fine," I replied.

"Sorry about that," he said, cocking his head toward his friend. "We're in group together." His voice lowered to a whisper. "Anger Management."

He went on ahead of me and I pointed to Jimmy's three shabby pieces. The grunter looked around the store, and then pulled a plain white envelope out of his back pocket. He handed it to me. I removed the stack of hundreds and began to count.

About halfway through, he interrupted me. "What, don't you trust us?"

The thin man nudged him and leaned over to whisper in his ear. The grunter took a deep breath and folded his arms. I continued to count.

There were fifteen crisp one-hundred dollar bills. I was relieved, because I'd have enough money to pay off Jimmy. But I also felt nervous. My debt to Mrs. Russo had just increased.

The thin man picked up the Chippendale chair in one hand and the tilt-top table in the other. The grunter grabbed the settee and hoisted it over his head as if it was light as an umbrella. Suddenly, I envisioned my heavy buffet floating effortlessly through the air to its new location. I followed them into the alley to watch as Jimmy's junk disappeared into the back of their nondescript white moving truck.

"Before you go, could I ask a favor?" I looked hopefully at the two. "Could you help me move some furniture around?"

The grunter took a step toward me. "Hell, no. Who do you think we are?"

The other man cleared his throat and the grunter stepped back and again took a deep breath.

"Sorry," he said, giving me a strained smile, "we're on a tight schedule today."

"Okay, thanks anyway." I waved the envelope at him to indicate there were no hard feelings.

"You might not want to do that," he growled, looking up and down the alley.

I tucked the envelope under my shirt.

The grunter gave one last grunt as he hauled himself up into the passenger side of the truck and slammed the door. The thin man smiled and waved goodbye.

"Okay, bye now," I called out. "Nice doing business with you."

After tucking the $1,500 safely away in the cash register, I decided to ask for help with rearranging the store. No matter how independent I wanted to be, I still couldn't move a two hundred pound buffet by myself.

I headed down to Jake's Body Shop. The morning fog had lifted and the sun felt warm on my skin. I entered the garage through a massive roll-up door. Large plate glass windows allowed views into two offices, sitting side-by-side. Jake talked on the phone, while his sister, Lily, filed in the adjacent room.

An assortment of banged up cars and trucks filled the bays. Jimmy's Cadillac sat next to an enclosed room which I assumed was the painting booth. The back of the building also had a large roll-up door that mirrored the front. A young guy with short sandy hair and wearing dark blue overalls used a buffer to gently polish the fender of a newer model Mercedes.

Jake glanced up and I waved to him. He ended his call and came out to greet me.

"Hi," he said.

"Hi. I came to ask a favor."

"Okay."

"I need some furniture moved in the store."

"Sure," he said and turned into the cavernous garage. "Reed!" he yelled, and then whistled loudly.

The hum of the buffer stopped and Reed stood up. Jake swung his arm up indicating he should follow us.

"Back in a minute," he said to Lily, who responded with a scowl.

We walked slowly out to the street until Reed caught up. Jake introduced us and I eyed his hands, worried they might be grimy. They weren't.

"What are you doing with Jimmy's Caddy?" I asked.

"He wants it painted black. It's going to look great." Jake grinned. He might pretend his job was ho-hum but he obviously liked his work.

When we arrived back at my store I pointed to two 1960s orange vinyl upholstered chairs. "Okay," I said. "These can be moved to the back wall."

Jake and Reed picked up the two pieces and placed them

where I'd requested.

"This armoire," I said, patting the plain pine door, "can go right next to those chairs."

The two men circled the large cabinet, but there was nothing to grab onto.

"Do you have a dolly?" Reed asked.

"Sure." I jogged off to retrieve it from the storage closet.

After a few minutes of struggle and maneuvering, the armoire sat next to the chairs. Reed wiped his brow with the back of his hand. Jake rolled up his sleeves, put his hands on his hips, and took a deep breath.

The last piece was the buffet. They pulled out the front drawers and grabbed the marble top, but the back edge of stone fit flush, so using pressure with their open hands they squeezed and lifted. Jake's biceps strained at his shirt sleeves. He shuffled past me and I inhaled his wonderful aroma. My mind went blank.

"Patricia?" Jake spoke to me.

"Hmmm?" I replied, my eyes barely able to focus.

"Is this where you want it?"

I nodded and tried to speak, but no words come out.

They pushed the buffet a few more inches until it hugged the wall. I looked around hoping I had other pieces to move, just to keep Jake in the store. I pointed at the secretary that I liked so much. The two men moved to each side. Jake turned his head to me, I gestured for them to move it over a foot, and then another foot. They kept inching over until Reed bumped into an end table.

"That's fine," I said, finally finding my voice.

Both men were breathing hard by now, and I noticed Jake

staring at me.

"Anything else?" Reed asked, as his eyes darted back and forth between the two of us.

I shook my head.

"Okay, I guess I'll go," Reed said.

I followed Reed to the door, thanking him profusely.

When I turned back I noticed a picture on the wall, visible now that the secretary had been moved. It was a black and white photograph of a young Sunny Russo. She looked to be in her mid-20s, with dark hair cut in the same page boy that she currently wore. She leaned up against someone very familiar.

I took the picture down. "It can't be. Is that Elvis?" I asked, tapping on the dusty glass.

Elvis Presley, dressed in his army duds, had his arm around Sunny's waist and he was smiling down at her. She gazed up at him, also smiling. How would she know Elvis? Groupie? Lover? An adoring fan? On the left side of the picture was a young man, with short wavy hair, leaning up against a convertible.

Jake leaned over my shoulder and I could feel his breath on my neck.

"I can't believe it. Sunny and Elvis?" I started to laugh. "I guess you never know about people's past."

Being so close to Jake made my toes tingle. I turned to face him and his cell phone rang.

"Hello?" He paused. "Okay, I'll be right there." He turned off the phone. "I have to go." He held my gaze for a few seconds and his eyes fell to my mouth. I thought he was going to lean in for a kiss, but my front door jangled open and he stepped back. "Well, I'd better be getting back," he said, a smile turning up the corners of his mouth ever so slightly.

"Okay," I said, catching myself before I fell over. He moved to the door, stepping around the customer who had come in. "Thanks for your help," I called out after him. I took a deep breath. I could feel my lust buzz sizzling in my chest.

Chapter Fifteen

Late that afternoon, I sat in my office and pulled out Julie's keys. Holding them tightly in my hand, I hoped for some kind of telepathic message. I felt silly and was about to toss them back into my purse when her mailbox key caught my eye. I jumped up. It was the only place we hadn't looked. But I had one unpleasant errand to attend to before I could go rummaging through Julie's letters and junk mail.

I took Jimmy's $1,500 out of the cash register, folded it in half once, and then a second time. Wrapping a rubber band around the bills, I tucked them into my pocket. I checked the time: five minutes to six. I locked the front door and peeked out the window. Across the street a creepy mannequin sat in a rocking chair in The Yarn Barn's store window. For a second I thought it was the real Ms. Barn, and my heart missed a beat. I berated myself. I really shouldn't be afraid of a woman just because she wears killer knitting needles in her beehive.

I went out the back and turned the corner from the alley onto Jimmy's car lot. Parked in front of his trailer was a bright yellow VW bug like Mrs. B's. I moved back and hid behind the wall, peering around the corner, just enough to see, but not be seen. Mrs. B emerged from Jimmy's office and drove off. I was starting to get a little uncomfortable with how chummy these two were. But I decided to give Mrs. B the benefit of the doubt. She could be in the market for another car.

I jogged across the parking lot, up the stairs to the trailer and knocked. The door opened a crack. Jimmy was on the phone and waved me in. The place smelled of oil paint. I looked around for my Monet. Harsh overhead florescent lights contrasted with dreary taupe colored paneled walls. Two folding chairs sat opposite Jimmy's dull green desk and matching filing cabinet. A red bowl filled with oranges sitting on a small corner table provided the only color.

Jimmy hung up the phone, leaned back in his chair and put his hands behind his head. He wore a white suit with a navy button-down shirt open at the neck.

"Patty, Patty, Patty," he said slowly, giving me the once over. "That Monet. It's beautiful."

I stared at him, my anger rising. "Give it back, Jimmy."

He slowly stood up and reached into an inside pocket of his jacket and removed a small test tube with a red plug on the end. Popping off the lid he slid out a toothpick and put it in his mouth.

"Pick?" he asked.

I glared at him.

He shrugged and put the container back into his pocket. "You're as good as Elsie," he continued. "Maybe even better. I thought you'd have to practice for awhile to get up and running." He wagged his index finger at me. "But I must say, I'm impressed."

I lowered my voice to a growl. "I want it back."

"Oh man, are we going to rake in the dough. I already have a buyer in Taiwan. How's a thirty-seventy split sound to you?"

"Give it back, Jimmy."

"No? Okay, forty-sixty, but you're going to have to throw in a frame for that."

"Jimmy, I want my painting back. And there is no way I'm going to help you con people."

Putting his hand to his heart, he looked genuinely hurt, "But Patty Cakes, you don't have a choice."

"Where is it? I know it's here."

"Take a look at this."

He pulled his phone from his pocket, pushed some buttons, and then turned it around to show me a picture. "See this guy?"

The tiny screen showed the inside of Elsie's Antiques. I stood behind my counter talking to a man wearing sunglasses, the one whose girlfriend asked about the pearls. Jimmy had shot the photo from outside on the sidewalk.

"Yeah," I replied.

"He's an undercover cop. And he's ready to claim you offered him an original Monet." He paused, his mouth turning into a sneer. "At a fraction of the price."

"It's my word against his," I snapped.

"Is it?" He showed me another picture. It was of me in my kitchen, painting the Monet. "Now who are the police going to believe? A suspected car thief or a cop?"

"How dare you," I said through gritted teeth.

He laughed. "Patty Cakes you are so predictable. Once you found out about your grandmother, I knew you wouldn't be able to resist following in her footsteps. But it happened so quickly. That's what amazes me. You're a natural. We have a great future ahead of us. Oh, and I have a buyer looking for a Warhol. How are you at painting soup cans?" He folded his arms in front of him, looking content.

A black cloud of rage engulfed me. I threw the only thing I had available to me, the wad of cash. Fifteen hundred dollars slapped against his chest and then flopped onto the desk.

"Mmm," he purred. "Cash and an angry woman. Two of my favorite things."

I stomped back to my car, drove like a mad woman to Julie's apartment, and then circled the block a few times to calm my nerves. My anger was transforming into resolve. I had to prove Jimmy Chang was responsible for Julie's murder. At any cost.

Julie's apartment mailboxes were close to the street and I wanted to get in and out without being seen. I parked in front and walked straight to the boxes, acting like I did it everyday. Envelopes and advertising mailers tumbled out as I yanked open the small aluminum door. I cradled them in my arms and shuffled through the stack. A bank statement, an electric bill, an ad for a dating service, and something from a company called U-Store-It. A note from the post office informed Julie that mail awaited pickup. The last piece was a check from the Finley Hotel, which I replaced since I didn't think that knowing Julie's salary would be of much help.

Dropping the rest into my purse, I turned around and slammed into a barrier. Shit! I jerked back and my head smacked up against the wall of metal mailboxes. It was a man. Jake's Uncle Pete, to be exact. He stuck a finger in my face, "You owe me an SUV!"

"Ah, Pete, I'm really sorry about that."

He pulled back and grinned.

"That's okay. Look what I've got now." He reached deep into the breast pocket of his blue and white Hawaiian shirt. I glanced around the complex, now hoping someone would see me.

He spun something small and green in my face. It was a four leaf clover.

"Nice," I said, forcing a smile.

"Now, all my problems are over," he said. Taking a step backwards, he shook his finger at me. "Oh, no you don't." He tucked the clover back into his pocket. "You're not going to ruin this one for me."

He glanced away and I thought I'd make a dash for the car. But his face contorted in anger. "Damn it!" he said, and his hand rose up.

I closed my eyes, preparing to be hit. But nothing happened.

"I've told the manager at least three times, to put a lock on this," he said.

I opened one eye.

"Such a ridiculous place to put a breaker box," he continued, his focus to the left of my head.

Taking a step away from the wall, I followed his gaze. He opened up a small metal door that fit between the mailboxes and the corner of the building and gestured to the electrical panel. "The kids get in here all the time and turn the lights off to the complex."

"The whole complex?" I asked, hoping I sounded equally outraged.

"No, just the exterior." He pointed a finger straight up. "The lights for the walkways and out in the bushes, the pool too. The teenagers like to go skinny-dipping." He sighed and his shoulders slumped. "That's why Julie died. The lights were out that night. She couldn't see the pool." He closed the electrical panel and took a step back. "And yet the door remains unlocked." He turned and walked away, shaking his head, seeming to have forgotten about me.

I let out a breath, ran to my car, and locked myself in. I closed my eyes trying to compose myself, but all I could see was a dark figure pushing Julie into a dark pool.

"Patricia, what a nice surprise," Mrs. Miller said. "Come in *mi hija*, we're all here." She pulled a red zinnia from behind her ear and tucked it behind mine.

A cloud of garlic enveloped me as I stepped into her house.

Mrs. Russo hovered over the stove, stirring a double boiler of what looked to be an Alfredo sauce. Mrs. T sat on the couch, engrossed in a movie. She smiled and waved to me across the room.

"Would you like to stay for dinner?" Mrs. M asked. "There's plenty."

"I'd love to," I replied.

Mrs. B stood at the sink, wearing a yellow apron, and rinsing lettuce leaves. She turned to greet me and then asked, "Is there something wrong, dear?"

My anger instantly returned. "Jimmy Chang has found another way to blackmail me." Four heads swiveled to look at me. Mrs. T muted the TV so she could listen.

"Tell us what happened," Mrs. M said.

"Remember the German couple you took pictures of?" I directed the question to Mrs. R.

She nodded.

"Jimmy took a picture of me talking to them. And Jimmy says the guy is an undercover cop."

"I knew it." Mrs. Butterfield said, waving wet romaine in the air. "Something didn't seem right about him."

"And you know the Monet I was painting?" I asked.

"The one that could pass for the real thing," Mrs. R said matter-of-factly.

I nodded. "Jimmy stole it." She stopped stirring. "And he claims this cop is willing to say I'd offered him a real Monet at a fraction of the price." The room went silent. "Jimmy took a picture of me painting the Monet." I suddenly felt ridiculously stupid.

"A dirty cop. Great. That's just what we need," Mrs. Russo said. She went back to stirring the simmering sauce. "So what does Jimmy want?"

"More paintings. With a thirty-seventy split."

"Thirty-seventy!" Mrs. B exclaimed and ripped a chunk of lettuce from the head. "The cheapskate!"

"I told him no."

"Good for you. That's a fifty-fifty venture if I ever heard one!"

"But, it's not about the money—"

"It's always about the money."

"Betty," Mrs. M said, "what Patricia means is that she doesn't want to do something illegal."

Mrs. B turned to me. "Oh. Sorry. I hadn't thought of that."

Mrs. Miller dropped fresh linguini noodles into a large pot of boiling water and poured me a glass of Chardonnay. I smiled gratefully and took a sip.

"Oh, I almost forgot," I said. "I went by Julie's today and picked up her mail."

"Can I see?" Mrs. Miller asked.

I dug through my purse and handed over the letters. Without looking at them, she held them over the steam. After a minute she ran a knife under the gummed edges, opening each one, leaving the flaps wrinkled but intact. She passed the envelopes around. I opened the electric bill. I looked it over, nothing unusual, Julie owed $58.50, but she was up to date with the payments.

"Nothing here," Mrs. Miller said, as she tossed the online dating ad on the counter and returned her attention to the pasta.

"I've come up empty as well," Mrs. B said and shook her head. "She used her debit card at Cooper's Grocery store and Copperfield's Books."

Mrs. Russo turned off the heat to her sauce and opened up the letter from 'U-Store-It'. "Oh, what's this?" She tapped her finger on the page. "Looks like Julie recently rented a storage unit."

"That could prove interesting," said Mrs. M. "But we don't have the key."

"This is getting us nowhere," said Mrs. B. "What we need is more information on Julie. Maybe you could talk to those close to her?" She directed the request to me. "Like family or friends?"

"I met her coworker at the funeral," I said. "He might talk to me."

"Good, we've got a plan," Mrs. B said. "Patricia will weasel information out of Julie's work pal. And Rita and I will break into Julie's storage unit."

I put the wine glass to my lips but stopped mid-sip, hoping to head off the inevitable choking.

"Kidding! I'm kidding!" Mrs. B said, turning away, her shoulders shook as she tried to hold back the laughter.

My mother showed up at my house later that night.

"Mom, what a nice surprise!"

"Oh my dear, dear, daughter." She swooped in and kissed my cheek. Her eyes were puffy from crying. "I was thinking about you and wanted you to have this." She held out a homemade double-layer chocolate fudge cake. It was one of her specialties and one of my favorites. "And this," she handed over a white plastic grocery bag. I took a peek, it was a half gallon of vanilla ice cream.

"How sweet of you. Let's have some."

As my mom served up dessert, I made coffee. The rich smells of vanilla and chocolate seduced me and even though I felt full, my mouth began to water. I took a bite and looked at her. A tear rolled down her cheek.

"If only I'd been a better wife, he never would have left me," she said. "Now you're a child from a broken home. How is that going to affect you?"

"Mom, I'm twenty-five years old," I said, trying to talk through the cake in my mouth. "It's not like you're going to have joint custody and be shuffling me back and forth between households."

She blew her nose on a paper napkin. "You're right. I just feel so guilty. Plus now you don't have a grandmother."

I sat back and studied her. Besides dark brown crumbs on

her lips and a bright red nose, she had a sadness around her eyes that I hadn't noticed before. The stress of two losses at once, her mother and her marriage, was taking its toll.

"Mom, it's okay." I handed her another napkin. "I know about Nana being in jail, and that Mrs. Taylor took care of you."

She sniffled and took a deep breath. "You can't imagine how awful it was as a child, having your mother in jail. I never wanted you to be a part of that world. But now," she covered her face with her hands, "now you have a criminal record!"

"Mom, I didn't steal that car."

She slumped in her chair. "It's okay. It's in your blood; you can't help it." She sniffled again. "You know, I shoplifted when I was in high school."

"A lot of kids do that."

"I stole a $4,000 Yves Saint Laurent dress from the Emporium. I never got caught of course. I still have it." I heard a hint of pride in her voice.

"Have I ever seen it?"

She shrugged. "It's in the back of my closet, the long black one?"

"You mean the one with the velvet skirt and the silver and black lace bodice?" She nodded. I was impressed, but I didn't think it was time for a compliment.

She blew her nose again. "I should have given it back!" Tears squeezed out from the corners of her eyes. "Then none of this would have happened." She dabbed at her cheeks, took a deep breath, and slowly regained her composure. "Here, I brought something to show you."

She reached into her tote and pulled out an old family photo album. I'd looked through it many times. The pages were black construction paper, and the sepia colored pictures were held in by decorative tabs at the corners. She turned to the front and pointed to a woman in a long white dress holding a parasol.

"This is your great-grandmother, Elsie's mother, Petunia Bradshaw."

"I know. I've seen the picture." I put another forkful in my mouth. She paused, waiting.

"What?" I asked.

"Swallow," she said and I did. She hated when I choked.

"What you don't know is she robbed the West County Bank in 1928, when she was pregnant with your grandmother."

"Really?" I was amazed. "Did she get caught?"

"Nope."

"How much did she get?"

"About $1,800. That money fed Petunia and your grandmother through the Depression."

She flipped to the back of the book and unfolded a yellowed sheet of paper. It was our family tree. I hadn't looked at it in years. She pointed to Matilda Bradshaw, who was Petunia's mother.

"Now your great-great grandmother, Matilda." She tapped on the paper. "She robbed a smelting company in Vallejo in the early 1900s. She and an ex-employee dug a tunnel under the building. They cut a hole in the floor under the vault and in one night took over half a ton in gold bars. At the time it was worth close to $300,000."

"Did she ever get caught?"

"No. But the guy did, although he never turned her in. Accounts vary, but supposedly the company recovered only half of what was stolen."

I leaned over the table. "Do you think Matilda kept the other half?"

"Who's to say?" My mother raised an eyebrow at me. She looked down and tapped on the paper again. "And Matilda's sister, Clara, dressed up as a man and robbed trains. Three different times she held up the Southern Pacific Railroad."

"By herself?"

She nodded and took a sip of coffee. Her nose had returned to its original color and she'd stopped sniffling. "My mother was the first to be convicted. Clara was arrested once, but they couldn't make it stick. Apparently she was sleeping with the judge, and he threw the case out." She folded up the family tree and closed the cover. "That's quite a legacy you're carrying."

"Mom, you can't really believe I'm predestined to be a thief because of a blood line?" I tapped my finger on the album. "Stuff like that isn't inherited."

My mom turned just enough to point over her shoulder at my paints on the side board. I lowered my eyes and using my fork, poked holes into a small hill of melting ice cream on my plate.

"That's different," I said.

"Is it? Done anything illegal lately?" Her voice was casual, not accusing.

I thought about stealing Julie's keys, possibly compromising a crime scene by rifling through her apartment and opening her mail. Not to mention giving Jason marijuana for information.

"Patricia, only a real thief thinks they're not going to get caught," she continued.

I sat up straight in my chair; maybe she was right. I was afraid of going to jail for something I hadn't done, yet believing I'd get away with the things I had.

Wow, maybe being a thief was in my blood.

Chapter Sixteen

The first thing I did the next morning was call my surfing bud Chris.

"'lo," he answered in a sleepy voice.

"See ya out there?" I asked.

"See ya," he said and hung up.

I grabbed my surfboard from the garage and strapped it down to the top of my Civic. I needed to clear my head and the best way for me to do that was in the water. As I drove, the cool morning air rushed in through my open window. The road to the coast meandered through rural pastures dotted with grazing dairy cows and sheep. The hills were green, but would be turning a deep golden color any day now.

Perched on a small cliff just north of Bodega Bay was a parking lot with a restroom. I changed into my wetsuit and walked down a narrow dirt path sinking into the soft sand at the bottom. Just before the ground turned solid along the shoreline, I dropped my bag and board and kicked off my flip-flops. A strong breeze blew my hair back and I waved at Adam and Chris, bobbing in the water.

I closed my eyes and took a deep breath, filling myself with the potent smell of the ocean's salty essence. A seagull called out and I envisioned it slowly flying by.

The rhythmic sounds of the waves hypnotized me and I relaxed. I heard uninhibited laughing, the soft pounding of a runner, and the panting of a dog. The wash of a wave encircled my bare feet, cool and foamy. Its retreat eroded the sand from around my soles and left me perched on two miniature islands. I sank a bit and felt something tickle my left big toe and imagined a sand crab digging its way downward.

I opened my eyes. The waves were three to four feet, perfect for a nice relaxing day. Adam was riding one in, a grin showing through the tangled mess of hair that hung over his face. A man standing on a deck of a blue and white fishing boat looked toward shore.

I pulled on my booties and tethered the leash to my ankle. I walked out as far as I could, laid belly down on the board and paddled out beyond the break. I turned back toward shore and sat up. Two women, deep in conversation, walked barefoot along the beach, both carrying sandals.

After a few minutes of floating I heard a motor behind me and twisted around catching sight of a wave runner, heading my direction. It turned sharply, spraying white water into the air.

"Hotdog!" I called out to Adam. He nodded in agreement.

A swell lifted me and again, I lay down on my belly and paddled. The instant I started moving faster than my arms could propel me, I put my hands on the sides of the board, pulled my knees up and my feet under me. Standing up, I slowly raised my arms, getting my balance. The wave was smooth and strong. Immersed in the moment, the natural world became my only world. I felt free. My confidence returned as I sailed across the surface of the water.

The ride was almost at its end when I heard the wave runner. The sound was deafening as the machine came up behind me and slammed into my surfboard. Its back end tipped up and I flew head first into the churning water, my right elbow smacking hard against the board. I twisted and turned under the wave, trying to right myself. The leash pulled one leg skyward at the same time my body hit the sandy bottom. I pushed off with my hands and put one arm above my head. I popped up into the air and gasped. My board spun toward me and I grabbed it before it sliced me in two.

"Patricia!"

I looked around and saw Adam frantically paddling my direction.

"Are you okay?" he asked, as he came along side of me.

I nodded, breathing too hard to speak.

He looked behind him. "Here comes another wave."

I let go of my surfboard and turned back toward the oncoming wall of water and dove into it, coming out on the other side. The leash tugged at my ankle and I used it to drag the board to me.

Adam again swam my direction. But I was pulled back with the momentum of the outgoing swell before he could reach me. I tried not to panic, but the urgency to touch solid ground suddenly became all-consuming.

The next incoming wave was smaller and just enough to push me and the surfboard forward without it coming over my head. My toes touched bottom and Adam finally came up along side me, putting his arm around my waist and my free arm over his shoulder. He helped me to shore, but didn't let go of me until the water was ankle deep. I fell forward onto my hands and knees and stared down at wet, foamy sand, still panting. Adam squatted, his hand on my shoulder. He pulled the leash off my ankle and dragged the board above the tide line.

"You okay?" he asked again.

I nodded.

"She okay?" I heard Chris yelling as he splashed toward us.

I crawled out of the surf and dropped down sideways onto dry sand. I flipped over onto my back and looked up at them, my eyes burning from the salt. They were looking out to sea.

"Did you see that?" Chris said. "That was way uncool."

"Way uncool," Adam repeated.

"Do you think that was on purpose?" I said, finally catching my breath.

They both nodded.

"She was aiming for you, Salty Sister," Chris said.

"She? I assumed it was a guy."

"Nope," Adam said, turning and pointing out to the horizon. "She came off that fishing boat."

"Did you see what she looked like?" I asked, reaching over and hugging my elbow.

"No, she had on a hooded wet suit with goggles."

"How about her build?"

"Hard to tell with her wearing a life jacket," Chris stated. "But I'd say more on the thin side."

I rolled sideways and propped myself up on my left arm. The boat was now a dot, heading south.

"That was totally uncool," Chris said again.

"Totally." Adam and I replied in unison.

I leaned up against my car after changing back into jeans and a T-shirt. Adam loaned me one of his sweatshirts, but my hair was still wet and I shivered in the wind. The three of us explained what little we knew to the sheriff.

"That's not much to go on," he said.

"I know," was my reply. But it was a scary thing that had happened, and I wanted it documented.

"I'll check back at the marina." The sheriff shook his head. "But it doesn't look good." He gave me the head-to-toe glance. "Having any personal problems? Maybe with an ex-boyfriend?"

"No," I said, looking down at my flip-flops.

The sheriff eyed Adam and Chris. "Good thing your friends were here."

I nodded in agreement. I had already thanked Adam and Chris profusely, with promises of a home cooked meal. I gave my two friends another thank-you smile. Good thing indeed.

I stopped at The Tides Restaurant in Bodega Bay for a large coffee but since it was too early for clam chowder, I opted for an apple tart. A row of drawings based on Alfred Hitchcock's movie *The Birds*, lined the walls next to the cash register. In one, Tippi Hedron raised both arms to ward off an attack of the crazed fowl, her mouth open in terror.

I went outside to the pier, the smell of creosote heavy in the air. I choose a picnic bench already occupied by a gray and white seagull, who eyed me suspiciously.

"There's room for both of us," I told the bird as I sat down. It stood up from its resting position and waddled over a foot, sitting sideways, keeping one eye on my pastry.

More gulls perched on the metal roof above me, stealthily on alert by my presence. I knew if I offered one a piece of tart, within seconds I'd be just like Tippi, fighting off dozens of screeching fowl.

The tide was in and a fishing boat unloaded its catch. A seal called out to the fisherman, asking for a handout. Everything seemed so peaceful. The idea of someone wanting to hurt me seemed absurd. But Chris and Adam were convinced she was aiming for me.

But who knew I was here? Was someone watching my house? Or bugging my phone? Mrs. Russo came to mind. Her apartment window looked directly into my driveway. She could have seen me leave with my surfboard strapped to my car. But if Sunny Russo wanted to get rid of me, poisoning a plate of cannelloni would be an easier way.

As my adrenaline started to recede there was one thing I couldn't ignore.

I was onto something.

My father and Cassandra stood on my front doorstep. Cassandra had on bright pink cropped pants and a white button-down shirt tied in a knot above her waist. She carried a large tote that matched the color of her pants. She looked a little pissed off, but it was hard to tell behind her oversized round sunglasses. My father crossed the lawn to meet me at the car.

"Cassie was listening to the police scanner and heard a woman surfer almost drowned. I was so worried it was you."

"Was it you?" Cassandra asked breathlessly over my dad's shoulder.

Did I detect a hint of hopefulness in her voice?

"Yes, it was me. I'm fine though, a wave runner clipped my board, that's all," I said. "And I didn't almost drown." I refused to show my fear in front of either of them.

"God, I wish you'd give up this stupid sport," my dad snapped.

I was glad I had on Adam's sweatshirt so my dad couldn't see my bruised arm. I walked around the two and went in the house, fighting an overwhelming desire to slam the door in their faces.

"Well, aren't you going to say something?" he continued.

"Like what Dad? Like I'm going to give up surfing because you say so? I play it safe when I'm in the water. Chris and Adam were there to help me." I didn't like being put in the position of defending myself in front of Cassandra.

"And what if they weren't there?"

"Then I wouldn't have been in the water."

He dropped his anger and his shoulders slumped. "Look, sweetie, I just hate to see you doing something so risky."

I glanced toward his girlfriend and had to bite my tongue as to who was engaging in risky behavior. Cassandra's crack about me being daddy's little girl echoed in my ears. Even though I was scared, I didn't want my father's help.

"Dad, I'm fine. Okay? I need to take a shower so I can get to work."

He looked defeated but nodded, "Okay, have it your way."

I still had a few errands to run before I opened Elsie's Antiques. The first was a quick trip by Julie's to replace her mail. Parking on the street in front of the complex, I checked my rear view mirror for strange cars. There were no faces peeking out at me from the windows and no sign of Jake's wacky uncle. I ran to Julie's mail box, opened it, jammed the wrinkled letters inside, and then ran back to my car. My breath quickened and my heart pounded in my chest, but it wasn't the physical excursion. It was paranoia.

My second errand was a visit with Matt. I'd been to the Finley Hotel many times and the lobby always surprised me, once inside the humidity rose perceptibly. It contained a two-story high fountain that poured quiet sheets of water down three tiers of black granite into a shallow round pool. Today, I had the urge to kick off my sandals and wade in.

Instead, I went to the front desk and asked for the accounting department and was directed down a long hallway. A small brass plaque told me I'd found the right place. I knocked and opened the door. File cabinets lined the wall directly in front of me. Matt sat behind a computer; his usual spiky hair lay flat against the top of his head. He seemed lost in the piles of folders on his desk.

"Can I help you?" he said, glancing up.

"Hi." I could tell from the look on his face that he didn't remember me. "I'm Patricia. We met at Julie's funeral."

"Oh, hi," he said. "How are you?"

"Fine, thanks." I gave him my best friendly smile. "Julie's mom wanted me to check to see if you had any personal items of hers." I surprised myself with a smooth lie.

He looked confused.

I gestured to the empty desk next to his. "Was that hers?"

"Yes, but she'd moved her things into her new office." He went to the desk and started pulling out drawers, finding only pens and sticky pads.

"How did she like her new job?" I asked.

"Okay, I guess."

Leaning up against Julie's desk, I acted as if I could listen all day.

"The Finley is trying to increase its convention business." He stopped searching and sat down, folding his arms. "You know, playing up the access to the wine country. Julie was helping to organize our first big convention of Pacific Rim businesses. We have guests coming in from Korea this weekend. She was arranging shopping trips and winery tours, that sort of thing."

"Sounds like she was putting in a lot of hours." What it didn't sound like was a woman planning a vacation. But why did she leave so much rat food with Jason? Did she have a clue as to what was about to happen to her?

"She seemed to enjoy it." He looked in the last drawer and shook his head. "There's nothing here. You'll have to check her office."

I gestured to the piles of folders on his desk and smiled, "Looks like you got stuck with some extra work when she moved up."

He finally smiled. "I didn't mind." I saw sadness flicker across his face.

"So how long did you work with Julie?"

"About a year."

"Do you mind me asking you a personal question?"

He shrugged.

"Julie's mom was concerned that she had started drinking again. Do you think she had?"

He nodded. "Yeah, I suspected something after her dad died. She came in late, red eyes, that sort of thing. But she never drank during work." He sounded defensive. "Then a few weeks ago I saw her in the bar."

I nodded, encouraging him to continue.

"I was working late that night and I went to get a soda. Julie was sitting at the far end with a drink, talking to Kwan, one of the bartenders. She was laughing. Then she started talking softly, and he had to lean over to hear her. She whispered something in his ear."

"And what did he do?"

"He laughed and she said, 'No, really.' And he dropped a glass he was drying." Matt looked away and shook his head. "Later, I saw them leaving together." He looked disgusted.

"Where's her new office?"

"Go back the direction you came and turn right at the first hallway. It's down at the end."

"Do you think I could take a look?"

"You'd have to ask Human Resources to open it. Their office is across the hall."

I thanked Matt for his time and left.

I skipped the HR department, walked down the hallway and made a right. A woman in a business suit strode toward me and made eye contact. I smiled, hoping that if I appeared to belong there, no one would question me. She returned the smile and walked on.

Julie's name plaque identified her office. An unopened package sat on the floor, with a return address of Bellisa's Winery. I quickly pulled out her keys and tried the lock. The first key didn't work; the second did. I went inside and locked the door behind me. An automatic light came on, illuminating a small, sparse office. A floor-to-ceiling bookshelf on the far wall was empty. Her desk had a computer monitor and a pile of brochures scattered over the top: Russian River rafting trips, hiking on Mt. Tam, plus numerous wine tours. I opened each drawer only to find the typical supplies of pens, pencils, copy paper and an extra cartridge for the printer.

There were no personal items, except for a tiny troll doll with blue hair, its arms opened wide inviting hugs. A red light on her phone blinked, and I picked up the receiver. I heard two beeps and then a dial tone. Her extension number was taped to the handset cradle, and I punched in the number. Hearing nothing, I hit the pound sign. Luckily for me she hadn't put a password on her messages.

"You have one new message," the computer voice told me. "Main menu. To listen to your messages, press one."

I pressed one.

"First voice message. Wednesday 10:30 am."

"Hi Julie," a woman's voice said. "This is Michelle from Bellisa's Winery. I dropped the brochures that you requested in the mail today, plus menus from our restaurant. Thanks again for thinking of us. Call me if you have any questions."

The computer voice returned and said: "End of messages."

There was a small LED screen that ran along the top of her phone, showing the current time. Next to it were up and down arrows. I scrolled down. The screen turned into a caller ID. The first was an outside call, with the date and time. The second was Matt's name, with the same information plus his extension number. The third was Roger Finley's extension number. He had called Tuesday at 5:15 p.m. That would have been after I heard Julie arguing with Jimmy Chang at his car lot. The night she died.

Voices in the hall reminded me that I was pushing my luck. When it was quiet, I opened the door and slipped out, making it to the lobby without being noticed. Just past the silent waterfall a hotel employee placed a movable signpost in the foyer. White plastic letters spelled out the words: 'Welcome Korean Friends.'

Chapter Seventeen

Red light bulbs, illuminated by the evening sun, accented the perimeter of a theater marquee sign. But this was no theater. The removable letters said 'Adult Book tore.' A bin near the entrance had a one dollar price tag hanging from the top edge.

"Mrs. Miller, are you sure you don't want to buy this over the internet?" I asked. "It's more discreet."

"I told you, I'm a touchy-feely sort of person. Besides I'm too cheap to pay for overnight shipping costs. And Mrs. B's birthday is this weekend. I need a present for her now."

"I don't want to be recognized," I said.

"*Díos mío*, what if you are? Whoever sees you is in the same boat." She reached up and patted a pink carnation tucked behind her ear.

"But what about their surveillance equipment?" I glanced around the parking lot. "There're probably cameras up all over the place."

"Well, wait in the car if you like," she said.

I rubbed my forehead. I didn't want her going in alone. But our only other choice was Cassandra, and buying sex toys from my father's girlfriend seemed even more embarrassing than this. I stepped out of the car feeling underdressed, since I'd left my trench coat at home.

The bin next to the front door was full of Groucho Marx's glasses, complete with nose, fuzzy eyebrows and mustache. Mrs. Miller reached down and grabbed two, handing me one.

"Here. My treat."

I put on the glasses and felt both ridiculous and relieved.

The sales clerk sat on a stool behind a counter left of the door. He was shaved bald, wearing a tight rust colored T-shirt with a tiger tattoo running down his forearm.

"Ladies," he nodded to us.

I smiled, but I wasn't sure he could see behind my oversized nose. Mrs. Miller reached into her tote, counted out eight quarters from her change purse and put the money on the counter.

Wooden shelves stacked with magazines divided the room in half. High gloss covers exposed every inch of flesh known to the human body. We walked around the divider and passed by a curtained doorway that said 'Video Booths' across the top. Low moans and B-grade music emanated from behind dark purple velvet fabric. The back wall was lined with oak shelves, carrying X-rated DVDs. We kept walking and made a circle back to the clerk.

"Could you point us in the direction of the vibrators?" Mrs. Miller asked sweetly. Her fake mustache fluttered as she spoke.

"Sorry, ladies. We're all out. Our shipment got hijacked." He shook his head. "Can you believe it? That delivery was going to seven Northern California stores."

"What's someone going to do with all those vibrators?" Mrs. Miller asked.

Before the clerk could come up with an answer I didn't want to hear, I pulled Mrs. Miller out into the sunshine.

I knocked on the door to Cassandra's hotel suite. Mrs. Miller stood beside me. I'd suggested to Mrs. M that she buy some scented soap, or maybe a romance novel for Mrs. B's birthday, but she was insistent. I wanted to wear the Groucho Marx glasses, but since I'd called Cassandra to let her know we were coming, she was bound to see through my disguise. The door swung open wide.

"Patricia, so good to see you again." Cassandra was all smiles, the consummate salesperson. "And you must be Mrs. Miller." She grabbed Mrs. M's hands, pulled her forward and pushed her cheek next to hers. "Welcome," she said enthusiastically.

We entered into a round marble-floored foyer. A circular table sat in the center, dwarfed by a fresh flower arrangement large enough to block out the view of what lay beyond. Three pairs of women's shoes lay lined up on the floor close to the wall. Cassandra was barefoot. I slipped off my sandals and placed them with the other shoes. Then Mrs. M held onto my arm for balance as she removed her espadrilles.

Cassandra led the way into the living room decorated with ornate white French furniture. The view through the floor-to-ceiling glass consisted of the river in the distance and the employee parking lot directly below.

"This way please," Cassandra said.

We followed her into the dining room which also had floor-to-ceiling windows, and a sliding glass door that opened onto a balcony. Instead of a table, the room contained four rotating display racks of vibrators in every shape and color imaginable.

Along the wall was a long buffet with a granite top. Sitting on it were three dildos of super-human proportions, their bases suctioned to the stone. Mrs. M stood at the edge of the room, her mouth open.

"I've never seen so much pent-up pleasure in all my life," she said.

"They are beautiful, aren't they?" Cassandra replied, tipping her head to one side and giving one of the racks a spin. "Mrs. Miller, what did you have in mind?"

"Something in yellow," she replied.

"Yellow, hmm." Cassandra pondered her wares. "Oh, here's one." She pulled out an exact replica of the neon pink dildo she'd shown me at the restaurant. The yellow seemed even louder than the pink. "This one glows in the dark."

"How does it work?" Mrs. M asked.

"Manually," Cassandra replied, "it doesn't have batteries." She held it out, but Mrs. M kept her hands clasped tightly together. Cassandra put it back in its holder.

"Maybe this is more your speed." She pulled out a vibrator that lacked the anatomical correctness of the last and popped it out of its plastic packaging. It looked more like a large bullet, similar to the one Mrs. M had found at Julie's place, but in a pale yellow color. Cassandra inserted two batteries, twisted the base and it began to buzz. This time Mrs. M took it from her and held it against her palm.

"This will do," she stated. "Does it come in other colors?"

"Let's see. Oh, here's one in Moroccan Mint. I also have Luscious Lavender and Precious Peach."

"I'll take another in lavender."

"Would you like them gift wrapped?"

"Just the yellow one, thank you."

I heard giggling behind me and turned to see a young Asian woman, wearing jeans and a T-shirt.

"Hello," I said.

"This is Min," Cassandra said, handing Min Mrs. Miller's purchases. "She's my cousin from Korea. She's staying with me." She spoke sharply to Min in what I assumed was Korean. Min hurried out of the room.

Cassandra turned back to me.

"And how about you, Patricia?" She took a step closer. "I know you had your eye on that beautiful acrylic piece from the other night."

Before I had a chance to respond, Mrs. Miller let out a yelp. I looked over at the buffet. One of the dildos had come to life. Its writhing was more than Mrs. Miller could take. She ran from the room, knocking down one of the racks as she exited. All that pent up pleasure was now sprawled on the floor.

"Damn!" Cassandra swore at the mess.

I went to help her pick up the rack.

"Look, some of the packaging's cracked."

"Don't you have extras?"

She let out a sigh, "Oh, I do somewhere. I'm going to have to rearrange this whole thing now." She stepped back and turned around. "Where did she go?"

I pointed down a dark hallway, "Is the restroom that way?"

Cassandra disappeared into the dim, swearing under her breath.

"I'm sure she's fine," I called out after her.

I tried to straighten the wayward dildos that were looking at me cockeyed. He-he, cockeyed, I laughed at my own pun.

"Miss?" I turned to see Min holding out a yellow gift bag and a plain brown bag using both hands.

"Thank you, Min," I said. "I'm Patricia."

She smiled.

"How long have you been here?" I asked.

She looked up at the ceiling.

"Two months."

"Are you working?"

She shook her head and spoke softly. "I want to, but—"

"Min!" Cassandra barked at her as she stomped back into the room.

Min jumped backwards and hurried down the hall.

Cassandra's lips tighten. "I can't find her," she snarled.

"Don't worry. She's probably down in the lobby or at my car waiting for me."

"Well, she'd better be." Her voice had a nasty edge.

"How much does she owe you?"

"Forty-nine-fifty."

"Is a check okay?"

"I usually take cash only. But since I know your father, I'll make an exception."

I wrote it out and promptly left, straightening up one more vibrator as I walked past. As I slipped on my sandals I noticed Mrs. Miller's espadrilles were still in the entryway.

The lobby was empty. I stood and stared at the water flowing in the fountain for a few moments before sitting down on its edge to wait. Mrs. Miller finally emerged from the elevator, looking perplexed.

"Where were you?" I asked.

"In Cassandra's suite," she said.

"Is something wrong?"

She ignored my question, pulled out a small notebook from her purse and jotted down a few words.

"Mrs. M?"

She shook her head, "It wasn't what I was expecting."

"Overwhelmed by the inventory?" I asked with a smile.

"Something like that," she smiled back. "I'd like to know if your dad's paying for Cassandra's room."

"What if he is?"

"I don't trust her, that's all."

"My dad's a big boy. He knows what he's doing." I mimicked Cassandra's words.

When we settled into the car Mrs. M reached into her purse and pulled out a bag of weed. "Could you take me by Jason's? I need to make a delivery."

While Mrs. M visited Jason, I stood in the courtyard of Julie's apartment. The square shape of the building allowed the neighbors easy viewing of Julie's door. I thought about the night she died. She'd worn a jacket, which meant she was either on her way out, or coming home. She didn't have a car, so someone picked her up or dropped her off. If she'd been out drinking, her driver would have parked on the street. But was Julie alone in the courtyard, or did she have company?

A burst of kid's laughter interrupted the quiet as two young girls came running from the street dressed in bathing suits with towels thrown over their shoulders. They made a sharp turn to get around the stairs to the pool and easily pushed open the gate.

"Wait, girls," a woman called out as she followed them. She carried more towels and a cooler.

She knocked on one of the apartment doors, opened it and yelled inside: "Hey, did you know the pool gate's not locked?"

"It's been broken for weeks," a female voice replied.

The two girls squealed as they jumped in. "Mom! Mom! Get in!"

I examined the stairs that stood in front of the pool. The concrete steps were supported underneath at their center point by a steel beam. This gave the peculiar appearance that they were floating in midair. Since the lights were out the night Julie died, she would have been maneuvering around the courtyard in the dark. One of the steps hit me about eye level. Julie was around five foot five. If she smacked her head on the edge of a concrete step, she could have stumbled through the unlocked gate and fallen into the pool. So it could have been an accident. But like Mrs. R said, the odds were against it.

"Okay, I'm ready, dear," Mrs. Miller's voice broke into my thoughts.

We walked to the car in silence.

"Talk to me, girl," she said, once we put our seat belts on. "You look worried."

"How do we catch Jimmy? I need to get out of this grand theft auto charge."

"A tracker on the Cadillac would help."

"How?" I asked.

"So we can find out where Chang is going. You never know where something like that can lead."

"You know, someone else may have a key to the Caddy," I said, as I started the car up and pulled away from the curb.

"After I drove it, I left Julie's key in my mailbox for her to pick up. But when I swiped Julie's keys at the funeral, the Cadillac key wasn't there. So either she never put it back on her key ring or someone else took it."

"The nerve of some people," she said, shaking her head. "Any idea where the Caddy is?"

"Jake's garage; it's being painted."

"Painted!" Mrs. Miller yelled. "What color?"

"Black."

"Oh no!" Her eyes opened wide and she covered her mouth with her hand.

"Why? Is that important?"

"Oh, Sunny's not going to like this."

"Why would Mrs. R care about its color?"

"Honey, at our age you never want to look out the window in the morning and see a long black car in your driveway."

"I don't understand."

"Oh, it's hard to explain. You'll have to ask her." She took a deep breath, reached into her purse and pulled out a cell phone.

"Hello, Betty," she said, after punching in some numbers. "Do you have time tomorrow to do that thing we've been wanting to get done?" She paused. "Good. Patricia will pick you up around eight." She closed the phone and repositioned her carnation.

I turned and glared at her.

"What?" She threw up her hands.

"You could have asked me first."

"Will you take Mrs. B to Jake's garage tomorrow to put a tracker on the Caddy?"

"Yes."

"Good. She's expecting you at eight."

I sighed.

Chapter Eighteen

The morning disc jockey on the oldies station spun *Little Deuce Coupe* by the Beach Boys as I sat in my car in front of Mrs. Gordon's house. A half an hour earlier I had called her, asking if I could come by. She sounded tired, and I hoped my questions wouldn't upset her.

She opened the door and held the screen for me. "Coffee's made," she told me and gave me a hug.

We settled at the kitchen table, and I held tightly to the mug she'd placed in front of me. Mrs. Gordon's face looked drawn as if she hadn't slept.

"I'm so glad you came," she said. "I have to tell you."

"Oh?" I asked.

She looked down into her coffee.

"The police think that someone killed Julie."

"Oh no." I sat back in my chair. So it was true. There was a part of me that so hoped we'd all been wrong.

She reached into her pants pocket and pulled out a business card. "An Officer Romano came by the night that Julie died." She looked out into the backyard. "He was very kind. He asked me questions about her, who her friends were, if she had a boyfriend, that kind of thing."

Her hand disappeared into her pocket again and reappeared with a well used tissue. "The autopsy report came back and they said her neck was broken." Her voice cracked and she took a deep breath. "And she had a large gash on her forehead. She was dead before she went into the pool. Murdered."

She broke down crying and I reached across the table and squeezed her hand. "Mrs. Gordon, I'm sorry." I waited a few moments until she composed herself before continuing. "This must be so hard for you. Has Officer Romano come back by?"

"No, I wish he had. He, at least, seemed to have an ounce of sense to him. No, it was two other police officers, a tall gal and a redheaded guy. I don't remember their names." She looked down and ran a finger along the rim of her mug. "I don't have much confidence in them. They went through her apartment a few days ago, but didn't find anything." She fixed her eyes on me. "So what did you want to talk to me about?"

"It's about the Cadillac," I said, taking a sip of coffee. "I confirmed that it's registered in Jimmy Chang's name." I paused, letting it sink in. "You think your husband borrowed money on the car, don't you?"

"Ex-husband," she corrected me. "And I do. He was a fool." Her lips pursed in a look of disgust. "He got himself involved with those people and that's why they murdered him."

"Murdered?" I slammed the mug down, sloshing hot liquid onto my hand. I had no idea they considered it murder. Two killings in one family? What were the odds?

"Hit and run in Cooper's Grocery store parking lot." She handed me a napkin to wipe my spill.

"And the police thought it was intentional?"

She shrugged. "It looked like an accident."

"What people are you talking about?" Did she mean Jimmy Chang?

She brushed away an imaginary hair from her forehead and clenched a fist around the handle of her cup.

"Nico Russo, and his cronies," she whispered.

"Sunny's husband?"

She nodded.

"Involved how?"

"My ex played cards with them. That's how he got the Cadillac."

I leaned forward, "Mrs. Gordon, I'm sorry, I'm not following—"

"He won the Cadillac off Nico Russo in a card game."

Finally it made sense! So that's why the car holds Mrs. Russo's interest.

"After you told me there was a lien on the car," she continued, "I was sure he was trying to pay off a gambling debt." She shook her head. "You might win once against those people one time, but eventually your luck is going to run out and his certainly did." Again she stared at something outside. "That's why I didn't want Julie driving the Cadillac. I figured it would only be a matter of time before they went after her."

"But Nico Russo's dead," I replied. "I can't see how the mob would have been involved with Julie's death. If they wanted the car, why not just steal it?"

She waved the tissue in the air, and her eyes started to tear up again. "Who knows the rationale behind murder?"

I shook my head. "You're right. There doesn't seem to be one."

* * *

"Hello, Sunshine!" Mrs. Butterfield sang, as she settled into my car.

I forced a smile, thinking no one should be so chipper in the morning.

"Oh, isn't this exciting!" she said. "Sneaking into Jake's garage?" She rubbed her hands together. "So have you thought of a diversion tactic? Maybe distracting him with your sex appeal?" She leaned over and looked at the front of my shirt. "You know, you really ought to buy some button-downs."

I liked Jake, and I didn't want to distract him with sex or any other way for that matter. "How's this," I said. "How about if we're honest with him? We'll tell him we'd like to look at the car."

"Honest?" Mrs. B said laughing. "Honest with a man? Oh, you young people and your wild ideas." Then she thought for a moment. "No, it definitely won't work, because he'll want to show off the car, point out all the details. And I'm going to need a few minutes alone with that beautiful hunk of steel." She patted her bulky yellow tote. "No, we'll have to sneak."

I pulled into the alley behind Elsie's Antiques and parked. We walked to the corner across the street from Jake's Body Shop. When the light turned green, Mrs. Butterfield took off in a trot, her purse flopping at her hip. In front of Jake's building, she put her back up to the brick wall and poked her head around the corner to look inside.

"Oh!" Mrs. B exclaimed. She put her hand on her chest, suddenly breathing hard.

"What?"

She pointed. I peered into the depths of the garage. Jimmy

Chang was examining the paint job on the now-black Cadillac. I ducked behind Mrs. B. I didn't want Jimmy to see me anywhere near the Caddy.

"Rita tried to warn me," she hissed and then shook her head. "The stock color on that car is Olympic White number 90, and that's what it should be."

I glanced back. "I like it. Gives it a sleek, cool look."

She turned back to me, "Cool, shmool! It has nothing to do with how attractive it is. Stock is stock."

Ish. I rolled my eyes.

"So now what do we do?" I asked her, trying to get back to the reason we were here. I peered back around the corner. Jimmy stood up and headed toward Jake's office. I could see Jake at his desk talking on the phone. He ran his hand through his dark curly hair, and I wished we were here under different circumstances.

"Jimmy's probably picking up the car," Mrs. B said, "so we only have a few minutes. Let's go around back. We're going to have to hurry."

We trotted down the side of the building and into the alley. The roll-up door at the rear of the building was open. I popped my head in to take a look just as Reed came walking toward me, holding a buffer.

"Hi," he said.

"Hi," I said, moving into the garage, trying to act nonchalant. Reed looked back to Jake's office.

"Jake's in with someone, but I'm sure he'll be done in a minute."

"What are you working on?" I asked.

"Trunk lid and back fender." He pointed to a newer model Lexus.

"Can I see?"

He shrugged. "Sure."

We walked behind the car and bent down. Reed explained the process while out of the corner of my eye I watched the trunk lid of the Cadillac open slowly and close just as slow. The last few inches shut mechanically, crunching down with a sickening finality. I stood up abruptly, interrupting Reed mid-sentence. I thanked him for his body work instructions and made a beeline to the back of the Caddy. A six inch piece of yellow silk scarf hung out from under the trunk lid. I put my hands on the back of the car and leaned over. I could hear Mrs. B tapping.

The convertible top was down, as were all the windows. I opened up the driver's door and slid in, pulling out the ignition key. The edges were smooth, worn down over the years, confirming Officer Romano's suggestion that Chang received a key from Mr. Gordon.

"Hey! What are you doing?" Jimmy yelled, as he jogged over to the car.

My stomach muscles clenched as I jammed the key back into the ignition. "Just wanted to take a look at the new paint job."

"From the inside?"

I got out of the car and moved to the rear, while he moved to the front. We continued this dance until he slid behind the wheel and I stood at the passenger door.

"Take me for a spin?" I asked, swallowing hard.

He looked at me for a long moment.

"Sorry, Patty Cakes, I got business to attend to." He adjusted the side mirror and put on his sun glasses.

I placed my hand on the door, hoping to stall him.

"Don't touch. You'll get fingerprints on the new paint job," he said. "This doesn't belong to you, remember? And it never will," he added with a sneer. He started up the car and pulled away.

As Jimmy turned out of the building, I stood and watched helplessly as the Cadillac's four torpedo-shaped brake lights went off, and Mrs. B's yellow scarf fluttered a farewell.

"Patricia," Jake called out, leaning out of his office.

I smiled at him, his handsome demeanor distracting me for a moment from my task.

"I'm sorry, I have to go," I sputtered and power walked by him. But after a few feet I realized that the day had gotten off to a bad start, and I needed to do something to change it. I turned and walked back to Jake and kissed him. It was meant to be a short, 'I'm off to save someone, wish me luck' sort of kiss, but the way he kissed me back took me by surprise. I grabbed his arms and pulled him to me, feeling his chest pressed into mine. I had to use all my will power to push him away.

"Sorry, I have to go," I repeated and took a deep breath.

"Good luck," he said, looking happily dazed.

I walked backwards a few steps wanting to stay and ask him why he said that, but the image of Mrs. B trapped inside that dark trunk made me turn and run. When I reached the street the Cadillac had vanished. I pulled out my cell phone and dialed.

"Mrs. Miller," I yelled.

"Yes?"

"It's Patricia. Jimmy just drove off with Mrs. Butterfield

trapped in the trunk of the Caddy."

"*Ay caramba!*" she swore. "Hold on."

"Hold on? Hold on for what?" I yelled again, but she was gone.

By the time I got to my car and pulled onto the street, Mrs. Miller was back on the line.

"Okay, they're going north on Lakeville Boulevard."

"How do you know that?"

"Because Mrs. B turned the tracker on."

I pulled the phone away from my ear and took a few deep breaths.

"Patricia, are you there?"

"Yeah, I'm here." I clicked on the speaker phone and put both hands on the steering wheel.

"Okay, they're going east over the freeway."

I started zigzagging between cars, pushing the speed limit.

"He turned right and he's stopped. Wait, he's moving forward. No he's stopped." Mrs. M narrated his movements.

"Turned right into where?"

"The shopping center."

I made a right and looped around the perimeter of the parking lot. I caught sight of the black car as Jimmy pulled up to the take-out window of a coffee house.

"He's stopped to get a drink," I told Mrs. M.

"Okay, stay back until you see him moving again."

After a few minutes he pulled away, sipping from a tall cup. He turned back onto the road, and by the time I exited, he was three cars ahead of me.

The stop light turned yellow. Just when I thought I'd have a chance to stay with him, he gunned the Caddy, veering to the right and onto the freeway onramp.

"Damn, it!" The cars in front of me stopped and I was stuck, staring at a red light.

"Don't worry," Mrs. M said. "I know exactly where he is."

"It's one thing to know where he is; it's another to know where he's going." I couldn't help but think about how much air Mrs. Butterfield had left.

I tapped my nails on the steering wheel. There was no way my wimpy little four cylinder engine could keep up with the huge V-8 the Caddy sported. After the light changed, I merged onto the highway. In the distance, the road made a gentle curve upwards and I saw the car crest the hill and then disappear. Mrs. M instructed me to continue northward. After about fifteen minutes, she told me the car had taken the River Road exit. I followed, heading west over the freeway.

The two lane road, leading to the Russian River and eventually to the Pacific Coast, was flanked on both sides by rows of grapevines. Strands of iridescent tinsel caught my eye as it blew in the wind, chasing the birds away from the tender fruit. I gunned my car and hoped that Jimmy had slowed down to admire the scenery, or even better, that he got caught in a speed trap and a cop had pulled him over.

I finally had him in view when he turned right into the far entrance of the Bellisa Winery's parking lot. I pulled in at the first driveway and gave Mrs. M an update. She paused as if writing everything down.

"Okay, let me know if you need anything else." She hung up.

I parked in one of the few empty spots between a stretch limo with dark tinted windows and a tour bus. The winery sprawled up a hill with terraced gardens between the parking lot and the second level. Yellow trumpet vines coiled through wood trellises and bright orange Iceland poppies spilled onto the walkways.

Jimmy nabbed a prime front parking space, next to the stairs leading to the main level. I sat in my car and watched him bound up the steps two at a time. He turned left onto a path. A small sign with an arrow indicated that he was heading for the tasting room. I raced to the Caddy while digging in my purse for Julie's keys. My hands were shaking as I suddenly remembered that the Cadillac key was missing from Julie's key ring. I called Mrs. M back.

"I don't have a key," I said, as I paced back and forth behind the car.

"Is the top down?"

"Yeah."

"Good. Look for a button in the glove compartment."

I sprinted to the passenger side and pushed in the compartment's shiny silver button. The little door popped open. Pushing another button released the trunk lid.

"Got it," I said and hung up.

I held my breath, terrified of what I might find. I pulled up on the trunk lid.

Mrs. Butterfield sat up and smiled.

"Where are we?" she asked, blinking up at me.

"Where are we?" I yelled, as she rolled over the edge of the trunk and stood up. "What the hell are you doing? You were just supposed to put a tracker on the car, not risk your life."

"Oh, don't get your panties in a bunch, Patricia." She looked around as she brushed herself off and adjusted her misaligned scarf. "Bellisa's. Nice." She nodded her head in approval and hoisted her huge purse onto her shoulder. "Okay, which way did he go?"

I pointed and she took off up the stairs.

"Wait," I called out, "where're you going?" I slammed the trunk lid and ran after her.

She turned left on the second level and I caught up with her as we passed a large brick building. Above the arched doorway a sign read: Bellisa Winery, Est. 1896.

"Now that we're here," she said, "we might as well see what Jimmy's up to."

"But I don't want Jimmy to see me," I said, glancing from side-to-side wondering where he might have gone. I assumed we'd start with the tasting room, but she veered to the right.

"This way," she said and pointed to an ornate black metal gate with a sign stating: 'Private Residence. Please Keep Out.'

I hesitated.

"Mrs. B, I really don't like to trespass."

"Come on," she said, pulling me by the hand.

I gently closed the gate behind me. But instead of following the path, Mrs. B plunged into the bushes and we fought our way through thick brush until we came to a Victorian home. A large porch ran along the front and the first floor was up at least six feet off the ground. We snuck around to the side of the house, but it was impossible to see in a window.

"How do you know he's here?" I whispered.

"Just a hunch," she whispered back.

The front screen door squeaked open and both of us ducked.

"One hundred and twenty-five thousand?" A male voice sounded incredulous. "We're talking about a car here, not a work of art."

"Wait till you see her. She is a work of art." Jimmy's voice was on the defensive. "There were only 1,300 made, and with its provenance, it's a steal."

"You have proof of this provenance?"

"I'll get it," Jimmy replied.

After they disappeared, we headed back into the bush and came out on the path just before the metal gate. I tried to keep myself hidden as I peered down the walkway toward the parking lot. The man walking with Jimmy wore blue jeans and a work shirt. His hands were casually tucked in his pockets. They stopped at the top of the stairs and looked down. Suddenly Jimmy threw his arms in the air.

"Where's my car?" he yelled. "This can't be happening! Not again!"

"Could you have parked it in the north parking lot?"

"No. It was right there." Jimmy pointed. "What kind of place do you run here when a car gets stolen in broad daylight?"

"Now, whoa there, Mr. Chang." He put up his hands and took a step back. "If your car's been stolen it's not my fault. We're right on the highway."

Panic flashed around my neck and into my jaw. Jimmy pulled out his cell phone and started to dial. While he and his companion were still facing away from us, I grabbed Mrs. Butterfield and pulled her across the walkway into the tasting room. A three-foot-high ceramic rooster glared at us from a crockery display case.

"This isn't good," I said, pulling leaves from Mrs. B's hair. "If Jimmy sees me, he's going to think I had something to do with the disappearance of the car, and the police will think the same thing." I peeked out the door. Jimmy stood at the top of the stairs leading to the parking lot. It appeared he wasn't going to budge until the sheriff arrived.

"Okay," Mrs. B said. "I have an idea. Let's get you on that bus."

I looked around the room in desperation. It was packed with seniors. No matter how you cut it, I couldn't age myself forty years to blend in.

"Mrs. B that's not going to work."

She ignored my objection.

"That's probably the bus driver over there." She pointed to a bored-looking man leaning up against the wall and wearing a short-sleeved white shirt, black tie and black pants. "I'll buy you a ticket. Go hide in the bathroom. I'll meet you there."

Mrs. Butterfield tottered over to the man, whose uninterested look seemed permanently etched on his face.

I exited through the heavy wooden doors, turned the opposite direction from Jimmy and followed the signs to the restroom. A fountain of lions spitting water into a pool stood in the center of a small courtyard. To my right was a restaurant. Ahead of me a stately California White Oak partially blocked the view of the highway and the vast emerald green vineyards belonging to the winery. I entered the restroom and stood at the back of the line.

Mrs. Butterfield walked in as a stall became available. She pulled me in and locked the door. We stood on opposite sides of the toilet.

"Here's the ticket," she whispered. "The driver thinks it's for me."

"Mrs. B, I'm going to stand out. Jimmy will see me."

"Try this."

She pulled a white Gilligan's hat out of her purse. I stuffed my hair up under it. She looked at me and gave it a tug on one side, "Okay, let's change coats."

I unzipped my black hoodie and handed it to her as she gave me her pale yellow suit jacket. I could almost wrap it around me twice. She put her arms through the sleeves of my sweatshirt, but couldn't get the zipper to come together in the front. I stretched the fabric and pulled up on the metal tab.

Mrs. B dug further into her purse and pulled out a mirror. I held it up and looked at myself.

"Rub off that lipstick," she said, examining my face, "and here, let's swap sunglasses." I cringed as I handed over the expensive Ray-Bans that my father had given me as a birthday present. She put them on top of her head and pulled out a pair of sunglasses for me.

"Here, I used these after my cataract surgery."

I tried them on. They wrapped around the sides of my head, blocking out so much light it was like wearing a blindfold.

"Good," she said, "you look good."

I looked in the mirror again, but I couldn't see a thing.

"You're going to need keys," I said, propping the sunglasses on top of my head. I dug in my pocket and dropped my keys into her hand.

She stared at them.

"Something wrong?" I asked.

"Nothing."

"Oh no. You don't have a driver's license do you?"

"Umm, yes and no."

I slapped my hand to my forehead.

"I have one," she continued. "It's just a little past its expiration date, that's all."

"Okay, I didn't just hear that." I put my hands up to ward off any more information.

"I SAID IT'S A LITTLE PAST ITS—" she yelled.

"I HEARD YOU!" I yelled back.

"I thought you said—"

"Mrs. B, let's focus on the task at hand. Did you find out where the next stop is?"

"Caprice Winery. It's in Alexander Valley."

I rubbed my eyes. That was at least a half hour drive.

"You know, you could get in the trunk of your car. It's really not that bad."

I mumbled under my breath.

"What dear?"

"I'm claustrophobic," I snapped.

"Oh. Well. I guess you'll have to get on the bus."

I put the sunglasses back on. "I'm going to need help getting out of the bathroom." I saw some movement and took it for a nod.

She grabbed my hand, and I followed her outside. My eyes adjusted to the glasses and we merged with the crowd of seniors as they flocked to the bus.

"You're too tall," Mrs. B whispered. "Slouch some."

I hunched over, the muscles in my neck and shoulders tightening into rocks. Jimmy paced back and forth in the empty parking space that previously held the Caddy. As we shuffled past him, his eyes stayed glued to the road.

My car was hidden from Jimmy's view, since I'd parked on the far side of the bus. Mrs. Butterfield held my hand until I stepped up into my new ride. I gave the driver my ticket, took a window seat and watched Mrs. Butterfield open my car door. As the seniors settled in, a gentleman in a cardigan sat down next to me.

"Cataract surgery, huh?" he said. "You'll be fine in a few days. Just remember don't lift anything heavy." He held out his hand, "I'm Clyde, by the way."

"Betty," I said.

The diesel engine came to life and we rolled forward. The bus and my Civic turned out of the parking lot just as the sheriff turned in.

Chapter Nineteen

Mrs. B and I swapped clothes again at Caprice Winery, and I turned back into a twenty-five-year-old. We indulged ourselves by tasting a variety of wines, along with some local cheeses, salamis and bread. I bought a bottle of Chardonnay and Mrs. B purchased a bottle of Rosé, her favorite. I drove Mrs. B home and stopped in at my mom's house to say 'hi.'

She didn't answer the bell, so I walked up the driveway to the backyard. The condition of her garden shocked me. Hundreds of bright yellow orange blossoms peaked out beneath every zucchini plant. Her mysterious fertilizer must contain steroids. I waded into the sea of squash, their prickly leaves scratching against my jeans.

My mother sat on the back porch, wearing a holey pink bathrobe, smudged with black paint. She smoked a cigarette, something I hadn't seen her do since I was in third grade.

"You want a drink?" she asked. "I just started." She held up a tumbler of golden brown liquid. Ice tinkled as she jiggled the glass back and forth.

"No, thanks. I came by to see how you're doing."

"I've been painting," she said flatly.

I was relieved. That was a good sign.

"Can I see?"

She shrugged. "Sure." She stubbed out her cigarette but held onto the drink. Swinging her legs over the side of the lounge chair, she shuffled into the house in her tattered pink slippers.

The bedroom she used as her art studio smelled of oil paints and turpentine. I opened up a window, thinking some fresh air might save our brain cells. Three easels sat in a semicircle, and paper towels smeared with dark paint littered the floor.

She pointed to the first canvas, which leaned against an old wooden chair. It was solid black.

"I'm calling this: 'It's All Over.'"

She pointed to the next canvas sitting on an easel. It was also solid black. "This one is called 'Death and the Abyss.'"

The third canvas was also black with maybe a hint of red in it, or maybe I was just hoping for a hint of red.

"This one is called 'Alone.' And this last one," she waved at the forth picture, that may have had a dollop of blue mixed in with the black, "is called 'Why Bother?'"

She handed me her drink, sat down on our old love seat, pulled her feet up next to her and flopped over sideways.

"Could you clean out my brushes? I don't have the energy."

"Sure, Mom."

I looked back to the canvases. The depression stage. What could I say? At least she was working through it.

When I arrived home, Jimmy was sitting in a brown Pinto in front of my house. Parked across the street in front of the elementary school was a police car. An officer stood on my front porch. He walked toward me as I exited the car.

"Patricia Schuster?" he asked.

"Yes."

"I'd like to ask you a few questions."

Jimmy Chang sprinted across my lawn. I positioned myself so the officer acted as a shield.

"Where is it? I know you took it!" Jimmy yelled.

The officer half-turned to him and put his arm out.

"Mr. Chang, just calm down."

"Arrest her! You know she took it!"

"Get off my property, Jimmy." I was angry and tired of being jerked around.

He stopped yelling, but his hand hung in the air pointing at me.

"Now," I said firmly.

The officer's back was to me and I peaked around him as he casually moved his hand to his gun holster. Jimmy looked at the weapon and backed up a step.

"Sir, I think it would be best if you left," the officer stated.

Jimmy turned, swearing under his breath.

"That car better turn up, Patty Cakes!" he yelled over his shoulder.

The officer waited for Jimmy to drive off.

Turning back to me he asked: "Where were you this afternoon, Ms. Schuster?"

"Wine tasting. What's this about?"

"Mr. Chang's car was stolen this morning."

"Which one?"

He consulted his notepad, "A 1959 Cadillac. He said you were at the body shop downtown."

"I went by to say 'hi' to the owner."

"Then you spent the rest of the day wine tasting?"

I nodded.

"Did you go to Bellisa's Winery?"

"No," I lied.

"Where did you go?"

"Caprices' Winery in Alexander Valley."

I looked at his sunglasses, but saw only my reflection.

"What do you do for a living, Ms. Schuster?"

"I own an antique store downtown."

"Was it open today?"

"No."

"You must be doing pretty good, if you can let your store sit closed and go off wine tasting." His voice held a challenge.

I let that one hang, wondering if the Yarn Barn lady had tattled on me.

He glanced into my car. "Is that wine you bought today?"

I nodded.

"Do you have a receipt for it?"

I pulled the wine bag out of the car, reached in and handed him a piece of paper.

"This is a phone number," he said, "for someone named Clyde."

I took back the slip of paper. "Sorry, that was a guy I met." I searched again, this time coming up with the receipt. I hadn't looked at it and hoped it didn't have the time of the sale. The officer read it over, jotted down a note, and handed the receipt back to me.

"Was there anyone else at the body shop with you?"

"Yes, Reed was there. He's one of Jake's employees."

"No, I mean, did you go to the shop with anyone else?"

"No," I lied again.

He snapped his notebook shut.

"Keep hold of that receipt," he said, as he walked away. "Thanks for your time. Give us a call if Mr. Chang comes back."

I let out a breath. I watched the officer pull away and hurried over to Mrs. Russo's. She took a minute to answer the door.

"Patricia, I'm glad you came over. Come on back."

I followed her into the bedroom. There was an open suitcase on the bed.

"I heard yelling," she said.

"That was Jimmy, and the police were here, too, asking questions about the Caddy."

A sly smile crept over her face. "Are you ready to go find it?" she asked, folding a blouse into the suitcase.

"Find it?"

"We need a driver."

Eeks. Did she plan on stealing it back?

"Where is it?" I asked, fear twisting my stomach.

"Last I heard it was heading to Bodega Bay." She opened her closet and pulled out a cream colored suit.

"Why don't you call the police and tell them where the car is?"

"Why would I do that?"

"Ah, because a crime's been committed and we have evidence—"

"Evidence that we came about illegally."

"We could make an anonymous phone call."

"Patricia, we need the tracker back. Betty's fingerprints are all over it." Her eyebrows pulled together as she tucked a pair of beige pumps into the open luggage. "Did you use gloves when you opened the trunk to let Betty out?"

"No, I didn't think of that."

"So your fingerprints are all over it, too."

I rubbed my arms, suddenly feeling a chill.

"What's the suitcase for?"

"We're going to the Finley Hotel for the weekend. It's Mrs. B's birthday." She snapped the latches closed. "They have great spa packages. Would you like to join us?"

"Sure." I immediately felt relieved. I wouldn't be alone. What could Jimmy do to me at a hotel? Plus after spending the afternoon hunched over, I could use a massage.

"Good," she said. "I'll call the others and tell them you're coming."

The five of us huddled around Mrs. Miller's computer screen in her study, staring at a small blinking light.

"I got it," Mrs. M said.

"Pull back some, I can't see where we're at," Mrs. R replied.

The picture gave the illusion we were moving away from the earth and I could make out a peninsula and a bay.

"What address is it giving?" Mrs. T asked. "I don't have my glasses."

"Bodega Head State Park," Mrs. M explained.

"There's a parking lot and a lookout point," I said. "But what if it moves again? It's a good thirty minute drive from here."

"I have a mobile tracker," Mrs. Miller said, pulling out a

small handheld device showing a tiny screen.

"Okay, let's go," Mrs. Russo said.

A half-an-hour later we drove through Bodega Bay and turned onto Bay Flat Road. Following the edge of the water, just past Westside Regional Park—an asphalt campsite for RVs—the road made a sharp upward climb. When we reached the top of Bodega Head, we found the parking lot. But I didn't see the Caddy.

"Mrs. Miller, what's the tracker say?"

"It says it's here."

There was no place to hide a car, large or small. Logs placed horizontally lined the perimeter of the parking lot, creating barriers to the cliffs. A dirt walkway, at least twenty feet across, marked the entrance to the lookout spot.

"Damn!" Mrs. Russo swore.

Then it hit me. The cliff. There was plenty of room to drive the Cadillac through the opening and over the edge to the rocks below.

I opened the car door, pushing it hard against the force of the wind. The Ladies got out along with me. We huddled at the rear of the car, Mrs. T holding onto the trunk lid for support.

"Sunny, I know it means a lot to you," Mrs. Butterfield yelled. "But remember, it's just a car."

Mrs. R nodded her head and pointed at the dirt. Tire tracks.

"I'll go," I volunteered.

I pulled my jacket up around my throat and stepped onto the dry soil. There were no hand rails here and it was a dangerous spot. The drop off was straight down into loud crashing waves.

The sun eased toward the horizon, but the long June days

allowed a few more hours before sunset. I went to the closest edge and looked up the rough California coastline. Blue-green water rushed into half moon shaped beaches below ochre colored cliffs. I peered over, the wind whipping hair into my eyes. No car. I moved to my left facing the Pacific Ocean and looked down, still no sign of the Caddy. I walked south, but saw only waves slamming up against black jagged rocks.

"Unless the waves pulled it out to sea," I explained to The Ladies when I rejoined them. "It didn't go over the edge."

Mrs. Miller stared at her tracker, tapping on the little screen. "What's wrong with this thing?"

"Nothing," Mrs. R said, "it's a ruse. Someone found the tracking device, came out here and threw it into the water."

I looked around the parking lot. One car was parked next to the outhouse and another four or five spaces away. Both were nondescript SUVs. Both empty. Walking trails off the asphalt headed in different directions for miles. Were we being watched? Had we been followed? I shivered inside my jacket and hurried The Ladies back into the car.

We drove to town in silence. I thought about never finding the Cadillac and spending years of my life in a jail cell, surrounded by cold cinder block and windowless walls.

Chapter Twenty

Inside the Finley Hotel's lobby, I hauled the first load of The Ladies' luggage past the giant waterfall. Mrs. Russo led the way, bobbing and weaving through a throng of guests. Most were Asian men and women, dressed in professional attire. I assumed they were visiting for the weekend's Korean Business Convention. We walked past the entrance to the bar and I noticed Roger Finley speaking to Kwan. Finley glanced our direction. He did a double take and stared. I wondered which of The Ladies caught his eye.

I also spotted Cassandra and Min sitting at a small table surrounded by three men in suits. Both wore hats with netting that covered their eyes, giving them a 1940s movie star look. I could hear Cassandra speaking in what I assumed was Korean and speculated on what delights she was offering.

When we arrived at our room on the top floor, I realized that we were next door to Cassandra's suite. Ours was as opulent as hers with a similar round foyer and marble floor. An oversized bouquet of orange tiger lilies and white spider mums greeted us as we entered. Modern maroon and black leather furniture arranged around a flat screen TV made an inviting living room. In the nook sat a rectangular glass and wood table with tan colored leather chairs offering a place to eat or play games next to a small kitchenette.

My room contained a king size bed and a sitting area. On top of a round oak table sat a fruit basket containing oranges, Asian pears, and shiny red apples. A mint the size of a hockey puck sat on my gold satin pillow. Floor-to-ceiling limestone decorated the bath. I dropped my overnight bag on the bathroom counter and decided to move in permanently.

Mrs. Miller handed me the keys to her car and I headed out for another load of luggage. The elevator moved slowly and stopped at the next floor down. The doors opened and Jimmy Chang stood in the hallway, arms crossed. A toothpick bobbed up and down between his front teeth. He stepped inside and the doors slid shut behind him. So much for the hotel being a safe haven.

"Where's the car?" he snarled.

"It's in my purse," I responded.

He glanced down at my hands and then back to my face. I grinned. He pulled the toothpick out of his mouth and pointed it at me.

"You're not in a position to make jokes, Patty Cakes."

"Well, what do you think I did with it, Jimmy?" I snapped back. "And why on earth do you think I'd even want it?"

His eyebrows popped up and he looked away from me. Was that desperation on his face?

The elevator doors slid open.

"Find the car and I'll drop the charges," Jimmy stated.

We were on the ground floor. He backed up a step and disappeared into the crowd. Now I knew what was going to be number three of my get-out-of-jail-free cards. But if I found the car would he honor his promise?

"Jimmy's here," I announced to The Ladies when I returned to our suite.

I explained his latest terms.

"He's not trustworthy," Mrs. Russo said. "But I can't blame him for wanting the car back."

"What's so special about this car?" I asked. "Is there gold under all that chrome? Uncut diamonds in the tail lights?"

"Well, in a way," Mrs. R said. "Cadillac made only 1,320 models of the 1959 Biarritz. They were the top of the line. They didn't advertise them; they didn't need to. They sold them to a special set of clientele, very exclusive."

Mrs. R glanced at Mrs. Miller, who'd pulled her lips into a thin line. I had a feeling I still wasn't getting the full story.

"And of those 1,320 Cadillacs, there were only ninety-nine that had bucket seats. And of those ninety-nine only a handful exists today. Last year one sold for $175,000."

I raised an eyebrow. No wonder she wanted it back.

Located off the lobby, Finley's main restaurant buzzed with activity. I ate steak and shrimp until I thought I would pop. Raising our champagne glasses high, we toasted Mrs. Butter-field's sixty-eighth birthday so many times I lost track of how much I drank.

When we entered our suite, I immediately noticed the smell of spicy cologne, but it was gone in a second, overpowered by the fragrance of tiger lilies. Uneasiness tightened around my jaw. I went into my room and opened my suitcase. My carefully folded clothes were now a mess. Back into the living room

Mrs. Russo sat on the couch, flipping through channels on the big screen TV.

"Someone's gone through my bag," I said.

Everyone scattered to check their rooms.

Mrs. M came back looking appalled. "My luggage's been gone through also," she said. "Thank goodness I kept my computer with me." She gestured to a large leather purse that she'd lugged down to the restaurant.

Mrs. T poked her head in from the bedroom. "Mine too."

"Is anything missing?" Mrs. R asked. She came back in fingering an emerald that hung on a gold chain around her neck.

"No, not from my stuff," I replied.

Mrs. B and Mrs. T shook their heads.

"I left a pair of gold earrings on the dresser. They're still there," Mrs. R said, "so they weren't looking for valuables. Rita, where's the surveillance equipment?"

Mrs. M walked over to a small blue and white cooler sitting in plain site on the kitchenette counter. She opened the lid and let out a breath.

"Still here," she said.

"Should we call hotel security?" I asked.

"No, I don't trust them any more than I trust Jimmy," Mrs. R replied.

The Ladies sat down to play cards, but my nerves felt pulled to their breaking point. I needed a distraction. I called Jake.

"Patricia, hi," he replied to my greeting.

"Want to listen to some music?" I asked. "I'm at the Finley."

"Sure, where should I meet you?"

"How about the Beastly Lounge. They have a band tonight."

"Okay, see you soon."

I told the Ladies my plans and headed downstairs. The hotel gift shop was still open so I popped in for some mints. The little store was crowded with other shoppers holding up T-shirts and trying on sunglasses. Min, Cassandra's houseguest, stood at the jewelry counter. She and the salesperson huddled over a gray felt-covered jewelry display tray on top of the glass counter top. Min picked up a ring and slid it on her finger.

"Hi, Min," I said.

She turned to me and smiled, "Hello."

The salesclerk looked up at me. "Can I help you?"

"I'd like some mints." I could see them on the shelf behind her.

"What flavor?" she asked, as she turned around.

"Hmm." I thought for a moment. "What are my choices?"

"Cinnamon, peppermint, wintergreen and ginger."

"Wintergreen," I replied and reached into my pocket for some cash. But a hand grabbed my arm, pulled it behind me and pushed me forward, pinning me to the counter. I winced, my elbow still sore from my altercation with the wave runner.

"Coming to look at the pretty lights, huh?" a male voice whispered into my ear.

His cologne was the same smell I'd noticed in our suite. I twisted around and saw enough of his face to recognize him as the security guard from the night I'd been in the parking lot with Mrs. M.

"You're under arrest for shoplifting," he hissed.

I felt something plastic being slipped onto one wrist.

"Shoplifting? I didn't take anything." He grabbed my other

arm and forced it into the synthetic handcuffs.

"No? Being an accomplice is the same thing."

"What are you talking about?"

I turned to Min and saw that she, too, had her hands in cuffs. The other guard pulled a diamond ring out of her jacket pocket.

"Oh, Min," I said.

She hung her head, not looking at me.

The guards took us downstairs into the hotel basement to the Security Department. They took my room key and phone, but left me my license and a twenty dollar bill. They separated Min and me and shoved me into the employee kitchen. The guard pushed me down into a metal folding chair in front of a table with a fake walnut Formica top covered with crumbs and bits of dried ketchup.

"So who's your friend?" the guard asked.

"Her name's Min."

"How do you know her?"

I didn't reply.

"So, you all in this together?"

"In what?" I asked.

"You're going to try and tell me you're not a gang?" he asked.

I laughed and he glared at me.

"We'll see if you're still laughing at the police station."

He slammed the door and locked me in. I tried to distract myself from my confinement by counting the acoustical ceiling tiles. I didn't want to think about Jake, who was probably at this moment upstairs searching for me.

When the police arrived they shuffled Min and me out a back door and up some steps to the parking lot. The arresting officers read us our rights as we walked to the patrol car. One put his hand on my head and pushed me into the back seat. Min sat next to me, her sophisticated hat now askew, tilting down and covering her right eye.

"Sorry, Miss Patricia."

"It's okay Min," I said, slouching down and leaning my head back against the seat. I closed my eyes. What was Jake going to think of me now?

The cinder block felt ice cold against my back. My hands were sweating and I took deep breaths, trying to reduce the ringing in my ears. This was the second time in as many weeks for me to be locked up in the hole, the slammer, the hoosegow, the big house. The cell door opened interrupting my thesaurus game.

It was Sherilee, the prostitute that shared my cell on my previous stay, being manhandled into the room by a female police officer. She struggled to stay upright on her stiletto heels.

"You really need to lighten up," she said, and a stream of swear words escaped from her lips. She turned and spoke to me, "We can't catch a break can we?"

The officer motioned for me to follow her. "Schuster, you're out of here."

Min sat in the corner. "Bye, Miss Patricia."

"Bye, Min."

Maria Sanchez, my lawyer and liberator, stood in the hallway. I followed her out into the main lobby. She looked like she was attending the Oscars. She wore a floor length, light blue gown, held up by spaghetti straps. A blue and purple shawl covered her upper arms. Her hair was piled high on top of her head, a mass of curls going every direction.

"Oh my God, you were out on a date," I said, feeling terrible that I'd disturbed her evening.

She shrugged it off. "I was at the opera." Her tone of voice made me think she wasn't in a hurry to get back. "I talked the hotel manager out of pressing charges. It didn't take much."

I retrieved my belongings and followed Maria out into the cool evening air.

"I was questioned about Jimmy's Cadillac again," I told her as we stood on the sidewalk.

"Oh?" She sounded surprised.

"Yeah, someone stole the Caddy from Bellisa's Winery. Something else happened too." I felt guilty. I was taking her away from her evening. She must have read my mind.

"Go ahead. Really, the last aria I've heard."

So I told her about being knocked off my surfboard at the beach, rummaging through Julie's apartment with The Ladies and Mrs. Butterfield being stuck in the Caddy's trunk. Then I told her that Jimmy said he'd drop the charges if I found the car. I also told her I didn't believe him.

"This isn't good Patricia," she said, shaking her head, "not with the arraignment coming up. The case was flimsy when Jimmy had the car in his possession. I expected it to be dismissed. But now that the car has gone missing, that doesn't look good for you."

I started biting a fingernail.

"With someone after you, you might be in over your head. I don't want you getting hurt." She paused. "I'm not sure about this Jimmy guy; he makes me nervous."

"I know. Me too."

* * *

Maria gave me a ride back to the hotel and I walked quickly through the lobby. Even though I was sure the security cameras alerted the guards to my arrival, no one jumped out from behind a silk ficus to stop me.

I could hear and feel a deep drum beat from the dance lounge. I looked inside, just in case Jake was waiting. Not seeing him, I went upstairs to our room and knocked softly. The door flung open and Mrs. Miller wrapped her arms around me.

"*Mi hija*, please tell me you had a rendezvous with Jake," she said, holding me a bit too tight. "We were so worried. I went down to the Beastly Lounge and you weren't there." She pushed me away from her, but held onto my arms, looking me over. "Oh dear, you're not wearing the I-just-had-sex-look."

"I wish. I was picked up for shoplifting in the gift store." I broke from her grasp.

Mrs. Butterfield appeared behind her. "Shoplifting? Oh dear, you should have come to us first, we could have given you some tips."

"Betty, hush. Let her speak," Mrs. M said.

"Ms. Sanchez talked the hotel out of charging me," I explained.

Mrs. B grabbed my hand, pulled me in the living room, and down onto the couch. "Rita, get Patricia some ice cream, quickly. The woman needs ice cream."

Mrs. Russo and Mrs. T were seated in the living room. When I had ice cream in hand I preceded to tell them about the arrest.

Chapter Twenty-one

The gold satin sheets did not help me sleep. I called Jake the night before, but it went directly to voice mail, so I left a message of explanation and a thousand 'I'm sorrys.'

After showering I joined The Ladies in the common area where a healthy array of breakfast food filled two large rolling trays. I helped myself to scrambled eggs, a bagel and coffee.

"We're getting pedicures this afternoon, Patricia," Mrs. Miller said, a piece of toast in her hand and a spider mum behind her ear. "Are you sure you don't want to play hooky from work?"

"I'd like to, but the Yarn Barn lady probably turned me into the Merchant's Association for not opening up yesterday."

"The Yarn Barn lady needs to have her skeins rewrapped," Mrs. Butterfield said, enunciating each syllable distinctly.

"I don't think she's the one you should be worried about," Mrs. Russo said.

"I know, but I don't want to think about it," I replied.

She leaned over and stared intensely into my eyes. "Don't let your guard down, Patricia."

"You're scaring me."

"You should be scared. I'm not sure who to trust."

She wasn't the only one.

When I propped open the front door to the store, I saw Jake walking down the street.

"Good morning," he called out to me.

"Jake," I said, as he came closer. "I am so sorry about last night."

He nodded. "I got your message. I'm glad you're all right."

"You're not mad?"

"I was last night. But I figured you'd have a good excuse." He smiled. "And that was a doozy."

"That's sweet of you to understand."

"I was headed over to the bakery for some coffee. Like anything?"

"Sure." I wasn't hungry but I knew he offered free coffee at his garage to his customers. So I assumed that he came by just to see me.

When he returned a few minutes later with my order, we sat in a pair of English rosewood side chairs. He plopped down a small white bag on a round marble end table and handed me a cup of coffee. I passed him an apple turnover and took one for myself. We sat in silence for a moment, lost in a cinnamon-sugar high.

"So how's life treating you these days?" he asked. He leaned back in the chair, looking comfortable, like he had all day to listen. So I told him. I told him everything. I didn't preface it with 'don't tell your dad,' and I didn't end it with 'please don't tell your dad.' I decided to trust him, and when I trust people I trust them completely. I paused every once in a while, looking for clues of boredom or pity, but saw none.

"So I'm stuck," I said, finishing up my story. "No Cadillac, no way out of the theft charges. I could spend the next four or five years in jail. And whoever killed Julie may be coming after me."

He stared at me for a few moments, but I couldn't read his face.

"I'll wait for you," he said seriously.

"What?"

"I'll wait for you." He stood up, leaned over and kissed me lightly on the lips. "It probably won't come to that. But from what I've seen you're worth waiting for." And with that pronouncement he left me sitting there with my mouth open. No 'I'll save you,' no pie-in-the-sky optimism of how 'everything was going to be all right,' just an assessment of the situation and how he felt. What he didn't say was proof of what he did say.

"Damn," I said out loud. My lust buzz was morphing into something more. Much more.

A constant stream of customers kept me busy throughout the day. The last purchase was a rocking chair that I helped load into the back of an SUV. As I locked my front door I indulged in a daydream about a relaxing massage at the Finley, lying around inhaling eucalyptus oil with hot stones on my back. But when I saw the Yarn Barn lady rushing across the street, I had a sinking feeling it was not to be. She grabbed the door handle and banged on the glass as if I wasn't right on the other side.

"Patricia, Patricia!" she yelled.

I opened the door with dread.

"Yes?"

"They've arrested Jimmy Chang." Her knitting needles vibrated with excitement. "What's the world coming to when the head of the Merchants' Association gets arrested?"

"Taking a turn for the better?" was the flippant response that I stifled before it left my lips.

Joining her on the sidewalk, I closed and locked the door behind me and ran to the corner. Chang's auto lot was almost empty save for two Mercedes and an Audi.

"Where did all the cars go?" I asked.

"Jimmy and some man loaded them up in a car carrier. After the man drove off, two police officers went into Jimmy's trailer and dragged him out. Handcuffed."

"Did you see a police car?"

"No, they took him into the alley."

Something didn't feel right. I leapt up the steps to Jimmy's trailer and opened the door. The water cooler stand lay on its side, spreading water that stained the thin carpet. His desk chair also lay on its side. My Monet hung askew on the wall above his desk. It was obvious that Jimmy didn't go down without a fight. With his knowledge of Kung Fu, I suspected whoever took him had a gun.

I rummaged through the papers on his desk. There was nothing but car contracts and loan applications. His word-of-the-day calendar told me today's word was *hubris*, which included the pronunciation and definition. I turned around to see a small cork board hanging low on the wall. Pushpins held up a monthly calendar, two coupons for Tony's Pizzeria and a sticky note. The note read: Oakland ro-ro 612. I grabbed it and stuffed it into my pocket.

The small corner table with the red bowl of oranges sat undisturbed. Next to the fruit a greeting card stood open and I picked it up. The top edge said: Year of the Rat. I was born the same year, as was Julie. I glanced over the broad adjectives used to describe us: hardworking, meticulous, and energetic. But the last thing caught my eye. 'They are choosey with their friends and trust few.' I looked at the rat, and then I looked at the word trust. And something finally connected.

Ten minutes later I was pounding on Jason's front door. He looked through the curtains before opening it. The smell of marijuana wafted out to greet me. I skipped the pleasantries.

"Did you open the envelope Julie left you?" I asked.

He looked bewildered.

"What envelope?"

"The one underneath Ferris' food bag."

"I don't know what you're talking about."

I ran around him, greeted his mom with a wave, and entered his room. I went to the bag, dug around for the envelope and handed it to Jason.

"Open it," I instructed.

He did and handed me a key and what looked like a credit card. One side had a magnetic strip and on the other side the words: 'U-Store-It'.

Then he pulled out a letter. "Oh man," he said.

"Read it out loud." My hands started to shake.

He took a deep breath, "Jason, if I'm not back by Wednesday, please go to my storage unit and e-mail my draft." He looked up. "Wednesday? We're a week-and-a-half late."

"Draft? What's she talking about?"

"I know," he said. "Come on let's go."

Checking my rear view mirror for cops, I sped through town to the 'U-Store-it' buildings. We stopped in front of a metal gate. I rolled down my window and looked at a small security box that resembled a miniature ATM.

"Here," Jason handed the card over to me.

I slid it into the available slot and pulled it out. A digital readout asked me for a pin number.

"Oh no." I turned to him.

"Three, five, five, zero, and the pound sign," he said.

Using the keypad, I punched in the numbers and the gate slid opened.

"Wow, I'm impressed. How did you come up with that?" I asked.

He waved the letter at me, "She wrote it down."

For the second time I felt embarrassed. I'd assumed that Jason was a typical teenager and could hack into any computer with barely a thought. But he was oblivious to my faux pas.

"It's storage unit three-eighteen," he continued.

Following the numbers through the mini-streets of orange roll-up doors, we found it quickly. Using the key from Julie's envelope, Jason unlocked the padlock and pulled the door up. A laptop sat in the middle of an otherwise empty room on the concrete floor.

"So there it is," I said. "I've been looking for that."

Jason squatted down next to the computer, popped open the lid and turned it on.

"Julie wanted to know how to write an e-mail and send it out at a set time," he explained as we waited for the machine to boot up. "I told her you needed special software to do that, but you could write the letter and save it as a draft. Then it would be ready to send whenever you wanted."

The machine chimed and Jason opened her e-mail software. Sure enough there was one document waiting to be sent. He double clicked on it. The address it was going to was: matt@accountslife.com.

"Matt's her coworker at the Finley," I told him.

The e-mail said: Matt, if you get this, I'm in serious trouble. I took these files from work. Please read through them carefully. Julie.

"There's an attachment," I said, pointing to the tiny paperclip icon.

Jason clicked on it and an accounting ledger opened. The file was over thirty pages long.

"Just send it to Matt. It'll take us hours to figure out what it means."

Jason's fingers tapped on the keyboard.

"Bet that's going to be a surprise," I continued.

"What?"

"Getting an e-mail from a dead woman."

Jason pushed a few more buttons and an error message popped up.

"There's no wi-fi connection here," he said. "We can take it to my house and send it from there."

"I'll take that," a voice said from behind me. I turned and looked up into the face of a police officer, his gun pointed at my head. The meter maid stood behind him, her gun aimed at Jason.

The male officer held out his hand. It was then I recognized him as the man from my store who'd pretended to be German, the one who Jimmy fingered as a dirty cop. The meter maid had been his companion. She'd cut her hair since the first day I'd seen her trying to run down the Yarn Barn lady with her motorized cart.

Jason's jaw tightened and for an awful moment I thought he might fight back. But instead he closed the lid carefully and handed over the computer. I glanced outside and saw the front end of the Cadillac. The two intruders backed out of the storage unit.

"Auf Wiedersehen, surfer girl," the meter maid sneered at me. She reached up and pulled on the corrugated door, it rambled down and crashed closed.

Darkness surrounded us. The click of the padlock catching stopped my heart for an icy second, before it started pounding again at a crazy speed.

"No!" I yelled, and rushed at the hot metal that now blocked my escape. I slammed myself against it and then moved sideways to the crack between the door and the wall, gasping for breath. The heat became stifling within seconds.

"Patricia," Jason said softly.

I knelt to the floor hugging my legs, I couldn't look at him. "We're never getting out of here," I said, staring at the small shaft of light.

"Patricia," Jason said again. I looked up, something shiny flashed in his hand.

"No, no." I tried to move farther away from him, but I was in the corner. Oh God, did he kill Julie?

"Look," he said, pointing to the object. "I've got a screwdriver." I looked closer. It was a pocket knife, the kind that comes with different types of attachments. "I'll take the screws out of the back side of the hasp." He moved away from me and started working. I heard a loud thud as the lock hit the floor. Jason rolled the door up and I squinted into the sunlight, surprised it still existed. He reached down for me, holding out his hand.

"Ready?" he said, pulling me up. He opened up the passenger door to my car, and as I slid in he went around to the driver's side.

"Where to?" he asked, as if I was as sane as the next person.

"The Finley Hotel," I instructed.

I took a few deep breaths, pulled out my cell phone, called information, and then the police department.

"Officer Romano, please."

After a moment I heard his voice, gruffer than usual. "Romano."

"It's Patricia Schuster, Officer Romano. Could you tell me if Jimmy Chang was arrested this afternoon?"

He paused. "Hold on, Ms. Schuster."

I tapped impatiently on the arm rest of my car.

"Why did she call you surfer girl?" Jason asked.

The realization made the hair on my arms stand up.

"The meter maid!"

Jason looked confused.

"Someone on a wave runner knocked me off my surfboard. It must have been her."

Officer Romano's voice came back on the phone. "Nope, we haven't had any arrests since this morning. Why are you asking?"

"I think Jimmy Chang has been kidnapped by the meter

maid. She's with a cop, and they're driving the Cadillac."

There was dead silence on the line.

"Jimmy's office has been ransacked," I continued.

He still didn't say anything.

"Officer Romano?"

"I'm here. Anything else?"

"Ask the Yarn Barn lady. She might have seen something."

"Ms. Schuster, you're going to need to come in and make a statement."

"You're breaking up," I replied. "Hello? I can't hear you." I heard him sigh and the line went dead. I turned to Jason. "I'm not sure he believed me."

Jason gave me a sideways glance. "I'm not sure I believe you."

Mrs. Butterfield met us in her bare feet and an oversized bright yellow terrycloth robe. She looked like a giant Easter Peep candy. She smiled warmly at Jason as I rushed through introductions.

"Patricia, you look flustered," she remarked.

"We were held up at gunpoint by a cop," I explained.

"Come, sit. Tell me what happened."

After I finished my story, Mrs. B had more information.

"The guy I pickpocketed in your store's not a cop," Mrs. B said. "At least not anymore. That condom I swiped from him came in handy, his fingerprints were on the wrapper."

"Fingerprints? How do you have access to run fingerprints?" I asked.

"It's a long story, dear. Maybe another time. But his name's Anthony Pachucca. He used to be a police officer in San Jose, but he got caught selling drugs." She stood up and started pacing the floor. "We'll need everyone back here."

"Where are they?"

"Rita went downstairs to go dancing. Mrs. T and Sunny are next door playing games at Cassandra's."

Games? I didn't want to imagine what kind of games they were playing at Cassandra's.

"Okay, here's what we'll do," Mrs. B said. "You two go next door and get Mrs. T and Sunny, and I'll go downstairs and get Rita."

"You'd better take Jason with you," I said to Mrs. Butterfield.

"But you have to be twenty-one to get into the dance," Mrs. B replied.

"I've got a fake ID," Jason said.

"Okay, I didn't just hear that," I remarked.

"HE SAID HE HAS—" Mrs. B yelled at me.

I held up my hand to stop her.

"Patricia, you really need to get your hearing checked."

I nodded my head indulgently.

"On second thought—Jason, why don't you stay here." I pointed to the TV remote. "We should only be gone a minute."

He nodded and we left.

There was a lot of noise coming from Cassandra's suite. I rang the bell thinking no one would hear it, but Min opened the door.

"Good evening," she said. "Nice to see you again, Miss Patricia. Please come in."

The foyer looked the same except the bouquet held purple iris and long white stemmed roses. A piece of rolling luggage leaned against the wall.

"The games are this way." Min gestured to my left, where double doors opened into a large room. "What would you like to play?"

"I came to see some friends," I replied.

I stood at the entrance dumbfounded as I watched small groups of people sitting around tables rolling dice and dealing cards. One couple played backgammon, another dominos. The boisterous crowd laughed and cheered. I let out a breath. When Mrs. B said games, she really meant games.

"Yoo-hoo!" Mrs. T called out, her arm waving in the air.

I walked sideways between the tables and chairs. Mrs. R and Mrs. T sat with two Asian men who rose and bowed to me. I smiled and bowed back, uncertain of the etiquette.

Mrs. Russo's long fingers shuffled a deck of cards and by the look of the pile of chips in front of her, she was winning.

"Care to join us?" Mrs. T asked. "We're playing Texas Hold-em."

"We have a situation," I stated.

Mrs. R stopped shuffling. I leaned down and whispered in her ear.

"I'm sorry gentlemen; we have to leave," Mrs. R said, gathering her chips.

The men stood and bowed again.

We gathered around Mrs. Miller in the common area of the suite. She sat in front of a laptop computer and next to it a small speaker and what looked like a portable radio.

"What's that for?" I asked, pointing to the speaker.

"It's a listening device. I planted a bug in one of Cassandra's display racks the day we visited her. And that," she pointed to the radio, "is a police scanner." As if on cue, the scanner crackled and a dispatcher's voice announced a prowler on Lake Street. Mrs. Miller turned the volume down.

"Hey," Jason exclaimed, as he pointed out the sliding glass door that opened up onto the balcony. "Isn't that Julie's Cadillac?"

We all ran to join him. The Caddy was parked in the employee parking lot. The front doors flew open and the fake cop and meter maid stepped out, each carrying a takeout soda drink. They walked casually through the parking lot and entered the hotel through the back entrance.

"What do you think they've done with Jimmy?" I asked.

"And where's Julie's laptop?" asked Jason.

"Hey, I'm getting something," Mrs. Miller said, from her post at the computer.

We huddled around the small speaker.

"I was expecting to find a den of pleasure. Naked woman waving dildos." It was a deep male voice.

"That's Finley," I whispered. "He's the owner of the hotel and Julie's boss."

Apparently Cassandra's guests were far enough away from her dining room for us to eavesdrop without any background noise.

"Five hundred vibrators I stole for you," Finley continued. "But what do I find instead? A room full of my guests playing games," he paused. "Board games. Monopoly, Clue, Jenga," he spit the words out as if they were dirt in his mouth, "and God only knows what else."

"Risk, Go," Cassandra's voice sounded confident.

"I don't care what stupid games they are!" Finley's snapped

back. "We had a deal."

"You said to provide entertainment," Cassandra said. "That's what we do for entertainment in Korea."

"You know damn well that's not what I was talking about. I have a business to run here, I already have clients lined up. You told me if I got you the Caddy, you'd get me girls. So where are they?"

"The Cadillac's here? Where?" There was excitement in Cassandra's voice.

"Out back."

I stepped back to the slider and stood in the shadows where I could see Cassandra on her balcony.

"The deal was the Caddy and the provenance," she said. "You were supposed to get it from Julie, remember?"

"It's in the trunk."

"What? Really?" She leaned on the railing looking down. "Why didn't you bring it up?"

"I thought it should stay with the car."

"He's lying," Mrs. B whispered.

"I can't wait to see it!" Cassandra sounded genuinely excited. She turned back into the room, and I joined the huddled group again.

"Okay, so I got you the car. Where are the girls?"

"I told you yesterday, the ship's late," Cassandra replied.

"I called about the ro-ro," Finley continued, "it docked this afternoon."

I took a sharp breath and reached in my pocket. Mrs. Russo eyed me as I pulled out the sticky note I'd taken from Jimmy's board. I read it again: 'Oakland ro-ro 612'. But on closer inspection, the 1 and 2 were close together. It could be 6 12, which might mean today, June 12th. I passed the note over to Mrs. R and whispered: "I got this at Jimmy's." She read it and nodded her head.

"Maybe I called on the wrong ship," Cassandra's voice sounded shaky. "Or maybe you called on the wrong ship."

A slap sounded through the speakers. Jason jerked back and the rest of us let out a collective gasp.

Cassandra didn't make a sound.

"I got the right ship," Finley growled. "That's the one thing I did get out of Chang."

"Out of Chang?" Her voice dropped and became difficult to hear. "Did you do something to Jimmy? Where is he?"

"Forget him. You're playing me for a fool." Finley's tone was cold and hard. "I see your luggage in the hallway. Where are the girls? Where are you hiding them?"

The sound of breaking glass came through the speakers and Cassandra cried out: "I'm not hiding anyone!"

I imagined her trying to get away from that huge beast of a man and a feeling of nausea came over me. "We have to help her," I said turning, but Mrs. R grabbed my arm and put a finger to her lips.

"He needs more information," Mrs. T said. "He won't seriously hurt her until he gets what he wants."

"Where's Kwan?" Finley continued. "I didn't see him down at the bar. Is your brother at the ship?"

"Stop it!" Cassandra cried out.

Finley's voice was unyielding: "You're taking me to the ship. Now."

We waited for more, but there was only silence.

"We have to follow them," Mrs. Russo said.

"I'm on it," Mrs. B said and scurried out of the room.

"Mrs. T, you stay with Jason and watch the equipment. Turn the police scanner up, and keep your eye on the GPS system."

"But there's no GPS tracker on the Cadillac." I pointed out the obvious.

"No, but I have one in my pocket. I want Mrs. T to know where we are. Plus there's another one on Jimmy Chang's car carrier."

"The carrier's at the Oakland dock," Mrs. M said.

My neck tightened, I didn't feel prepared for this. "Shouldn't we call someone?" I asked. "Like the police?"

"Mrs. T will take care of that." Mrs. R looked around at our small group and called out: "Mrs. B you ready?"

She reappeared in the doorway. "Yep." In her hand she held a long narrow piece of luggage I'd seen before. It was her rifle.

"We'll take Patricia's car," Mrs. R stated.

"My car?"

"Come on, dear." She grabbed me by the elbow. "We need a driver."

Chapter Twenty-two

Mrs. R opened her wallet and thrust it past me to the Port of Oakland's security guard. He shined his flashlight over it and then into the car. Returning the ID he waved us through.

"What did you show him?" I asked.

"My library card," she replied sarcastically. "Turn your headlights off."

The fog from San Francisco Bay created a fuzzy glow around the oversized street lights. We slowly cruised into what looked like a massive parking lot. Rows of identical compact Hyundais filled the space, the mist dulling their shiny exteriors.

"Turn right," Mrs. R said, pointing to a break in the line of vehicles.

Ahead of us, the long starboard side of a massive ship hugged the dock. Like a petulant child sticking out a mammoth tongue, a ramp protruded from its back corner. Three or four car lengths from the ramp, flood lights glinted off the Cadillac's excessive chrome.

"Park here," Mrs. R said.

I slid into an opening between two rows of the new vehicles and we piled out. Mrs. B took her rifle out of its case and held it loosely at her side, the barrel pointing toward the ground. Mrs. R tucked a gun into the back of her waist band. My shoulders tensed up, and I took a few deep breaths. I could smell diesel until a slight breeze brought a hint of fresh sea air. Mrs. R waved and we followed her single file, crouching down, using the cars as cover.

"Kwan! Kwan!" It was Finley's voice.

We stopped and poked our heads up. Finley stood next to Jimmy's car carrier, his hand firmly entangled in Cassandra's hair.

The front end of Jimmy's old Pontiac pointed up the ramp, ready to be loaded. A brown Ford Pinto sat alone on the upper rack of the carrier.

"Those are Jimmy's cars," I whispered.

Kwan jogged down the ramp from the hull of the ship as Finley moved forward, dragging Cassandra.

"Come on," Mrs. R whispered.

We made it to the back of the Caddy, where Mrs. R pulled out a set of keys and opened the trunk lid a few inches.

"Mr. Chang?" she asked.

"Yeah," Jimmy's voice sounded weak.

A small flashlight on Mrs. R's key chain lit up the trunk compartment. Jimmy lay with his arms behind his back. One eye squinted at the light. The other eye was swollen shut with a blackish half moon bruise forming under it.

"What's Finley doing?" Mrs. R whispered to Mrs. B who peered around the car.

"Still looking the other direction."

Mrs. R spoke to Jimmy.

"Are you hurt?"

"A little," he replied.

Mrs. M opened the lid further and we helped Jimmy out. Mrs. R pulled up her pant leg and removed a switchblade strapped to her calf. She cut the plastic that held Jimmy's hands together.

"Can you walk?" she asked.

He nodded as he rubbed his wrists.

Mrs. R turned her attention to the car. "Betty, hit the kill switch. I don't want the Caddy going anywhere."

Hunched over, Mrs. B opened the driver's door. The interior light came on for a split second before going dark.

Mrs. R whispered to me, "You stay with Chang." She gestured to the other two. "Let's move in closer."

Jimmy and I leaned around opposite sides of the Cadillac, trying to see while staying hidden.

"Where are they, Kwan? You promised me girls!" Finley yelled, towering over the diminutive man.

"Let go of her," Kwan said sternly.

Finley yanked Cassandra's head around like a rag doll while she pawed at his arm.

"Are they in here?" Finley motioned to the cab of the truck.

He threw Cassandra to the ground and momentarily disappeared from view. Returning he held a man and a woman by the arms. Cassandra struggled to her feet and reached out to the woman, who was wrapped in a blanket. The woman turned on Finley. She struck him on the arm, yelling at him in an Asian language. Finley didn't acknowledge her—she was like a gnat attacking an elephant. Kwan spoke softly to the two people, and the woman stopped her assault.

Finley let the two go and reached out his large hand,

encircling Kwan's neck. "I expected girls. And instead I get—"
He swung his free arm toward the two. "Who are these people?"

"My parents," Kwan squeaked, through his half-closed throat.

"Parents?" Finley shouted at him. "You mean I paid you to smuggle your family into the country? Why, I ought to kill you right here, you double crossing little rodent." He paused and leered at the visitors. "Better yet, I'll have you and your sorry ass kin deported."

Kwan reached up and grabbed Finley's hand that was around his neck, pried it off and twisted it outwards.

"Ouch," Jimmy whispered. "He must have found a pressure point."

Finley grunted in pain, leaned sideways and went down hard on his knees. His free arm came out swinging and Kwan took a step back, easily dodging the punch. Before Finley could recover from his wayward strike, Kwan kicked him hard in the chest, pushing him backwards.

"Damn you!" Finley gasped.

Kwan reached under his jacket and pulled out an automatic pistol and pointed it at Finley's head.

"I could get you into a lot of trouble, Finley. I know you killed Julie Gordon."

Finley shook his head.

"Cassie and I went to her apartment that night looking for her," Kwan continued. "We saw the two of you come into the complex. She was drunk and hit her head on those concrete stairs. We thought you were helping her upstairs, but instead, you dragged her to the pool and snapped her neck."

"I had to protect myself," Finley retorted. "She was blackmailing me, that little bitch. First, she wanted a promotion, and then she demanded twenty grand. It was never going to end."

I heard a whimper next to me and turned to see Jimmy crumpling onto the asphalt like a pair of blue jeans failing off a clothes line. He'd fainted.

"Oh, for the love of Pete," I said, kneeling next to him and patting his hand. "Jimmy, Jimmy," I whispered.

Finally his one good eye flicked open. "It's my fault. I wanted to pay off that stupid car carrier." He stared off into the distance. "I thought she could get the money from her mom. I never thought she'd…" He took in a deep breath. "It's like I killed her."

"You didn't kill her Jimmy, and you didn't force her to blackmail Finley. She'd already hit him up for a promotion. If it wasn't the car, it would have been something else. Now, try and sit up."

He did as he was told. He rubbed the back of his head and took a deep breath.

"You okay?" I asked.

"Yeah, I think so." He reached out and put his hand on my arm. "Patricia, I want to tell you something."

"Can't it wait Jimmy? There's a lot going on here." I sensed a confession coming from him, and I really wasn't in the mood.

"I want you to know, I've always had a thing for you."

"That's sweet, Jimmy." I pried his hand off my arm. "But this probably isn't the time."

"No, you don't understand. I took your Monet because you painted it. I wanted something of yours. I wasn't going to sell it."

"No? So you were going to force me to make more so you could wallpaper your office with them?" Now I was angry. "You have an odd way of showing your affection."

He winced. "Sorry. I'll give it back. I promise."

"Are you going to drop the theft charges against me?"

"Yeah, I always was."

Looking at his swollen lip I felt sorry for him, but only for a moment—it was a fleeting emotion. We hadn't heard anything for a few minutes so I looked around the fender. What I saw made my stomach churn.

The three Ladies were being marched toward Finley at gunpoint by Pachucca, the ex-cop. The meter maid carried Mrs. B's rifle, pointing it at her back.

"Oh crap!" I swore and hunkered down behind the car again.

"What?" Jimmy asked.

I pointed for him to see for himself.

"Oh crap," he repeated after looking. He sat down on the ground and leaned up against the car. He started patting his pockets, looking for something.

"Do you have a gun?" I asked hopefully.

He gave me a look, like I'd just asked the stupidest question in the world. "No, I don't have a gun."

I guess he was over his crush. He pulled out his toothpick container, opened it, and popped a pick in his mouth.

"What do you know about the ex-cop and the meter maid?" I asked, hoping for some insight to the situation.

"They're for hire," he scrunched up his face like he tasted something bad. "The gal's his girlfriend. Kwan told me about them, and he probably heard about them through Finley."

"Drop it." I heard a male voice say.

We peeked around the car. Pachucca had his firearm pointed at Kwan's chest. Kwan's gun hit the pavement with a thud.

"Stick 'em in the Cadillac trunk," Finley said, as he stood up, brushed himself off and picked up Kwan's weapon. "Let's send them all to Korea."

"They're not all going to fit, sir," Pachucca said. "Not with Chang still in there."

"Oh yeah, I forgot about him."

Cassandra whimpered, her hand covering her mouth.

"Worried about your boyfriend?" Finley asked with a sneer.

"I have an idea," I told Jimmy. "I'll distract them and you grab the guns."

Jimmy rolled his eyes. "Distract them with what? Your female charms?" He huffed. "Besides, there are at least three guns. I can't grab them all at the same time. They'll shoot me."

"As soon as you make a move, the others will jump in."

"And how am I supposed to get that close to them?"

"I hate to be the one to tell you this, but they're going to come looking for you as soon as they realize you're not in the trunk."

I dove into the field of cars, leaving Jimmy to fend for himself. When I got to the car carrier, I moved to the far side of the cab. Inspecting the last vehicle waiting to be unloaded, I could see the tie-downs had been removed from the old Pinto and it was ready to be backed off.

"Damn it!" Finley swore. "Find him!"

I turned to look. The group stood by the Cadillac's open trunk lid.

"Get in!" Finley yelled.

Mrs. Russo stood her ground, looking defiant with her chin held high. Finley raised his arm and hit her on the side of her head. She went down, disappearing from view.

I recoiled almost as if I'd been hit. My legs trembled as I scrambled up the ladder to the top deck of the car carrier and crawled to the Pinto on my hands and knees. The door opened with a horrible screech, but when I looked to the group, no one seemed to have heard. I couldn't see Mrs. Butterfield and with a sinking feeling, realized that she was probably in the trunk. My hands shook as I lowered the emergency brake. Pushing in the clutch I used the gear shift knob to put the car in neutral.

From this elevated view I could see that the fake cop had found Jimmy and was marching him to the Caddy. It looked like Pachucca had a gun pointed at Jimmy's back. I got out and moved to the front of the car.

Putting all my weight into the Pinto I gave the front end a push. The car moved a few inches. I pushed again, this time harder. It moved a few feet, and then the back end tipped downward. As gravity caught the Pinto it picked up speed, rolling off the car carrier faster than I imagined. I jumped on the ladder and started moving down.

I was expecting a loud crash when it rammed into the rows of Hyundai's. But what I wasn't expecting was an explosion. Fire shot up through the fog, illuminating the dock like a fireworks show. For a moment I closed my eyes as if that would block out the deafening noise. Burning debris fell around me as I touched ground and crawled to safety under the bottom rack of the car carrier. I could hear men from the ship yelling, even through the din.

When the remains of the Pinto settled onto the pier, I crawled out to see the explosion had the desired affect. Finley was on the ground with Kwan pointing a gun at his head.

Heat emanating from the blast prickled my skin as I ran to the Cadillac. Jimmy and Pachucca were locked in hand-to-hand combat. Jimmy's knowledge of Kung Fu appeared to be an even match with the ex-cop's police academy training. Mrs. Miller kicked Pachucca in the shin and Jimmy took the advantage, pinning Pachucca's arm behind him and getting a choke hold around his neck.

I looked for the meter maid and saw a head bobbing and weaving in the distance, she was running for the exit, making her escape.

Mrs. Miller knelt beside Mrs. Russo, who lay behind the Caddy, unconscious.

"Where's Mrs. B?" I asked.

Mrs. Miller pointed to the closed trunk lid. On it sat a steaming twisted circle of metal that was once the Pinto's steering wheel.

"Finley pushed her in the trunk and when it started raining Pinto parts she pulled the lid down. The impact of the steering wheel must have pushed it shut."

"Hello? Hello?" It was Mrs. B's muffled voice from inside the trunk. "A little help, please."

I tapped on the lid. "Just a minute, Mrs. B." I moved toward the driver's door, figuring I could use the keys or the glove box release.

Cassandra sat in the driver's seat of the Caddy, the rifle lying across her lap.

"It won't start. What's wrong with it?" Her foot pumped

the accelerator as she tried to turn over the ignition. Gas fumes burned my nose as the engine flooded.

"Cassandra, pop open the trunk lid. The release is in the glove box."

"This car's getting on that ship."

I didn't like the sound of that. "But Mrs. B's locked in the trunk."

Cassandra stepped out of the Caddy and pointed the rifle at my chest. "What would you do to make sure your grandmother had food?" she spat the question at me.

I wanted to focus on what she was saying but my flight response was suddenly screaming and the only thing I understood was that Cassandra had lost a wing nut.

"Look, Mrs. B is in the trunk, let's get her out—"

"Food!" She yelled. "No luxuries, just enough to eat so you can think straight and sleep at night. That's all she wants and that car's going to get it for her."

"Cassandra, what are you talking about?"

Sirens screamed in the distance, and I hoped I could keep her chatting until they arrived.

"Kim Jong-Il is going to let my grandmother go when he gets the Cadillac." She lapsed into Korean.

"Kim Jong-Il," I repeated, "as in the leader of North Korea?"

"Is there another one?" she shot back. "You have no idea how hard it is to get someone out of that hellhole."

Then I understood her fury. Family members starving to death would be enough to send anyone over the edge.

"But an old Cadillac?" I asked. I wanted to keep her talking, but amusing repartee alluded me.

"He loves Elvis," she shrugged. "Go figure."

"What does Elvis have to do with this?"

"We're running out of time." She jabbed the rifle into my throat. "Start the damn car."

"Cassandra," Jimmy spoke softly. "Open the trunk." He couldn't move since he still had Pachucca by the neck.

"Shut up, Jimmy," she snapped at him.

"She's dead!" Mrs. Miller wailed. "Sunny! No!" She started to sob.

Cassandra turned to look, and I stepped forward grabbing the barrel of the gun, pushing it away from me, but Cassandra pushed back and for a split second I saw her eyes overflow with rage. The gun went off with an explosion that reverberated through my whole body. I fell backwards, staring at blackness.

Chapter Twenty-three

I woke up groggy and disorientated. My head ached worse than a wine and beer hangover. My left ear buzzed like I'd spent hours in front of a speaker at a rock concert. I stared at a ceiling made of white acoustical tiles and then glanced around. The walls were white, the furniture was white, and the linens on my bed were white. This must be the jail's hospital. Visions from the previous evening swept over me. I squeezed my eyes shut but the tears still came. Sunny was dead and I could only assume that the Hyundai corporation was pressing charges for destruction of property.

The door opened and a woman wearing pale green scrubs walked softly across the room.

"Good morning," she said. "How are you feeling?"

"My head hurts," I whispered, as I used the back of my hand to wipe my wet eyes.

"Well, you got a nasty bump." She checked my vitals and seemed satisfied that I was still alive. "Why don't you try getting up?"

I winced when my bare feet touched the cold vinyl floor.

"Dizzy?" she asked.

"No, just sore."

"Do you need help getting dressed?"

"I don't think so."

"When you're done, come on out. There's someone waiting for you in the hall."

After freshening up, I slowly eased into yesterday's clothes. I took another deep breath before opening the door. Leaning up against the wall was a woman dressed in a navy blue suit and a white blouse. She spoke with a slight Indian accent and her large brown eyes looked at me with compassion.

"Hungry, Ms. Schuster?" she asked.

I shrugged.

"This way, please."

We walked down a long carpeted hallway to an elevator. I moved slowly, more from emotional pain than physical. We ascended a few flights, and upon exiting I looked outside and could see buildings on hilly terrain that I recognized as San Francisco, beyond that lay the dark blue of the Pacific Ocean.

I smelled coffee as we entered a sunny corner room. Next to a buffet table sat The Ladies, all four of them, along with an African-American woman I'd never seen before. They stopped talking when I entered.

"Sunny," my voice was a whisper.

She stood up and walked to me arms outstretched. "I'm sorry I gave you a scare, dear. Distraction techniques sometimes have unfortunate consequences." I fell into her arms, tears once again squeezed from the corners of my eyes. I'd never felt so relieved.

"Patricia!" Mrs. M and Mrs. T called out in unison.

"Dear, so good to see you," Mrs. B said. "Come. Sit."

I sat down and glanced around the table. The Ladies looked, well, they looked, how can I put it? Professional. Mrs. Butterfield didn't have on a stitch of yellow. Mrs. Taylor sat up straight in her chair, hatless and without her cane. Mrs. Russo lacked her usual excessive jewelry. And Mrs. Miller seemed like herself, but she was missing a flower that would normally adorn her hair.

"How's your head, Mrs. Russo?" I asked.

"Throbbing," she said. "And yours?"

"The same."

"Lucky for you, Patricia, that Cassandra's a bad shot."

"Oh, I remember the first time I got shot at," Mrs. B chimed in, looking like her old self.

The other ladies gave her a reproachful glance, and Mrs. B stopped talking.

"Patricia, this is Beatrice Johnson." Mrs. R gestured to the woman sitting next to her. "She's an old friend of your grandmother's."

"Nice to meet you, Ms. Johnson," I said.

"It's nice to finally meet you, Patricia. I've heard a lot about you," she replied, smiling.

Swimming in confusion, I raised my eyebrows and looked questioningly around the room. "So?" I asked.

"Let's start with last night," said Mrs. Butterfield. "Do you remember hearing sirens?"

I nodded.

"That was the Oakland police and Officer Romano arriving. They arrested Finley, Anthony Pachucca, and Cassandra."

"Cassandra too?"

"She shot at you, remember, dear?" Mrs. B said.

"Yes, I remember."

"She was arrested for assault and because she had an unregistered firearm in her possession."

Ms. Johnson slid a sideways glance at Mrs. Butterfield.

"They never did find that horrible meter maid," Mrs. B said. "She got away."

"So that explains last night." I folded my arms and landed my stare on Mrs. Russo.

"Well, we have some fessing up to do." Mrs. R said, tapping the side of her coffee cup.

"Give Patricia some coffee for gosh sakes, Sunny. Let's ease her into this," Mrs. B said.

All conversation stopped as they filled my cup. I looked over at the long food table pushed against the wall. The smell of bacon made my mouth water.

"Let's have something to eat!" Mrs. Russo offered.

I knew they were stalling, but I was suddenly too hungry to care.

We all filled our plates and once again sat down. For a few minutes there was no talking. After I ate a couple of bites, I couldn't take it any more.

"Okay, spill it," I said to the group.
They all looked to Mrs. R.

"Well, Ms. Johnson isn't just a friend of your grandmother's."
"Oh?"

"She's our liaison."

"Liaison with whom?" I asked, crunching down on a bagel smothered in cream cheese.

Mrs. Miller held up her finger to the group. "Wait till she swallows."

I chewed quickly, hoping they wouldn't want proof.

Mrs. Russo took a deep breath. "The FBI," she said firmly.

I put down my fork and looked from one sweet face to another, trying to grasp what was happening.

"You're FBI?"

"She is," Mrs. M gestured to Ms. Johnson. "But the rest of us aren't. Since we all have records. You can't work for the FBI if you're a felon."

Mrs. Russo cleared her throat.

"Well, everyone has a record but Sunny," Mrs. M corrected herself.

"We do contract work," Mrs. Taylor said. "We're like freelancers. The FBI hires us to do a job, and we do that job however we see fit."

"Patricia," Ms. Johnson said, "let me introduce you to the best group I've got. This is Betty Brewer," she gestured to Mrs. Butterfield. "Ms. Brewer speaks five languages, is an expert shot and has a vast knowledge of cars. We approached Ms. Brewer in 1983, after she turned state's evidence against the owner of an auto dealership in Southern California."

Mrs. B explained: "The auto dealer and I had a good insurance scam going, but he promised me he would leave his wife and he didn't. What else was I supposed to do?"

"And this is Rita Martinez," Ms. Johnson gestured to Mrs. Miller. "Ms. Martinez is a surveillance expert. We asked her to come to work for us after she turned in the President of Regency Savings for mortgage fraud, in the mid-'80s. She was the first to draw attention to the Savings and Loan crisis."

"And Mrs. Taylor's real name is Audrey Thatcher. She's a fingerprint expert, has a doctorate in Behavioral Psychology and is knowledgeable in the world of counterfeit art. She and your grandmother came to our attention when they gave us a tip about a stolen Picasso in South America."

Mrs. T leaned over to me and whispered, "That was just after you were born. Your grandmother was trying to make amends."

"And Sunny approached us recently after finding out that her husband, Nico, was linked to organized crime."

Mrs. Russo gave a dismissive wave. "A woman needs a hobby."

"Okay," I said, trying to digest this new information. "You're going to have to start at the beginning."

"This particular job started when Jimmy Chang bragged to your grandmother implying he stole cars from Nevada," said Mrs. R.

I nodded my head. Jimmy liked to boast, whether it was true or not.

"So Elsie told Jimmy about her past, trying to gain his confidence."

"But it wasn't until Julie's death," said Ms. Johnson, "that we realized we might be dealing with something larger than car theft."

"Kwan needed money to transport his relatives into the country," said Mrs. T. "He and his sister Cassandra were scamming Finley by telling him they could deliver girls to him for a price."

"So what happened to Kwan?" I asked.

"Kwan and his parents were taken in for questioning last night," explained Ms. Johnson. "But their paperwork was in order, so they were released."

"And Jimmy?" I asked.

Mrs. R shrugged. "He's perfectly legit. But we're still curious as to why he wanted you to sell pearls and furniture."

I busied myself with adding more cream cheese to my bagel. I didn't want to share Jimmy's confession from the night before. If they knew Jimmy had a thing for me, I'd never hear the end of it.

"How does the Cadillac fit into all this?" I asked.

"Julie told Kwan about its history and when Cassandra heard the story, she got the wild idea of using it to get her grandmother out of North Korea." Mrs. B explained.

"What story?" I said looking at Mrs. Russo.

"Sunny's Cadillac was a wedding gift from Elvis," Mrs. B spit out.

"Elvis? The Elvis?" I asked. Then I remembered the photo of Sunny. "I found a picture of you and Elvis and another man."

"That was taken in New York, right before Elvis left for Germany to do his stint in the army," Mrs. R said. "The man who was leaning on the Cadillac in the picture was my first husband."

"How on earth did you meet Elvis?"

"I sang in one of his movies and we became friends."

"So you two were never..." I raised an eyebrow, letting the sentence trail off.

"Of course not, we were just friends."

"Why didn't you tell me all this before?"

"A few reasons," Mrs. R explained. "Our job was to find out if Chang was stealing cars out of Nevada. It didn't have anything to do with finding the Cadillac. That was my own personal agenda."

"Plus, we were afraid you wouldn't believe us," Mrs. Miller said. "We needed you, and if you thought we were all dotty, well, that wouldn't be in our best interest."

I stared out the window and rubbed my temple. "What about the provenance that Cassandra talked about?"

"Hopefully it's still with the car," Mrs. R said. "It's hidden under the back seat."

"Did your husband really lose the Cadillac in a poker game to Julie's dad?"

Mrs. Russo nodded. "That's when I turned Nico in, and with the help of your grandmother, he went to jail for racketeering. He crossed the line. He knew how much I loved that car."

"There's one more thing," Ms. Johnson said. "I was heartbroken when your grandmother died, not only for losing a great colleague, but also for losing a dear friend. And given your contribution in catching Finley, I think The Ladies might have an offer for you."

"We need someone with spunk," said Mrs. M.

"Someone who's loyal," said Mrs. T.

"Someone who's smart," said Mrs. R.

"And someone who can drive at night," said Mrs. B.

The five ladies beamed at me, and my food gurgled in my stomach. I took another swallow of coffee, I had a feeling I was in for a gnarly ride.

Epilogue

I watched Jake and Jason playing Frisbee in the sand. Well, mostly I watched Jake, since he was wearing only shorts. Adam and Chris were out on the water, sitting on their boards, waiting for the next perfect wave. Two abutting canopies provided shade for our gathering. Jason's mom joined us, taking advantage of a break in her chemotherapy. She wore a blue and yellow scarf around her head and smiled broadly behind her sunglasses. Mrs. T and Mrs. B strolled barefoot down the beach, each holding onto big floppy hats.

"Surfers sell seashells by the sea shore."

"What?" I turned and looked at Mrs. Miller.

She had her binoculars out, pointing them up at the cars parked on the cliffs. I thought she had been obsessively watching the Cadillac. Mrs. Russo had bought the Caddy back from Jimmy, and where she came up with the money I'll never know. Apparently, the provenance that everyone spoke of was still hidden under the back seat. It consisted of the original pink slip and the purchase contract with Elvis's signature, both framed under glass. Jake removed the dent in the trunk lid and re-painted the car to the original stock color of Olympic White

Number 90.

"He's naked," she said.

I glanced up at the cars. A male surfer changed out of his wetsuit.

"Naked as a jay bird," Mrs. Miller said.

I swear she was purring.

"Let me see," my mom said, looking through the binoculars. "You're right. He is." She giggled. My mother's mood had improved considerably when she found out that my father broke up with his new girlfriend. I hadn't seen her this relaxed in years. For our outing she wore a blue sarong over a matching one-piece bathing suit. Her legs stuck out from under the canopy, soaking up some rays. She put the glasses down and turned to me. "Do they always do that?"

I nodded.

"No wonder you like it here so much."

The
Zucchini Fairy
Murder
By
Ann Philipp

A Salty Sister Mystery
Book Two

Read on for an excerpt…

Salty Sister Publishing

Chapter One

"Mom," I whispered into the darkness. "How many more cars?"

"Two," she whispered back.

"Where's the next one?"

"Across the street."

I squinted into the dim light. An old wood-paneled station wagon stood helpless in a driveway, unaware of the bounty it was about to receive.

A fluttering above our heads startled me. "What's that?" I sputtered.

"An owl," my mother responded. "Patricia, if I'd known you were going to be so edgy, I would have left you at home."

It took all my self-control not to let out an exasperated sigh. The last thing I wanted was my mother prancing around a suburban neighborhood at night by herself.

"Come on," she said, "we're almost done."

We sprinted to a large tree next to the sidewalk and then darted across the street to the station wagon. She turned and I unzipped the huge pack on her back. I took out five slender green vegetables and placed them on the front seat of the car.

"Did you get one with a face?" she asked.

Of course, my mother couldn't garden the usual way. She forced her produce to grow in plastic molds, creating creepy gnome-like faces as the vegetables grew.

I checked. "Yes, Mom."

"Give 'em the big one too," she said. "With a car this size, they must have a lot of kids."

I reached back in and grasped the inedible three-foot-long squash that must have weighed ten pounds and placed it next to the others. A siren wailed in the distance, and I longed to be at home watching TV and scarfing ice cream.

"Okay. Next?"

My mother had plotted out every open car window—at least those without alarms—within a six-block radius. But that was at 7:00 this evening; it was now almost 10:00. So far they'd all still been open. She consulted her map using a penlight.

"Five houses to the north."

We dashed to a low fence, stepped over it, and crunched across a gravel driveway onto a freshly mown lawn. A dense six-foot hedge blocked our path, so we veered for the sidewalk. A fluffy white dog on a leash appeared from around the barrier, pulling a man who was tying a knot at the end of a plastic bag.

We stood perfectly still, smack dab in the middle of the grass, as if being motionless would hide us.

"Genevieve?" the man called out. "I almost didn't recognize you. How nice to see you!"

My mother had picked out my clothes for the night: a black turtleneck, black cargo pants, black running shoes, black leather gloves, and a black baseball cap, but I drew the line at black and green camouflage makeup. She wore the same—except with the camouflage makeup.

I stared at this man, baffled that he could identify her with all that goop on her face. He was tall, wore glasses, with a clean-shaven face and a strong jaw line. A shapeless overcoat hid his physique.

"Richard," my mother said. Her back stiffened, and I could tell that this was not a welcome encounter. A month ago my father left my mother for a much younger woman. Since then, a load of single middle-aged men had honed in on her; she was like a beacon of sexuality.

We sauntered over to him and stood awkwardly, his non-descript terrier sniffing our feet.

"This is my daughter, Patricia," my mom said.

I would have reached out to shake his hand, but his bag of poop made me hesitate.

"Hello," I said.

"This is my dog, Cleopatra." He gestured to the panting mutt who'd plopped down on the lawn. "Beautiful night for a walk, isn't it?" he asked.

"It is," my mother said.

"Boy, those are some big packs you're hauling," Richard said.

We both carried camping backpacks, the kind you use for long hikes into the wilderness. Mine started out the night weighing close to 30 pounds.

"Hmm, yesss," my mother said. I could tell she was searching for a lie.

"We're in training," I intervened.

"Yes. Training," my mother repeated. "For a marathon."

"Oh, which one?" he asked.

"Bay to Breakers." I blurted out the first long-distance race that popped into my head. My mom shot me a look, and I knew what she was thinking. Except for a few masochists, Bay to Breakers was more of a moving street party than a marathon.

"Oh." He sounded surprised.

"We're going dressed as campers," I said.

"Oh." More surprise.

Richard studied my mother's face, and before he could ask about the makeup I gave her arm a tug. "Well, we better keep walking. Nice meeting you."

"Have a nice evening," he responded. "Maybe I'll see you at Café Lattes tomorrow, Genevieve."

We headed up the sidewalk, and I could see our last recipient: a small black sedan with an open rear window. Headlights turned the corner, and I instinctively pushed my mother away from the street.

A shadowy area between two homes looked like a good place to hide, so we squatted behind a low bush. Besides my heart pounding in my chest, I could hear the sound of a TV. I imagined those inside lounging on a soft couch eating luscious bowls of ice cream. Probably coffee flavored with homemade chocolate sauce.

A low, menacing growl behind us startled me, and I turned to see two tall wood gates, side by side. The one closest to us banged as a dog jumped against it, barking loudly to announce our presence.

"Dang," my mother swore. She stood up, reached over the far gate, and found the latch. It swung open and we stepped behind it. The canine continued to bark until the owner opened a side door and yelled, "Buster! Come!"

My mom peered between the slats of the gate. "Oh, crap,"

she said. "It's a cop, and he's stopped in the middle of the street."

With my luck it would be Officer Marc Romano—father of my "almost boyfriend," Jake.

"We'll have to go over the back fence," I said.

I heard a snort and realized we were not alone. I held out my arms, positioning myself between my mother and whatever beast had us trapped. From behind a stack of firewood came an unenthusiastic "woof." A dog's head appeared, and he lumbered toward us. He was large, black, and had a white spot just above his nose.

"Max?" I whispered.

He wagged his tail and softly woofed again.

"Mom, it's Max! I can't believe he's still alive. That means we're right behind your house." Between the ages of ten and twelve, I'd spent a lot of time climbing in the neighbor's magnolia tree by way of a large branch that hung over the fence. Back then Max was just a pup, and I'd lob pretzels or grapes into his yard for him to chase.

I gave Max a quick ear rub and peered around the corner into the backyard. On a large wood deck sat a BBQ grill and numerous types of mismatched outdoor furniture. The rest of the yard was lawn. In the corner, straight ahead of us, was our escape—the magnolia tree. We sprinted to it and I scrambled up the trunk. Reaching down, I grabbed my mother's arm and pulled her up with me. A branch stabbed me in the shoulder and I shifted sideways, ripping the arm of my turtleneck.

I found the limb that had provided my secret childhood passage, but at some point the branch had been cut off at the fence line. I looked down at an eight-foot drop into my mother's backyard, far enough to break an ankle.

Max stood at the base of the tree, a tennis ball in his mouth, still wagging his tail.

"Oh, look, he wants to play," my mom said. "Patricia, get down and throw the ball for him."

"Mom, this isn't a good time." I glanced back to the gate we'd come through, expecting a police officer to appear with gun drawn.

My mother dug around in her cargo pants pocket and threw something into the yard.

"What was that?" I asked.

"A liver-flavored doggie treat."

One thing I could say for my mom, she came prepared.

Max dropped the ball and chased after his quarry, which happened to land next to a trash can. As my mother tossed another treat in the opposite direction, I climbed down and ran to the can. It was made of indestructible plastic and full of weeds. I turned it upside down, dumped its contents, and ran back to the tree.

"Patricia, throw the ball," my mom said.

I tossed the tennis ball onto the deck, glad that my gloves protected me from the inevitable dog slobber. The back door opened and I crouched behind the can. A husky voice yelled, "Max!"

The old dog whined a goodbye, plodded up to the house, and disappeared inside. I returned to my task of heaving the garbage can up the tree. After struggling with branches and backpacks, I was high enough to drop it over the fence upside down. It landed on a shrub, a little cockeyed, but it would do. I put one foot on the two-by-four that held up the fence rails, held onto the cut branch, and reached out my other leg, touching the top of the can.

As I shifted my weight, the can sank into the bush and then caught. I stepped down with my other leg, and then jumped onto the ground. Turning around I took hold of my mother's outstretched arm and helped her to safety.

I leaned up against the fence, breathing hard. My mom brushed leaves off her arms, barely winded. A sea of thigh-high squash plants running from fence-line to fence-line surrounded us. I gestured to the lush greenery.

"Mom, why can't you just sell your zucchini at the Farmer's Market?"

"Farmer's Market," she scoffed. "Where's the sport in that?"

I really couldn't fault my mother for her odd behavior. Besides my father leaving her, she'd also recently lost her mother—my Nana. So what's a woman to do with all that anger and grief, if not take up an extreme hobby?

We slogged our way through the large, sticky leaves to the house. I was so tired I didn't even care about ice cream anymore; I just wanted to lie down on the couch and sleep the night away.

Dropping our packs on the back porch, we went in through the kitchen door. Flashing lights illuminated the hallway. Without saying a word we ran to the front door and peeked out the window.

"It's the police!" I said.

"They're on to us," my mother replied. "Oh, your father's going to have a field day with this."

My father worked as an estate attorney. A few weeks ago, I'd been arrested for grand theft auto. The charges were dropped, but that experience brought out some interesting facts about my not-so-pretty ancestry. I come from a long line of female criminals. My grandmother was an art counterfeiter, my great-grandmother robbed banks, and my great-great grandmother stole gold from a smelting company. My mother's indiscretion was stealing a $4,000 designer dress when she was in high school. Only my grandmother had done hard time. My father was embarrassed by this family history, as if it somehow tarnished his profession.

I glanced out the window again. Officer Romano stood next to his police car.

"It's Jake's dad." I turned and looked at my mom. "Hurry, wash your face."

I followed her back to the kitchen, where she poured dish soap in her hand and rubbed at her camouflage makeup.

My overnight bag sat on the counter, and I pulled out a towel to wipe sweat from my forehead. I took off my gloves, hat, and turtleneck and slipped on a t-shirt. I ran my fingers through my short, curly blond hair, which I knew would be sticking up in odd directions. I turned to my mom; her face was covered in lather.

"Rinse, Mom, rinse!"

She stuck her head under the faucet, spraying water everywhere. When she stood up, I handed her a wad of paper towels.

We hurried back to the living room window; Officer Romano was talking on the police radio.

"Looks like he's calling for backup," I said.

"Maybe he'll go easy on us. I hate being manhandled by cops." My mother plunked herself down onto an easy chair and dropped her head into her hands.

I sighed and looked again. Officer Romano was standing over something in the street.

"Oh, no. Mom, I don't think he's here for us."

At the officer's feet lay a body.

About the Author

Ann Philipp lives in Northern California with one husband and five cats. Others that share her space are greedy squirrels, ninja gophers and clairvoyant vultures.

She writes humorous murder mysteries, short stories, funny screenplays, and any type of humor that will make her laugh.

You can visit her website at annphilipp.com.

www.ingramcontent.com/pod-product-compliance
Lightning Source LLC
Chambersburg PA
CBHW031228120726
47905CB00002B/506